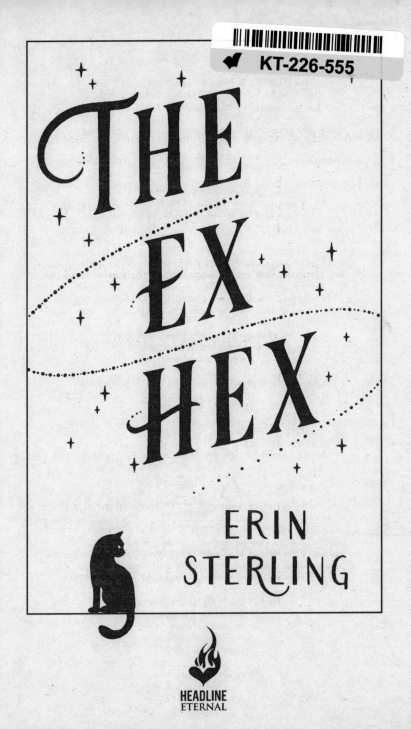

THE EX HEX

ERIN STERLING

HEADLINE
ETERNAL

Title page and chapter opener art © Kuznetsova Darja / Shutterstock, Inc.

Published by arrangement with Avon,
an imprint of HarperCollins Publishers.

First published in Great Britain in 2021
by HEADLINE ETERNAL
An imprint of HEADLINE PUBLISHING GROUP

11

Cataloguing in Publication Data is available from the British Library

ISBN 978 1 4722 9028 1

Offset in 12/17 pt Garamond Premier Pro by Jouve (UK), Milton Keynes

Printed and bound in Great Britain by Clays Ltd, Elcograf S.p.A

HEADLINE PUBLISHING GROUP
An Hachette UK Company
Carmelite House
50 Victoria Embankment
London EC4Y 0DZ

www.headlineeternal.com
www.headline.co.uk
www.hachette.co.uk

*To Sandra Brown, Jude Deveraux, Julie Garwood,
Judith McNaught and Amanda Quick, the writers who
made me want to be a romance novelist when I was
twelve. It took thirty years, but I'm finally here!*

PROLOGUE

Never mix vodka and witchcraft.

Vivi knew that. Not only had her aunt Elaine said it about a thousand times, but it was also printed on dish towels and T-shirts and, ironically, shot glasses in Something Wicked, the store Aunt Elaine ran in downtown Graves Glen, Georgia.

It might've actually been the closest thing the Jones family had to a family motto.

But, Vivi reasoned as she sank deeper into the bathtub and took another slurp of the vodka and cranberry concoction her cousin Gwyn had made her, there had to be exceptions for broken hearts.

And hers currently felt very thoroughly broken. Shattered maybe. Little bitty pieces of heart, rattling around in her chest, all because she got sucked in by a cute accent and a pair of very blue eyes.

Sniffling, she flicked her fingers again, filling the air with the smell of Rhys's cologne, something citrusy and spicy that she'd never managed to put her finger on, but had clearly imprinted on her brain enough that her magic could just summon it up.

Even now, slumped in Gwyn's claw-foot tub, she could remember how that scent made her head spin when she buried her face against his chest, how warm his skin had been.

"Vivi, not again!" Gwyn called from the bedroom. "It's giving me a headache!"

Vivi slid farther into the water, letting it slosh over the sides of the tub, nearly extinguishing one of the candles she'd put around the rim.

Another one of Aunt Elaine's lessons—the best cure for anything was candles and a bath, and even though Vivi had put plenty of rosemary and handfuls of pink salt in the water, lit just about every candle Gwyn owned, she wasn't feeling any better.

Although the vodka was helping, she allowed, leaning over to take another sip through the bright purple crazy straw.

"Let me live!" she called back once she'd drained the glass, and Gwyn stuck her head around the door, pink hair swinging over her shoulders.

"My darling, I adore you, but you dated the guy for three months."

"We've only been broken up for nine hours," Vivi said, not adding that it was actually nine hours and thirty-six minutes, almost thirty-seven. "I get at least another fifteen hours before I have to stop sulking. It's in the rule book."

Gwyn rolled her eyes. "This is why I told you not to date Witch Boys," she said. "Especially Penhallow Witch Boys. Those assholes may have founded this town, but they're still fucking Witch Boys."

"Fucking Witch Boys," Vivi agreed, looking sadly at her empty glass as Gwyn disappeared back into the bedroom.

Vivi was still a lot newer to the whole witch thing than Gwyn. While her cousin had grown up with Aunt Elaine, a happily practicing witch, Vivi's own mom, Elaine's sister, had kept her witchery under wraps. It was only after she'd died and Vivi had gone to live with Elaine and Gwyn that she'd started tapping into this side of herself.

Which meant she hadn't known about Witch Boys and how meeting one at a Solstice Revel on a warm summer night could be both the best and worst thing that had ever happened to you.

Lifting her hand, Vivi wiggled her fingers, and after a moment, a hazy, wavering image rose above the water.

The face was handsome, all good bone structure, dark hair, twinkling eyes and rakish grin.

Vivi scowled at it before flicking her hand again, sending a miniature tidal wave up out of the bath to splash down, the face vanishing in a shower of sparks.

Would've been nice if she could've erased his memory just as easily, but even in her sad and vodka-soaked state, Vivi knew better than to mess around with that kind of magic. And a couple of those little pieces of her heart didn't want to forget the past three months, wanted to hold on to the memory of that night they'd met, the musical way he'd said her name, always *Vivienne,* never Vivi, how that first night he'd asked, *May I kiss you?* and she'd said, *Now?* and he'd smiled that slow smile and said, *Now is preferable, but I'm open to whatever your schedule allows,* and how was any woman supposed to resist that? Especially a nineteen-year-old one at her first Solstice Revel? Especially when the man saying those words was tall and ridiculously handsome, and *Welsh*?

It was illegal, was what it was, and she was going to lodge some kind of complaint with the Witches Council as soon as she—

"Vivi!" Gwyn yelled from the bedroom. "You're making the lights flicker."

Oops.

Sitting up, Vivi pulled the plug in Gwyn's tub, hoping some of her misery was swirling down the drain with the water.

She carefully stepped over the candles, and pulled the robe Gwyn had lent her off the hook on the wall, feeling a little bit better as she tightened the black silk belt around her waist. This was why she'd come to Elaine and Gwyn's cabin in the woods high up in the mountains above Graves Glen instead of back to her dorm room at the college. Up here in this cozy little space with its candles and cats, every room smelling like woodsmoke and herbs, Vivi was home.

Maybe she and Gwyn could do face masks or something. Have another drink or five. Listen to Taylor Swift.

Or, Vivi amended as she walked out of the bathroom to see Gwyn pouring a salt circle on the floor, they could do . . . whatever this was.

"What are you doing?" she asked, waving a hand toward the bathroom. After a second, her glass floated out, crazy straw bobbing, and Vivi closed her fingers around it before heading to Gwyn's desk to pour herself another drink.

"We're cursing this dickbag," Gwyn replied with a grin.

"He wasn't a dickbag," Vivi said, chewing on the end of her straw and studying the circle. "Not at first. And to be fair, I was the one who called it off, not him."

Snorting, Gwyn began gathering her hair up in a ponytail. "You called it off *because* he was a dickbag. He came to Graves Glen, seduced you, and all the while, his dad was back in Wales, arranging his marriage to some fancy witch. And he knew! And didn't bother to tell you! No, dickbag ruling stands, so say we all."

"'We all' meaning just you."

"Me and Sir Purrcival," Gwyn said, gesturing to the tiny black kitten currently curled up on her bed. At his name, he lifted his little head, blinking bright green-yellow eyes at Vivi before giving a tiny mew that *did* kind of sound like agreement.

And Rhys *had* been engaged. Well, almost engaged. He hadn't used that word. He'd said "betrothed." Just dropped it on her this morning while they'd been snuggled up in the warmth of his bed, him kissing her shoulder, and murmuring that he had to go back home for a week or so, get some things sorted.

"Some things" apparently meaning, "Tell my dad to call off *my actual wedding to a stranger,*" and then he'd had the nerve to be shocked that *she* was shocked, and actually, yes, they should definitely curse this dickbag.

"Fair enough," Vivi said, folding her arms over her chest. "What do we do?"

"Open the windows," Gwyn said, moving to her desk and picking up a candle in a glass holder that Vivi had somehow overlooked for her ritual bath.

Vivi did as she was told, the late September air cool and smelling like pine trees as it rushed in the room. Over the top of the nearest mountain, the moon shone full and white, and Vivi gave it a little drunken wave before sticking her head out the window to look up Elaine's mountain.

Up there, somewhere in the darkness, was Rhys's family home, the one he'd never even visited before this summer. It was dark now because Rhys was gone.

Gone.

Back to Wales and whatever life he'd lived there before coming to take summer classes at Penhaven College.

And they were over.

Her eyes stinging again, Vivi turned back to her cousin.

Gwyn sat just outside the circle, the candle now in the center, the flame flickering, and for a second, Vivi hesitated. Okay, so yes, Rhys had broken her heart. Yes, he hadn't told her his father was in the process of finding him a wife. No discussion, no warning, no care for how she might've felt about the whole thing. One Hundred Percent Dickbag Moves.

But cursing?

And cursing while drunk?

Maybe that was a little bit much.

And then Gwyn closed her eyes, held her hands out and said,

"Goddess, we beseech you that this man shall never again darken Vivi's door nor her vagina."

Vivi nearly choked on her drink, giggling even as the alcohol seared her sinuses, and flopped down on the opposite side of the circle from Gwyn.

"Goddess," Vivi said, taking another sip, "we beseech you that he never again use his dimples for evil against unsuspecting maidens."

"Nice one," Gwyn said before adding, "Goddess, we beseech you to make sure his hair never does that thing again. You know the thing we mean."

"She totally does." Vivi nodded. "Goddess, we beseech you to make him the sort of man who will forever think the clitoris is exactly one-third of an inch away from where it actually is."

"Diabolical, Vivi. Truly dark magic."

Her head spinning, but her heart not feeling quite so piece-y, Vivi smiled and leaned over the circle, closer to the candle. "You broke my heart, Rhys Penhallow," she said. "And we curse you. You and your whole stupid, hot line."

The candle flame suddenly shot up high, startling Vivi so much that she knocked over her drink as she scrambled back, and from his spot on the bed, Sir Purrcival hissed, his back arching.

Gwyn leapt to her feet to pick him up, but before she could, both windows suddenly slammed shut, the drapes blowing back from the force.

Yelping, Vivi stood up, her foot smudging the salt circle, and when she turned to look back at the candle, its flame seemed to rise impossibly higher, taller than Gwyn, before abruptly extinguishing itself.

Everything was quiet and still then except for Sir Purrcival, still hissing and spitting as he backed up against Gwyn's pillows, and Vivi wasn't sure she'd ever sobered up so fast in her life.

"So that was . . . weird," she ventured at last, and Gwyn walked over to the window, cautiously lifting it.

The frame slid up easily and stayed put, and when Gwyn turned back to Vivi, some of the color was returning to her face.

"You made the lights flicker earlier, remember? Probably just, like, a power surge. A magical one."

"Can that happen?" Vivi asked, and Gwyn nodded, maybe a little too quickly.

"Sure. I mean . . . we were just goofing around. None of that was real curse magic. That candle came from Bath & Body Works, I think."

Vivi studied the label. "Yeah, I'm pretty sure 'Orchard Hayride' isn't in league with darkness."

"Right," Gwyn said. "So yeah, no harm, no foul, except that we scared baby boy here." She had managed to coax Sir Purrcival into her arms, and he snuggled in even as he seemed to glare in Vivi's general direction.

"Don't know my own strength, I guess," Vivi said, and then, as one, she and Gwyn added, "Never mix vodka and witchcraft."

Laughing a little sheepishly, Vivi set the candle back on Gwyn's desk.

"Feeling better?" Gwyn asked. "Fake-curse that man right out of your hair?"

It was going to take more than one bath, several drinks and some magical silliness to forget about Rhys, but for now, Vivi nodded. "I think so. And you're right, it was just three months, and now he's back to Wales, so it's not like I'll ever have to see him again. He can go back to his life, I can go back to mine. Now, let's clean up all this salt before Aunt Elaine comes up here and figures out we were drinking and magicking."

Vivi turned away and neither she nor Gwyn saw the candle briefly ignite again, the flame sparking, the smoke curling back toward the open window and the full moon.

CHAPTER 1

Nine Years Later

Of course it was bloody raining.

For one, it was Wales, so rain literally came with the territory, Rhys understood that, but he'd driven from London that morning through sunshine with the occasional cloud. Gorgeous blue skies, rolling green hills, the kind of day that made one want to take up painting or maybe develop some kind of poetry habit.

It was only once he drove into Dweniniaid, the tiny village where his family had lived for centuries, that it started pissing down.

He was fairly sure he knew why.

Grimacing, Rhys parked his rental car just off the High Street. He didn't have to drive, of course. Could've used a Traveling Stone, been here in the blink of an eye, but his insistence on driving everywhere irritated his father, and Rhys liked that more than he liked the convenience of magical travel.

Although, he thought as he got out of the car and frowned up at the sky, today it felt a little like cutting off his nose to spite his own face.

But what was done was done, and Rhys tugged the collar of his coat up a little and set off into the village proper.

There wasn't much on the High Street—a few shops, a church at one end and at the other, a pub. That was the direction he headed in now. There were only a handful of people out this afternoon, but all of them crossed to the other side of the street when they saw him.

Lovely to see the family reputation was still robust as ever.

At the end of the street, The Raven and Crown beckoned, its windows warm rectangles of light against the gray day, and as soon as Rhys pushed open the front door, he was assailed with some of his favorite smells—the malty richness of beer, the sharp tang of cider and the oaky warmth of aged wood.

God, he'd actually missed home.

Maybe it was just because he'd been away for so long this time. He usually tried to drop in every few months, more frequently if he thought his father was away. It put him right in between his two older brothers in terms of familial loyalty.

Llewellyn, the eldest, ran this pub and stayed in close contact with their father. Bowen, the middle brother, had fucked off to the mountains of Snowdonia two years ago, and they got occasional communications from him, mostly to alarm all of them with how intense his beard seemed to be getting.

So Rhys was, for once, not the most disappointing son, a title he was happy to hang on to until Bowen decided to stop doing whatever it was he was doing up there.

He was never going to be the favorite, though. Wells had won that role long ago, and Rhys was happy to let him have it. Besides, it was kind of fun being the black sheep. When he fucked up, that was taken as a given, and when he managed not to fuck up, everyone was pleasantly surprised.

Win-win.

Taking off his jacket, Rhys went to hang it on the coatrack by the door, the one just under an old advertisement for Strongbow cider, and as he did, he caught a glimpse of the man behind the bar watching him.

And when Rhys turned around, he realized the man behind the bar—his eldest brother, Llewellyn—was the *only* person in the pub.

Llewellyn was their father minus thirty years: same stern expression, same Roman nose—well, to be fair, they all had that nose—same thin lips. Only slightly less of a prick. But equally committed to staying in this tiny little village where everyone was terrified of him and running this pub that only the occasional tourist—and erstwhile brother—wandered into.

"Hiya, Wells," Rhys said, to which Wells only grunted in response.

Typical.

"Business still booming, I see." Rhys sauntered over to the bar, grabbing a handful of peanuts from a glass bowl there.

Wells shot him a dark look over the polished mahogany, and Rhys grinned, tossing a peanut into his mouth.

"Come on," he cajoled. "Admit that you're delighted to see me."

"Surprised to see you," Wells said. "Thought you'd abandoned us for good this time."

"And forgo such warm fraternal bonding? Never."

Wells gave him a reluctant smile at that. "Father said you were in New Zealand."

Nodding, Rhys took another handful of peanuts. "Until a couple of days ago. Stag do. Bunch of English guys wanting the full *Lord of the Rings* experience."

Rhys's travel company, Penhallow Tours, had grown from a small, one-man business run out of Rhys's London flat to a ten-person operation, running multiple trips all over the world. His customers routinely called his trips the best of their lives, and his reviews were full of people gushing over how they never had a single day of bad weather, not one delayed flight, not a solitary case of food poisoning.

Amazing how much the smallest bits of magic could do.

"Well, I'm glad you're back," Wells said, resuming his cleaning. "Because now you can go talk to Father, and get him out of this mood."

He nodded at the windows, and Rhys turned, seeing the truly abysmal weather in a new light.

Fuck me.

He'd been right, then. No ordinary storm, but one of his

father's making, which, yes, meant Rhys had undoubtedly irritated him. His brothers had never provoked a storm from his father.

Rhys had caused . . . twenty? Two dozen? Too many to count, really.

Turning back to Wells, Rhys went to reach for the peanuts again only to have his hand swatted at with a damp towel.

"Oi!" he cried, but Wells was already pointing at the door.

"Go up there and talk to him before he floods the main road and I never see a customer again."

"Am I not a customer?"

"You're a pain in my arse is what you are," Wells replied, then sighed, hands on his hips. "Seriously, Rhys, just go talk to him, get it over with. He's missed you."

Rhys snorted even as he got up from the barstool. "I appreciate that, Wells, but you're full of shite, mate."

AN HOUR LATER, Rhys was wondering why he hadn't at least stayed at the pub long enough to have a pint. Possibly three.

He'd decided to walk up to the house rather than antagonize his father with the car—a real show of growth and maturity on his part, he thought—but the closer he got, the worse the weather became, and even the protection spell he'd thrown up over himself was struggling.

For a moment, he considered dropping it, letting his father see him pathetic and bedraggled, but no, that kind of thing would only work on a father who had a heart, and Rhys was fairly certain Simon Penhallow had been born without one of those.

Or maybe he'd removed it himself at some point, some sort of experiment to see just how much of a bastard one man could be.

The wind howled down from the top of the hill, making the trees that lined the road creak and sway, and honestly, Rhys knew his father was an incredibly powerful witch, but he didn't have to be such a cliché about it.

Also a cliché: the Penhallow family manse, Penhaven Manor.

Rhys sometimes wondered how his family had managed to avoid being murdered over the five hundred years that they'd called the hulking pile of stone and obvious witchcraft home. They might as well have put signs in the front yard, HERE THERE BE WITCHES, for fuck's sake.

The house didn't so much sit on the hill as it crouched on it, only two stories tall, but sprawling, a warren of dark hallways and low ceilings and shadowy corners. One of the first spells Rhys had taught himself had been a basic illumination spell just so he could sodding well *see* things when trying to get to the breakfast table every morning.

He also sometimes wondered if the place would've been a little different, a little . . . lighter, if his mother had lived. She'd hated the house just as much as Rhys did, according to Wells, and had almost talked their father into moving to something smaller, something more modern and homier.

But then she died just a few months after Rhys was born, and any talk of moving out of this monster of a house had been squashed. Penhaven was home.

A terrifying, uncomfortable, medieval wreck of a home.

It always looked slightly crooked on first approach, the heavy wooden doors slouching on their hinges, and as Rhys climbed the front steps, he sighed, smoothing a hand over the air in front of him.

The Henley, jeans and boots he'd been wearing shimmered and rippled, transforming into a black suit with his family crest embroidered on the pocket. His father preferred they all wear robes in the house, but Rhys was only willing to go so far in the name of tradition.

He didn't bother knocking; his father would've known he was there the second he set foot on the hill, possibly even when he'd gone into the pub. There were guardian spells all over the place up here, a source of endless frustration to Rhys and his brothers whenever they'd been even a little bit late for curfew.

As Rhys placed his hand on the door, it swung open, groaning ominously on its hinges, and the wind and rain picked up, gusting strong enough that for just a second, Rhys's spell slipped.

Icy water slapped him in the face, trickling down the collar of his shirt and plastering his hair back against his head.

"Wonderful," he muttered. "Bloody wonderful."

And then he stepped inside.

CHAPTER 2

No matter what the weather looked like outside, the inside of Penhaven was always dim.

Rhys's father liked it best that way. Heavy velvet drapes covered most of the windows, and the few windows that were left uncovered were made of thick stained glass in dark shades of green and red, distorting the light that came through them, making strange shapes on the heavy stone table just inside the front door.

Rhys stood there in the entryway for a moment, looking up at the massive staircase and the life-size oil portrait that hung over it of Rhys, his father, and his two brothers. They were all wearing robes, all watching the front door solemnly, and every time Rhys saw the portrait he remembered being twelve and posing for it, hating how still he'd had to be, how sweltering and uncomfortable his robe was, how ridiculous it was that his father wouldn't let them just take a picture and have some painter paint from that.

But no, Father liked his traditions, and sweating one's balls off while sitting for a massive oil portrait was apparently right up there with cutting your own Yule log and attending Penhaven College in terms of Things Penhallow Men Do.

"Don't keep me waiting."

The voice boomed out from everywhere and nowhere, and Rhys sighed again, running a hand over his hair before jogging up the staircase.

His father would be in his library, the chosen theater for almost all confrontations between father and sons throughout the years, and as Rhys opened the heavy double doors leading to that room, he felt immediately transported back in time.

Not just in his own memories, although he had plenty of those from this room, but literally. His father's library was somehow, impossibly, even more Gothic than the rest of the house. There was black wood, more velvet, heavy silver candelabras covered in years of hardened wax. Overhead, a chandelier made of stag antlers cast gloomy light on the parquet floor, and Rhys had never longed for the bright light of his flat in London more. The open windows, the white linen on the bed, the comfortable couches that didn't dispel clouds of dust whenever anyone sat.

Not one velvet item—not so much as a fucking *pillow*—in the whole place.

No wonder he never came back here.

Simon Penhallow was standing in front of the large mirror he used for scrying and communicating with fellow witches, his hands clasped behind his back, wearing, as Rhys had predicted, his robes. Black ones, of course. His hair was black as well, although sprinkled through with gray, and as he turned around, Rhys thought he looked a little older now. A few more wrinkles around his eyes, more white in his beard.

"Do you know how long it's been since you were last in this house?" his father asked, and Rhys bit back a sarcastic reply.

He had at least three of them, but his father was never the biggest fan of Rhys's wit, so he just stepped into the room, mimicking his father's posture, hands behind his back. "I'm not sure, exactly."

"Half a year," his father replied because why say a normal thing like "six months"?

"It has been half a year since you last visited your father and your family home."

"Okay, but in my defense, that's still got to be better than Bowen, right?"

Rhys offered his father a grin, but as always, Simon was the one person Rhys had never been able to charm. "Bowen is involved in something that actually benefits this family. As opposed to you, living the bachelor life in England."

Rhys's father had a tendency to say "England" as though he meant *a sordid pit of debauchery*, and not for the first time, Rhys wondered if his father's idea of what his life must be like was not actually far more interesting than Rhys's actual life.

All right, to be fair, there was a bit of debauchery, but on the whole, Rhys lived as normal a life as most young men in their late twenties. He ran his travel business, he watched rugby at the pub with his mates, he dated.

Nothing out of the ordinary except for the role that magic played in all of those things.

His customers always had a smooth and easy trip. His favorite team always won. And while he never used magic on the women he dated, he might've used the occasional charm to make sure he could get a reservation at the restaurant he wanted, or that traffic would never be a hassle.

He didn't abuse his powers, but there was no doubt that magic made the path smoother, something Rhys had always appreciated.

"You are wasting your potential as a warlock," Simon went on, "engaging in all this frivolity."

"*Warlock* isn't a thing anymore, Father, I've told you, we're all witches now. Have been for literal decades."

Ignoring that, Simon continued, "It is time for you to likewise do your duty for this family, Rhys. Which is why I'm sending you back to Glynn Bedd."

Glynn Bedd.

Graves Glen.

Vivienne.

He didn't think of her that often. It had been years; what they'd had burned hot but brief, and there had been other, more serious relationships since her.

But every once in a while, she came to mind. Her pretty smile. Her hazel eyes. The way she'd tug at the ends of her honey-blond hair when she was nervous.

How she tasted.

No, definitely not a helpful memory right this second.

Better to remember her angry tears, her arms crossed over her chest, the pair of jeans she'd thrown at his head.

Christ, what a wanker he'd been.

Shaking himself slightly, he stepped closer to his father and said, "Graves Glen? Why?"

Simon scowled at him, the hollows beneath his cheekbones deepening.

"It's the anniversary of the founding of the town and the college," Simon said. "A Penhallow must be there. Your brothers have other responsibilities, as do I, so it will be you. You should leave as soon as possible, and I'll see to it that the house is prepared for you."

He waved one elegant, long-fingered hand. "You are dismissed."

"I fucking am not," Rhys countered, and Simon straightened up. Rhys was over six feet, but his father, like Wells, had him beat by an inch or two, something Rhys felt profoundly in this moment. Still, he held his ground.

"Da," he said, reverting to the name he hadn't used since he was a child. "You know their whole 'Founder's Day's' thing has nothing to do with us now, right? It's basically a Halloween party. They sell pumpkins, for Christ's sake, Da. Little painted ones. I think there are stuffed bats involved. It's nothing that requires our presence."

"And yet our presence will be felt because you will be there," his father said. "Every twenty-five years, a Penhallow must return to strengthen the ley lines, and this year, that Penhallow shall be you."

Bollocks.

He'd forgotten about the ley lines.

A hundred years ago, his ancestor, Gryffud Penhallow, had founded the town of Glyn Bedd in the mountains of North Georgia in a spot where the veil was weak and magic was strong. Naturally, the town had called to witches over the years, and the college there, named after the Penhallow family home, taught both regular classes to humans and the arcane arts to witches.

Not that the humans who attended the college knew that. They just assumed the Historical Folklore and Practice major was exceedingly hard to get into and also accepted a fuckton of transfer students.

Rhys had been one of those transfer students nine years ago, just for summer classes, and he had several reasons—well, one very big one—not to want to go back.

"How do you know that, by the way?" his father asked now, narrowing his eyes slightly. "About Founder's Day. You didn't stay long enough to witness it the last time you were there."

Because I occasionally have one whisky too many and see what The One Who Got Away is up to and she still lives there which is why I definitely don't want to go back was the truth, but, Rhys suspected, not the answer to give here.

"That town is our family legacy, Da," he said instead. "I've kept up with what's going on there."

Rhys was certain the look on his father's face wasn't pride

because he was equally certain that Simon taking pride in anything Rhys said or did would cause a rip in the fabric of space
and time, but at the very least, his father didn't look actively irritated with him, and that was something.

And he hated that that still mattered to him. The last time
he'd tried to win his father's approval, it had ended up costing
him Vivienne.

All right, so part of that had been his own utter idiocy in not
bothering to mention that he'd agreed to let his father find him
the perfect witch bride, but all of it had felt so far away, and Vivienne had been right there, real and immediate, not some abstract
concept of a woman, and it had been so easy to put off telling her.

Until it wasn't and she had, quite rightly, called him every
name in the book, including some he'd never heard of, and
stormed out.

And now his father was asking him to go back.

"Do this for your family. Do this for me," Simon said, coming
over to lay his hands on Rhys's shoulders. "Go to Glynn Bedd."

He was nearly thirty years old. He ran a successful business
that he'd started all on his own, lived a life he loved, was a goddamn *adult* and did not need his father's approval.

And still Rhys heard himself say, "Fine. I'll go."

"I TOLD YOU not to go to a Solstice Revel, I told you they were
nothing but trouble."

Head still on the bar, Rhys lifted a hand to give his brother a
double-fingered salute.

He heard Llewellyn sniff. "Well, I did."

"Yes, and I ignored your brotherly advice to my peril, thank you, Wells, very helpful."

He'd made his way back to the pub after his chat with Simon, and this time, he'd actually managed to have that pint.

Which was probably the only reason he'd confessed all to Wells. Not just that Da was sending him to Graves Glen, but about that summer nine years ago.

About Vivienne and all the ways he'd mucked it right up.

Rhys lifted his head to see that Llewellyn had moved over to the taps, pouring another pint that Rhys very much hoped was for him. This was clearly a Two Pint Conversation.

"Did you love her?" Wells asked.

Rhys fought very hard not to squirm on the barstool. His family didn't usually go in for this sort of thing, talking about feelings and such. Wells didn't even have feelings, as far as Rhys could tell, and any emotions Bowen might have were reserved for whatever it was he was doing out there in the mountains.

"I was twenty," he said at last, draining the rest of his lager. "And it was summer, and she was beautiful."

So beautiful. And so bloody sweet. He'd felt like someone had hit him solidly in the chest when he'd seen her there at the Solstice Revel, standing under a violet sky, a flower crown crooked on her head. She'd smiled at him, and it had been . . .

Instant. Irrevocable.

A fucking disaster.

"I . . . felt . . . ," he said now, remembering, "as though I might . . . have loving feelings."

St. Bugi's balls, that had been hard. How did people just go about talking like this all the time?

Wells folded his arms on the bar, leaning in. He had their father's slightly austere features and a sort of resting glare face that Rhys had always found a little alarming, but his eyes were the same clear blue as Rhys's own. "Maybe you won't even see her," Wells offered. "You'll just be there for what? A day, maybe two?" His smirk turned wry. "That's about the maximum you can give to one location, correct?"

Ignoring the jab, Rhys nodded. "I'm going to leave tomorrow. Founder's Day is the day after. Get in, charge the lines, get out."

"Easy-peasy, then," Wells said, spreading his hands, and Rhys nodded again even as another vision of Vivienne's tear-stained face seemed to float in front of him.

"The peasiest."

CHAPTER 3

The stack of papers on Vivi's desk was screaming.

Well, wailing, really, a sort of high-pitched shriek.

Frowning, she turned away from her computer and the email she'd been sending her department head to study the papers there on the corner as they emitted a high sort of wailing sound.

With narrowed eyes, Vivi reached for the essays, tossing one after another onto her desk until she found the one she was looking for. Not only did it appear to be shrieking, but the typed letters were slowly bleeding into red.

"Cheater, cheater, pumpkin eater," she muttered as she checked the name typed in the top corner.

Hainsley Barnes.

Ah yes, Mr. Lacrosse. No shock there, then. He'd missed her last few classes, and apparently no one from last semester had bothered to tell him that Ms. Jones was particularly good at sussing out cheaters.

Being a witch had so many unexpected perks.

Smoothing her hand over the paper, Vivi removed the spell,

watching the words turn back to black as the piercing whine slowly faded away, then flagged it with a red Post-it before tossing it in a drawer.

"What in god's name was that sound?"

Vivi's favorite colleague in the history department, Ezichi, stood in the doorway, wrinkling her nose, and, as the paper continued to whimper in Vivi's desk, she gave the drawer a discreet punch.

"Alarm on my phone," she answered as the sound abruptly cut off. "Reminding me that I was supposed to wrap up here, uh . . ." She checked the time on her computer.

Shit.

"Thirty minutes ago."

It was the third time this week she'd been late for the family dinner her aunt Elaine was so fanatical about, but such was midterm.

Vivi shot up from her desk, grabbing her jacket from the back of the chair and her purse as Ezi pointed at her.

"Girl, do not disappoint the woman who makes my favorite bath salts," she said, and Vivi reached into her bag, pulling out a small muslin sack.

"Speaking of, she said to give these to you, so thanks for reminding me."

Ezi took the bag from Vivi like it contained precious gems, holding it to her chest and taking a deep breath. "No offense, Vivi, but I love your aunt more than I love you."

"None taken," Vivi said. "She's magic."

Literally, not that Ezi knew that. Vivi had made the decision when she'd finished her undergrad at Penhaven College that she'd do a master's in history. Regular, human history, and that she'd teach regular, human kids, as opposed to the witches that took Penhaven's other, slightly more secretive classes.

So far it was a decision she hadn't regretted even if she did suspect she worked a lot harder teaching Intro to World Civ than she would have if she'd been teaching Ritual Candle-Making.

As Vivi jogged up the steps and out of the basement that housed the history department's junior lecturers' offices, she pulled on her jacket and attempted to text Gwyn at the same time.

Runing latr.

As soon as she hit the doors, her phone pinged in her hand.

I speak Vivi, so I know that means you're running late. Don't text and drive. Or text and walk, either.

Grinning, Vivi headed out into the quad. It wasn't dark yet, and the October night was pretty mild even up here in the mountains.

Nestled in the valley, Penhaven College was a little gem of redbrick buildings and green grass, tall oak trees and neatly trimmed hedges, and Vivi loved it more than a person should probably love her workplace.

But she did love it. Especially now with the first hint of fall in the air, the leaves orange, the sky purple. Penhaven was always at its best in the autumn.

So was all of Graves Glen. Vivi noticed that the decorations for tomorrow's Founder's Day, the beginning of Graves Glen's big Halloween season, were up. There were the electric candles in the window of The Written Wyrd, the town's bookshop, and plastic pumpkin decals stuck to the door of Coffee Cauldron. Of course, Elaine and Gwyn's store, Something Wicked, was all decked out, and Vivi was pretty sure she even spotted a dangling bat in front of her accountant's office.

She hadn't grown up in this little slice of perfection in the North Georgia mountains. Her parents had lived in Atlanta, and while Vivi missed them both a lot, she'd always be grateful she'd landed here in this spot that felt tailor-made for her somehow. This perfect small town where she could balance being a witch *and* a regular woman. Best of both worlds.

Elaine's house was set high on a hill at the end of a winding road, and as Vivi drove up under the bright orange and red leaves, her tires bumping on the dirt road, she felt her shoulders start to relax a little, and once the cabin came into sight, she actually sighed with happiness.

Home.

Once she'd parked behind Elaine's ancient Volvo, Vivi jogged up the front steps, past the grinning pumpkins and dangling bats and little lights in the shape of purple witches.

Aunt Elaine always went all-in for Halloween.

Just inside, Vivi stopped to pet Sir Purrcival where he was curled up in his basket. He was massive now, a hulking mass of black fur and green eyes who adored Gwyn and tolerated Elaine and Vivi, and she considered herself lucky when he only took the laziest of swats at her hand before settling back into sleep.

"I know, I'm late again!" Vivi called out as she gave him one last pet.

Elaine drifted into the hallway, her ash-blond hair piled messily on top of her head, her black skirts brushing the floor.

If Stevie Nicks taught middle school art was the way Gwyn always described her mother's look, and that was not far off. But it worked on Aunt Elaine in a way Vivi never could've pulled off. She'd stick to her floral prints and polka dots.

"You know," Aunt Elaine said, placing a beringed hand on her hip, "if you'd just come to work for me, you would be around all the time and never have to worry about being late."

An old argument, and one that, as usual, Vivi waved off. "You two do fine without me."

Something Wicked sold various witchy things, from candles to scarves to soap, with the occasional homemade jam thrown in. Business always picked up this time of year, thanks to Founder's Day, but it wasn't unusual for them to go days without a single sale, so Elaine and Gwyn could easily run the place by themselves.

"We might do even better with you, though," Elaine said as Vivi moved down the hallway and into the kitchen.

Of all the rooms in the house, this one always felt the most witchy. Copper pots hanging from hooks on the ceiling, little pots of herbs all along the windowsill, Elaine's candle-making supplies cluttered on the table.

The effect was only slightly spoiled by Gwyn standing by the stove, wearing a T-shirt that said, *Witch Don't Kill My Vibe*, and eating macaroni and cheese out of the pot.

"Business has picked up so much in the last few years," Elaine went on, languidly moving back toward the table. "Gwyn can barely keep up with the online orders."

Gwyn nodded, her messy bun of red hair nearly coming undone. "Everyone's a witch these days," she said, mouth full. "We sold, like, a hundred sets of tarot cards last month alone."

Vivi raised her eyebrows as she went to the fridge to grab a bottle of wine. "Jeez, seriously?" Her aunt's business had always been more of a hobby than an actual moneymaker, but Elaine had refused to get anything resembling a real job, and Gwyn wasn't all that inclined to join the workforce, either.

"Self-care and all that," she said now, placing the pot back on the stove and crossing one foot over the other. Glancing down, Vivi could see she was wearing the bright-green-and-black-striped socks that were perpetual bestsellers at Something Wicked.

"Tarot cards, crystals, candles, grimoires . . ." Gwyn ticked the items off on her fingers. "We can barely keep things in stock. I'm going to have to hire someone just to handle the online store. You could totally do that."

"I like my job," Vivi insisted, and the truth was, she did. Sure, there were the occasional Lacrosse Cheaters, but she could more than handle them, and she loved going to work on Penhaven's campus. She loved going to the big cafeteria for lunch, loved her office with its comfy chairs. Loved sharing her own love of history with her students. All in all, it was a good fit, and it made her feel . . . stable. Safe.

Two of Vivi's favorite words.

As Vivi opened the wine, Gwyn's phone buzzed, and she sighed.

"I swear to the goddess, if this is another text about Founder's Day shit, I am going to go full Carrie on this town."

"The mayor," Elaine said to Vivi in a stage whisper. "She keeps texting Gwyn about Founder's Day because she has a crush on her and this is her way of getting Gwyn to pay attention to her."

"A solid move," Vivi allowed, pouring herself some wine, and Gwyn rolled her eyes.

"I've already slept with her, Mom, it's not that."

"Also a solid move." Vivi lifted her glass and, distracted, Gwyn clinked her own against it.

"No, she's just freaking out because it's her first Founder's Day as mayor and she wants everything to go well," Gwyn said, her fingers moving rapidly over the phone, "and she's a normal human, not a witch, so you can see where these kinds of things stress her out."

"Does she know you're a witch?" Vivi asked, and Gwyn blew a raspberry.

"God, no. That is privileged information one only gets after the fourth date."

"You never go on a fourth date, darling," Elaine said, lining up her candles on the table.

"Exactly," Gwyn said with a wink.

She went to put her phone back in her pocket only to have it buzz again, and she groaned. "Jane, honestly, you're hot, but the sex was not good enough to warrant—oh, shit."

"What?" Vivi and Elaine asked in unison as Gwyn stared at her phone, her eyes wide.

"Um. Nothing. Nothing at all. She sent me a nude. I'm shocked and scandalized. By the nude."

Hastily shoving her phone in her back pocket, Gwyn picked up her wine and turned her attention to Vivi. "So! How is teaching the normies going?"

"Uh-uh," Vivi said, placing a hand on her hip. "You are the worst liar in the entire world, Gwynnevere Jones. What did Jane say that made you make that face?"

Gwyn looked between Vivi and Elaine, who was watching her with eyebrows raised, and finally groaned, wine sloshing out of her glass as she threw up her hands.

"Because it's the hundredth anniversary of the town's founding, they're sending a Penhallow."

For a long moment, there was nothing but silence in the kitchen as all three women took that in.

A Penhallow.

Vivi sipped her wine. There were lots of Penhallows. Okay, there were four that she knew about. Simon Penhallow, Terrifying Witch, and his three sons.

One of whom had shattered her heart into a billion pieces when she was nineteen.

Which had been a long time ago.

And was a thing she had completely moved past.

Mostly.

"It might not be him," Elaine finally said, turning back to her candles. "Might be that nightmare of a father of his."

"Probably is," Vivi agreed. "One hundredth is a big deal. And while Rhys might have changed a lot in the past nine years, I still don't see him as being the one you'd send for big ceremonial things, right?"

"Oh, totally," Gwyn said, nodding and pouring more wine into her glass. "You send in Rhys for the fun shit like Solstice Revels and those weird summer courses the college offers. You don't send him in to charge the ley lines."

"Of course you don't," Vivi said.

"I'm sure they wouldn't dream of it," Elaine declared, tapping the table for emphasis.

"But," Gwyn added slowly. "Maybe we should check?"

CHAPTER 4

"We haven't done witchy shit together in ages!"

Vivi stood in Gwyn's bedroom feeling the oddest sense of déjà vu.

It wasn't like she hadn't been in here tons of times since the night of all that weirdness after Rhys. She had.

But it was the first time she'd been back up on an autumn night with a salt circle on the floor and magic afoot.

"Gwyn, our entire lives are witchy shit," she reminded her cousin as she attempted to sit on the floor in her pencil skirt, but Gwyn just shook her head, turning around with her arms full. Vivi spotted at least three candles, an altar cloth, a silver bowl and a small black bag done up with a gold clasp.

"No, I mean the real-deal kind of witchy shit," she said, lowering herself to the hardwood. "Coven-type stuff. Getting our *The Craft* on."

Smiling, Vivi hiked up her skirt, crossed her legs, and took a sip of her wine.

"Not since the night Rhys and I broke up," she said, and Gwyn waved her off.

"That didn't count. That wasn't real magic. The last time we did *real* magic was . . . senior year? Maybe? That Beltane."

Remembering, Vivi nodded. "Okay, well, as long as we don't accidentally summon demons, I'm in."

"It was just that once, and technically it was a very pissed off elemental spirit."

Vivi shot Gwyn a look over the rim of her glass. "Do you remember how long it took my eyebrows to grow back?"

Dropping her pile of supplies onto the little rug in the middle of the floor, Gwyn heaved a sigh. "Vivi, if you bring bad energy into this, it's not going to work."

"I feel like you're just saying that to get out of the Eyebrow Conversation."

Gwyn didn't reply to that, opening the little black bag and pulling out a deck of tarot cards.

"Ooh," Vivi said, reaching for the deck, but Gwyn batted her hand away.

"No touching! Not until I'm ready."

"But I haven't seen this one before," Vivi said, and Gwyn grinned, spreading the cards out on the floor. Even in the dim lamplight, their colors practically glowed, and Vivi caught a glimpse of a diaphanous white gown on The Empress, bright butter yellow on The Sun.

Gwyn had been painting her own cards for years, ever since they were teenagers, and not for the first time, Vivi felt a little pang in her heart looking at her cousin's handiwork. Not just because the cards were beautiful, although they definitely were, but because Gwyn always seemed so connected to her craft in a way that Vivi had just never felt. Sure, she liked doing the occasional spell, and her little apartment over the store contained more candles than was probably wise, but she'd never had this. Never had what Gwyn and Elaine had, this ease with magic. Both of them did spells, big and small, as easily as breathing, and yet every time Vivi used magic, even the little things like her anti-cheater spell, something in her . . . paused.

Held back.

There were times she wished her mom had been a little more open about the whole witch thing. Maybe if she'd grown up doing magic, she'd feel more comfortable with it now.

Shaking her head, Vivi pushed that thought away.

It didn't matter now. She had exactly as much magic as she liked, no more, no less.

Gwyn had set the silver bowl on the rug and affixed a fat white candle to the bottom of it. Now, she ran her hands over her cards, humming softly as she slid one from the deck.

The Magician was dressed in bright red robes, a white crystal crown on her head, and Vivi smiled as she realized the figure was clearly modeled on Elaine. She could even spot Sir Purrcival winding himself around her ankles, his eyes a glittering green.

"So," Gwyn said before taking a sip of her own wine. "First things first, we find out if you have any bad luck right now. Bad luck, they send Rhys. Good luck, it's one of his brothers or his dad. Maybe a hot cousin."

"That seems much more likely," Vivi admitted, as Gwyn lit the candle in the silver bowl. "I mean, Rhys hated dealing with family stuff. I can't imagine he'd want to come back here."

Not after I threw his own pants at him and called him . . . something bad?

"We'll soon find out," Gwyn said, pulling four more cards from her tarot deck.

She slid The Magician in with them, her long fingers dexterous as she shuffled the five cards, sliding them back and forth over one another until Gwyn had no idea just where The Magician had ended up.

"Okay. The simple part. Turn over these cards one at a time," Gwyn said, laying the cards facedown on the floor. "If The Magician pops up in the first three, bad luck."

Frowning, Vivi studied the cards in front of her. Gwyn had painted the backs, too, a swirling pattern of green and purple spirals, and Vivi let her fingers dance over them for a moment before turning over the first card.

A man stood at the edge of a cliff, one foot lifted like he was seconds from stepping off, his eyes blue over the rim of a pair of sunglasses, his shirt unbuttoned to the middle of his sternum.

Vivi's heart did a little flip-flop in her chest because that sure was a familiar face.

Then she looked at what card it was.

"The Fool?" she asked, lifting her eyes to Gwyn's.

Gwyn just shrugged, leaning back on her hands. "I take inspiration from everywhere, and when it came time to paint that one, he just . . . leapt to mind. Am I wrong?"

The Fool was all about risks and chances, leaping without looking, so no, Rhys was not necessarily a bad model for that card. Still . . .

"So is this bad?" Vivi asked. She lifted it between her thumb and index finger, shaking the card slightly. "Does this mean it *is* him?"

"No," Gwyn said firmly, shaking her head. "Well. I mean. Probably not? I don't know. Let's see what the next card is."

Vivi turned over the next one.

The Magician, wearing her aunt's calm face, stared back up at her.

"Rhiannon's tits," Gwyn said, sitting up so fast that her knee nearly clocked her glass. "They are sending him."

Vivi wished her pulse hadn't suddenly sped up at that, wished her hands weren't trembling slightly as she reached out to flip over the last three cards.

The Star, which was clearly Vivi, standing on a desk in a classroom in a polka dot dress, an apple in one hand, a glowing orb in the other; The Tower, Elaine's cabin, but with a massive crack up the center of it, half the house sliding off a cliff; and last, The Moon, which was a . . .

"Werewolf?" Vivi asked, holding up the card for Gwyn, who rolled her eyes and plucked it from Vivi's fingers.

"Do not question my artistic vision, Vivienne," she said, sliding The Moon along with the other four cards back into her deck.

The two of them sat there on the floor, staring at the candles, and finally Vivi said, "So this is dumb."

Gwyn glanced up. "Which part? Him coming? Us finding out he's coming? You feeling weird about him coming? How many times I've said the word 'coming'?"

"All of the above," Vivi said, rising to her feet and sliding her skirt back into place. "Look, this was always bound to happen. His family founded this town and the college, the college where, let me add, I happen to work. He's part of this place. I knew that when I got involved with him. And!" She lifted a finger in the air. "I have had many boyfriends since him!"

"To be fair, you've had three."

"Which is more than two, which is 'a couple,' so therefore is many, Gwyn, *whose side are you on*?"

"Yours," Gwyn hastily acknowledged. "One hundred percent."

"It's no big deal," Vivi went on as she searched for her shoes near Gwyn's bed. "He'll come, he'll do his whole Founder's Day 'Ooh, Look at Me I'm Fancy' thing, and stuff will go back to how it was. I can continue to live a Penhallow-free life."

"Except for the part where there's a statue to his ancestor downtown and also your workplace is literally named after his house."

"Except for that."

"Remember when we pretended to curse him?" Gwyn asked, grinning as she shuffled her cards, and Vivi snorted.

"Something about his dimples and never being able to find a clitoris again."

"Which," Gwyn said, tilting her head to one side, "now that I think about it was actually more a curse against any women he dated, and I kind of regret that. For the sisterhood."

Laughing, Vivi shook her head. "It doesn't matter anyway. I may have done the occasional light social media stalking, and he seems . . . fine."

Better than fine, really. He was still handsome, apparently ran some super chic travel business that took groups all over the world to do various glam things and probably still knew *exactly* where the clitoris was. She and Gwyn had just been two silly, drunk witches, joking around and lucky that no actual magic had been employed. Whatever had happened with that candle had been a fluke, clearly.

Vivi had just reached down to slip on her boots when Gwyn's bedroom door flew open.

"Mom!" Gwyn yelped, leaping to her feet. "Did the Daniel Spencer Incident teach you nothing?"

Elaine just waved a hand at that even as Sir Purrcival lurched into the room, meowing balefully at all of them. "Well?" she asked, and Vivi walked over to Gwyn's desk, leaning against it.

"Cards say yes," she said, and Elaine looked briefly at the ceiling, muttering something under her breath.

"*But,*" Vivi said, pointing with her empty wineglass, "as I was just telling Gwyn, it's actually not that big of a deal. We're all grown-ups here, and it's not like he'll stay long. I'm telling you, I bet I won't even see him."

CHAPTER 5

Rhys wasn't sure what he'd done to the universe to deserve this day.

First there'd been the flight. That had gone well enough, but it had been long, and getting a rental car in Atlanta had been frustrating, though no more so than navigating Atlanta traffic to make his way north had been. There had been one point, feeling profoundly discombobulated on the wrong side of the car on the wrong side of the road, staring at the back of a semitruck in front of him, that Rhys had nearly broken and called his father to grudgingly ask for a Traveling Stone for his return journey.

He hadn't ended up sacrificing his pride on that particular altar and had survived the drive to Graves Glen with his sanity intact, but once he'd gotten into the town, it had been one clusterfuck after another.

He'd gotten a speeding ticket roughly five seconds after he'd passed the sign welcoming him to Graves Glen. Annoying and expensive (and, to his mind, slightly unjust, given that he was only going ten miles over and the town wouldn't bloody well exist without his family), but not enough to ruin his day.

No, that had come just half an hour ago when, halfway up the hillside leading to the Penhallow home, he'd blown a tire.

By that point, his patience had been too low to do something so perverse as change it himself, so he'd waved his hand at the thing to repair it only to have the tire blow up to twice its normal size before popping like a goddamn balloon.

And when he'd attempted to float the spare out of the boot of the car, it had gone madly spinning into a tree before rolling down the hill.

Which meant that he was stuck in the woods at night, a good half mile from the house, mud covering his best boots, and his magic apparently on the fritz.

Marvelous.

This, Rhys thought as he reached into the back seat to pull out his bag, was why he should've stayed in Wales. Hell, he could've run the pub while Llewellyn dealt with all of this. Wells probably wouldn't have insisted on flying and driving. Wells would've been sensible and used the Traveling Stone, been in and out in a flash, and Rhys might have discovered some heretofore undiscovered talent for pulling pints. Might've changed his whole life.

But no, Wells was back at The Raven and Crown, and Rhys was here, on a hillside in Georgia with a completely useless car, and he would bet the entire contents of his wallet that his father hadn't seen fit to stock the house with any kind of alcohol.

He had just started the trudge up the hill when he heard the sound of a car approaching.

Sending up a prayer to the goddess that his luck had actually turned for the better, Rhys shouldered his bag, waving his arms over his head as the headlights coming down the hill nearly blinded him.

Rhys made sure to stand near the edge of the road and look as affable as possible, smiling even as he squinted in the glare, and he was still smiling even as the car . . . didn't stop.

And not only did it not stop, it seemed to be veering slightly to the right.

He was on the right.

Rhys had only a moment of dazed thought—*this person is going to hit me, I am going to die on a hill in Georgia, what an utterly shite way to go*—before he dove out of the way. Distantly, he heard the squeal of brakes, smelled burning rubber, but given that he had just thrown himself down the side of a steep hill, he had slightly more pressing concerns.

Like stopping this slide into darkness and, if possible, saving his leather jacket.

The jacket was clearly not going to make it—he heard a truly awful tearing sound as he threw one arm out and clutched at a stray root—but the rest of him was all in one piece as he came to a stop several yards down the hill from the road.

Above him, he could still see the glow of headlights, and he heard a car door open and slam shut, and then the crunching of leaves underfoot as someone rushed toward the hill he was currently at the bottom of.

"Oh my god, oh my god, oh my god," a very familiar voice breathed, and ah, yes, yes, of *course*.

The universe still clearly hated him.

"I am so sorry!" Vivienne cried as she made her way down the hill, and Rhys turned his head to see her making her way toward him, her arms out to one side. She was just a silhouette, a dark figure against even more darkness, but even if he hadn't heard her voice, he would've recognized her, would've known that shape anywhere.

Even after nine years.

Even in the dark.

Fuck's sake.

Rhys let his head drop back to the ground as he studied the sky above him and waited for the inevitable moment when she'd figure out who she'd almost hit and possibly get back in her car and finish the job.

"I didn't even see you until you'd jumped," he heard her say from very close now. "And it was the weirdest thing, it was like the brakes just locked up, and the steering wheel had a mind of its—oof!"

Rhys's hands came up automatically as Vivienne tripped over his prone form, but it was too late to catch her, and now he got to add a seriously sharp elbow to the testicles to his list of grievances.

"I'm sorry!" she said again, scrambling to push herself up, her body half draped over his even as he attempted to curl in on himself.

"No worries," he managed to wheeze, and then her hands were on his chest, her hair hanging down in his face, brushing his lips.

"Rhys?"

Some of the pressure on his chest eased as she lifted a hand, and with a flick of her fingers, a soft light hovered over the pair of them there on the ground.

Any hope he'd had that whatever he'd felt for her nine years ago had been a mad mix of summer and magic and hormones was immediately squashed as he looked into those hazel eyes, took in her flushed cheeks and her parted lips.

Likewise, any hope that she might have forgiven him in the intervening years died a groaning death as she narrowed her eyes and said, "I shouldn't have tried to slow down."

"Good to see you, too, Vivienne," he said, still a little breathless from his slide down the hill and near emasculation.

Pushing herself off him, Vivienne rose to her feet and began brushing the leaves and various debris from her skirt.

Her polka dot skirt.

Her whole dress was polka dot, he saw now, little orange ones on a black background.

Had he always found polka dots so instantly, intensely erotic?

Wasn't really a thing he'd considered before, and it was possible he'd hit his head somewhere in his fall, but there was nothing for it now. Polka dots had replaced black lace and red satin in any sexual fantasy he might have for the rest of his life.

The light she'd conjured up still floated by her head, and as she picked the last stray leaf off her black jacket, she looked back down at him.

"Why were you on the road?" she asked, and he nodded back up the hill.

"Flat tire."

Vivienne snorted, pulling her jacket tighter around her as another gust of wind rustled the trees. "So you couldn't change it magically *or* physically?"

"Having a bit of a night, to tell the truth."

"Same."

"And why were *you* on this road, Vivienne? Did you hear I was coming back?"

"Don't flatter yourself. My aunt still lives on this road, and I was heading home from dinner with her and Gwyn."

"Ah, Gwyn," he said, remembering her cousin, a pink-haired witch who, he suspected, had hated him on sight.

Smart girl.

"How is she? And your aunt?"

Vivienne sighed, tipping her head back to look at the sky. "How about we not do this?" she said, and Rhys rolled onto his side, propping himself up on one elbow.

"What, talk to one another?"

"Make small talk," Vivienne said, looking down her nose at him. "Neither of us is any good at it."

For a long moment, they stared at each other, Rhys still on the ground, Vivienne standing above him, and he remembered they'd been in a similar position the last time he'd seen her, right after she'd leapt out of his bed when he'd told her that he had to go back to Wales to get out of his betrothal.

Looking back on it now, it was easy to see that he had perhaps not handled that conversation as well as he could have, but he'd thought she'd understand. She was a witch, too, after all; she knew all about betrothals.

As his jeans hitting him in the head had swiftly taught him, Vivienne did *not* in fact know all about betrothals, and that whole magical summer had come to a literally screaming halt.

Until now.

"I'm here for the ley lines," he finally said, sitting up and shaking the twigs out of his hair.

"I know that," she replied, crossing her arms over her chest. "Cutting it kind of close, aren't you? Only showing up the night before Founder's Day?"

"I didn't want to spend much time here," he said, then gave her a sardonic grin. "Can't imagine why, given the warm welcome and all."

Rolling her eyes, Vivienne turned to head back up the hill. "Okay, well, I'd say I was sorry about nearly killing you, but we both know that's a lie, so I'll leave you to find your own way home."

"Or," Rhys offered, coming to his feet, "you could be the absolute darling I know you are and give me a ride?"

She spun around, that light still bobbing like a demented fire-fly. "And why would I do that?"

"Well," Rhys said, lifting a finger, "for one, I *am* in town for altruistic purposes that benefit you and your family. Two"—another finger—"when you were on top of me, I did not make a single pervy reference to other times we'd found ourselves in that position."

"Except that you're doing that now, but continue."

"And three . . ." Rhys lifted the last finger, then looked down at his hand and frowned. "Actually, number three *was* going to be a pervy reference to our past, so probably best you leave me here to die."

To his surprise, the corner of her mouth ticked up a little at that.

Not quite a smile, certainly nothing as robust as a laugh, but it was something. She had liked him once, after all. Quite a lot, really.

And he'd liked her, too. That had been the worst part of it all when it ended. Rhys had never met anyone he liked just as much as he lusted for, and it had made missing her ten times worse.

Even now, battered and bruised and possibly standing in squirrel shit, he was . . . happy. Glad to see her, brush with ve-hicular homicide aside.

Maybe coming back wouldn't be so bad after all,

And then she turned away with a "Sounds good!"

The light above her blinked out and Rhys stood, dumbfounded, as she marched up the hill, never once looking back at him.

He was still standing there when he heard her car door open and close, the engine start, and the tires crunch down the dirt road.

In the aftermath, the only sounds were the wind picking up yet again and the faint skittering of some nocturnal animal.

"Fair play, I suppose," Rhys said to the darkness. "Fair play."

Sighing, he looked back up the hill and picked up his bag from where it had landed, and slinging it over his shoulder, lifted his free hand to summon up his own light.

His fingers sparked, and a bolt of flame suddenly shot out, hitting the nearest tree limb and sending it crashing to earth with a crack and a smell suspiciously like burned hair.

"Right," Rhys said, stomping on the smoldering leaves and actually grateful that he could feel the first fat droplets of rain start to fall.

The sooner he was out of Graves Glen, the better.

CHAPTER 6

"So you just left him there."

"Gwyn, I've told you the story three times already. And that's just today. I texted it to you, *and* called you about it last night."

Vivi reached up to readjust the little papier-mâché witch hanging over the cash register at Something Wicked, and Gwyn, standing behind the counter, leaned forward, putting her chin in her hands.

"I know, but it's my favorite story. I want it played at both my wedding and my funeral. I want to do it as a dramatic monologue at an open mic night. I want—"

"I get it," Vivi said, laughing as she held up her hand, "but seriously, it wasn't that big of a deal."

"You almost ran your ex-boyfriend over with a car, and then left him lying in the literal dirt on the side of the road. It is *such* a big deal, you absolute queen."

Vivi smiled again, but if she were being honest, she still felt a little . . . well, not guilty, exactly. Rhys was a powerful witch, and he'd been maybe a half mile from the Penhallow house. He could take care of himself.

But maybe it had been kind of bitchy to just leave him there, especially after he'd been surprisingly chill about the whole "nearly run over" thing.

Of course, that wasn't actually surprising. "Chill" was Rhys's default setting, after all.

And charming.

He'd been really freaking charming last night.

Suppressing a sigh, she moved over to the display of crystal balls, running her hands over the nearest one.

Elaine's store was just as cozy and perfect as her house and today, decked out for Founder's Day, it was at its absolute best. Candles had been lit, filling the store with the smell of bay and sage, and crystals were spilled out on black velvet tablecloths like recently discovered jewels.

Even Gwyn looked magical and mystical today, decked out in a clingy black dress and knee-high suede boots, her long red hair curling around her face.

Vivi was a little more subtle in her black pants and purple striped sweater, but then she was just the local history teacher, not the proprietress of the town's witch shop.

Besides, she'd been distracted this morning.

She'd spent a solid ten minutes in the shower replaying last night, and for all the time that had passed, for all the tears she'd cried over the awful way it had ended, when she'd looked down into those blue eyes, that same hank of dark hair falling over his forehead, that same lazy grin, her heart had knocked solidly against her ribs, her stomach had dropped and she wasn't even going to *think* about what certain other parts of her had done.

Needless to say, her body definitely remembered how much it had liked his, which was deeply unfair and, quite frankly, treasonous of it.

Taking a deep breath, she closed her eyes and reminded herself of the mantra she'd come up with driving away from him last night.

He is the worst, he is the worst, he is the actual, literal worst.

It probably wasn't that enlightened a mantra, but it got the job done, and when she opened her eyes, it was a little easier to remember there were good reasons she'd left without a second glance, both nine years ago and last night.

"Were you just picturing having sex with him?"

Vivi glared at Gwyn. "No," she lied, and was saved from any more questions by the ringing of the chime over the door.

"We're not open yet!" Gwyn called out, but it wasn't an early Founder's Day customer coming in, it was the mayor.

Vivi looked over at Jane Ellis, a tiny brunette who had a seriously great stiletto game. Today's pair were bright orange, working nicely with her black suit and the skull studs in her ears.

"Have either of you seen Rhys Penhallow?" she asked, her fingers moving over her phone even as she looked between Gwyn and Vivi.

"I haven't," Gwyn said slowly, looking over at Vivi.

Clearing her throat, Vivi stepped forward and, with supreme

effort, kept from fidgeting with her hands. Gwyn always said that was her tell.

"I bumped into him last night?" she offered. "He was on his way up to the house."

With a frustrated sound, Jane looked down at her phone. "Well, he's due to give the Founder's Day speech in twenty minutes, and he has yet to check in at the welcome booth."

Vivi relaxed a little. Okay, if that was the only cause for concern, maybe Rhys wasn't actually lying dead in a ditch on the side of the mountain. The words "welcome booth" were probably up there with "fiscal responsibility" and "ethical monogamy" in terms of phrases he'd shy away from.

"I haven't been able to reach him on his phone, but maybe I'm fucking up the whole international number thing, I don't know," Jane went on. "In any case, Founder's Day can't start until we do all the speeches, and he's on the program."

She looked up at Gwyn, beseeching. *"He's on. The. Program."*

"He'll turn up," Vivi said, laying a reassuring hand on Jane's arm only to step back slightly because, good god, the woman was actually vibrating; how much coffee had she consumed this morning?

"Vivi could go look for him," Gwyn said, and Vivi wondered if some witches had the power to kill with their minds because that sure would be handy right about now.

"I mean," Gwyn went on, barely suppressing her grin, "you've never met him, Jane, and he and Vivi are old friends."

"Really?" Jane turned to Vivi and for the barest second, her fingers stopped typing. "Why didn't you say?"

Vivi sniffed and waved a hand. "Oh, it was ages ago, and we haven't kept in touch. And like I said, I'm sure he'll be here. Tradition is really important to the Penhallows, and he came all this way just to do this."

And he's definitely not dead, I did not actually leave him to die or get eaten by wolves, there aren't any wolves left in Georgia, I'm pretty sure. Although there are bears ...

"You know what, I will just go mill around, see if I can find him, okay?"

As Vivi hustled out of the shop, she heard Gwyn say to Jane, "See? Problem solved!"

Vivi definitely hoped so.

The main street through Graves Glen's downtown was already starting to fill up even though the sky was gray and the temperature had dropped overnight, going from pleasantly autumnal to downright crisp.

As Vivi looked up, clouds moved quickly overhead, and she hoped the whole thing wasn't about to be rained out. They'd had hot, humid Founder's Days before, but usually, the magic thrumming under everything kept bad weather at bay.

A gust of wind blew down the street, rattling the plastic pumpkins hanging from the old-fashioned gas lamps, and Vivi wished she'd grabbed her coat from the back room of Something Wicked.

Hopefully she'd spot Rhys pretty quickly, get him over to the welcome booth, and then she could spend the rest of the day helping Elaine and Gwyn out at the shop. She'd be damned if she was going to stand in the crowd and watch Rhys make a big speech about the history of the town, his family honor or whatever it was he was actually planning to say.

As she passed a family all dressed up like witches, complete with the pointy hats, Vivi smiled. She loved Founder's Day, even when it involved her ex. It kicked off the whole Halloween season, and the town filled up with people really committed to having fun. According to Aunt Elaine, in the past, Founder's Day had been a more somber affair, a recognition of the sacrifices the Penhallows had made in founding this little village, tucked away in the mountains. Gryffud Penhallow had died his first year here, after all, and there was a legend that his ghost still roamed the hills above the town.

But over the past decade—and after a series of mayors like Jane—Graves Glen had transformed itself into a Halloween hotspot. There was the name, of course, but also the whole *charming small town* thing, the trees glowing bright orange, the apple orchards just on the edge of the village. And since Founder's Day was October thirteenth, it had slowly morphed into the natural starting point of their busiest season.

Sorry, Gryffud.

There were already booths set up selling everything from candy apples to "Halloween trees," little miniature Christmas trees painted black and decorated with wooden pumpkins, witch hats and ghosts.

Vivi waved at several people she knew, including Ezi, who was buying a giant bag of kettle corn with her boyfriend, Stuart, and kept her eyes peeled for that familiar lanky gait, that rumpled hair, those broad shoulders.

Finally, just when she was about to think he might actually be in a bear's stomach somewhere between her aunt's cabin and the bottom of the mountain, Vivi spotted him.

He was standing just outside Coffee Cauldron, a truly enormous paper cup in hand, and as Vivi approached, he pulled the coffee in even closer.

"Vivienne, I have already had a morning; if you're here to attempt to kill me again, I warn you, it will be very unsporting of you."

His eyes were hidden by sunglasses despite the gray day, a look that would've been douchey on any other man, but one that he was, unsurprisingly, pulling off.

It helped that the rest of his outfit was equally great. Gray trousers, a white button-down unbuttoned just so, a deep charcoal vest and around his neck, a silver pendant with a dark purple jewel.

Vivi had a sudden, explicit memory of that same pendant dangling against her chest as he'd moved above her, inside her, and felt her face flame hot.

She hadn't even *liked* jewelry on men before him, but that

necklace suited him, the delicacy of the chain emphasizing the width of his chest, the adornment making him somehow more masculine, not less.

Rhys sipped his coffee and didn't say anything, but she felt like he probably knew what she was thinking.

Which might have been why her tone was a little sharp when she said, "You need to go to the welcome booth."

He pulled a face. "The fuck is that?"

Rolling her eyes, Vivi took him by the elbow, steering him away from the coffee shop and toward the row of tents set up in the side street between Something Wicked and The Written Wyrd.

"The mayor is freaking out that you haven't checked in yet, so go check in."

"Were you worried?" he asked, and she didn't like how delighted he sounded. "Did you think I'd died? Did you think your callous actions had resulted in my death?"

"I think you need to go check in, make your speech and go home, Rhys."

He stopped, pulling them up short, and as he turned to look at her, Rhys reached up to slide his sunglasses down his nose.

"I need to check in, make my speech and charge the ley lines. Then I can go home."

Vivi could feel a few heads turn their way. She only spotted a handful of other witches in the crowd, people she knew from the college, so most of the people looking at them had no idea who Rhys was. He was just the kind of person who attracted stares.

She'd really liked that about him. Once.

Now, she leaned in and said, "Okay, maybe don't announce that to the whole town and half the tourists in Georgia, but yes, *that,* and then home. The going home part is really what I want you to focus on."

Vivi went to tug him back down the street again, but he stood firm, and she'd forgotten that for someone who looked so rangy, he was a pretty solid guy. He definitely wasn't moving.

"Come with me."

She blinked. "To Wales?"

That slow smile had once completely undone her, and now made her want to smack it off his face.

Or kiss it.

One or the other.

"I certainly wouldn't object to that, but what I meant was to the lines. After my speech, after this . . . charming festival is over."

In spite of herself, Vivi felt a little thrill at that. She'd never visited the ley lines, which lay in a cave on the mountain opposite from Elaine's mountain. The cave was a sacred space, only ever visited, as far as she knew, by Penhallows.

She'd be lying if she said she'd never wanted to see them. To get close to that kind of power.

"You said you wanted to. Before," Rhys went on, pushing his sunglasses back into place.

And then she remembered it. The Solstice Revel, the two of them in a tent, her head spinning with magic and desire and the sheer thrill of this man, that night.

You know, we're not far from the ley lines here, he'd said, kissing the tip of her nose. *The source of all the magic in this valley. My ancestor laid them down himself.*

Oh, I didn't realize I was making out with visiting royalty, she'd teased, and he'd smiled at her, kissed her again.

I've always wanted to see those. Later, whispered against the warm skin of his neck.

I'll take you there.

He hadn't. They hadn't lasted long enough for that little trip.

But now he was offering it again.

Was it a peace offering? Or a deeply misguided seduction attempt?

She looked into his blue eyes, and realized she really had no idea.

And at the same moment, she realized she also didn't care. Getting up close and personal with the ley lines was an honor few witches got, and she was taking it.

"Okay, sure," she said, and then, just in case he got the wrong idea, she added a poke to his chest. "Besides, you owe me."

"I don't know, after the attempted murder, I'd say we're at the very least even," Rhys replied, and then, when he saw her look, drained the rest of his coffee. "Fine. I owe you. Now, show me to this 'welcome booth,' and let's get this over with."

CHAPTER 7

"You don't think we have the same nose, do you?"

Rhys studied the head of his ancestor, currently lying at the base of its statue. Whoever had sculpted the unfortunate Gryffud Penhallow had gone into a lot of detail—the curling hair over the brow, the slight frown and expression of Noble Suffering in the eyes, and an absolute beast of a nose.

The mayor, Jane, was still unspooling a line of caution tape around the broken statue with one hand, and barking into a cell phone held in the other, so she didn't answer, and Rhys sighed, touching the bridge of his own nose.

"Bad luck, old man," he said to Gryffud's head, then looked back up at the top of the plinth.

The speech had been going so well, all things considered. Rhys figured the accent did most of the heavy lifting for him, plus the novelty of having an actual Penhallow, all the way from Wales. And he'd understood that this was the kind of thing people liked kept brief—let's be honest, they were really here to buy candied apples and hand-dipped candles, not listen to him blather on about his dead ancestor.

So thanks for the warm welcome, a quick acknowledgment of the beauty of the town, a few sentences in Welsh, always a crowd-pleaser, and he'd been done, one duty discharged.

And then he'd nearly had his own head knocked off his shoulders by Gryffud's.

As soon as he'd stepped onto the little steps leading off the stage, he'd heard the crack, then the gasp from the crowd, and had some instinct not urged him to freeze, he would've been directly under the plummeting stone skull of Gryffud Penhallow.

"I am so sorry," the mayor said for what, Rhys thought, was at least the thirty-fifth time. "I don't even know how this happened."

She was still holding the bright yellow tape, her cell phone shoved back into a holster at her waist. In her heels, she barely came up to his chin, and even though Rhys suspected she'd replaced all of her blood with Red Bull, she was definitely attractive with her big dark eyes and flushed cheeks.

However, being nearly killed for the second time in twenty-four hours had something of a dampening effect on the libido, so he didn't even attempt to flirt as he replied, "Hardly your fault. Probably just ol' Gryffud letting it be known he would've preferred a different Penhallow, and I can't blame him for that. I'm just glad no one else was standing nearby."

He was smiling as he said it, but as Rhys glanced back and

forth between the statue and the head on the ground, something cold settled into his chest.

Last night had been one thing—a series of mishaps that it was easy to chalk up to a strange run of bad luck, his magic thrown off by crossing an entire bloody ocean.

This? It felt . . . different.

Heads didn't just break off statues, certainly not exactly as he was walking under them, and after assuring the mayor one more time that he was fine and didn't plan on enacting some extravagant revenge for this insult, Rhys headed across the street to Vivienne's family's shop.

A chime rang as he pushed open the door, something slightly off-key and haunting, and just above him, some sort of animatronic nightmare of a raven began to squawk and flap its arms, its eyes blinking purple.

"Subtle," he said, and from her spot at the cash register, Vivienne's cousin, Gwyn, raised her middle finger at him.

"We're closed."

"You very obviously are not."

"We're closed to any and all exes of Vivi's, and you qualify, sooooo . . ."

Nearby, a group of young women was looking at a display of leather journals. Rhys saw a hand-painted sign advertising them as grimoires, but he couldn't detect even the faintest hint of magic coming off them. Probably best not to sell the real thing to tourists, though, and as Rhys looked around, he realized that very few things in the shop radiated any sort of real power except for Gwyn herself, decked out in full witchy regalia today.

He'd met her a handful of times during that summer he'd lived in Graves Glen, back when her hair had been pink. It was red now and long, hanging nearly to her waist, and while she didn't look that much like Vivienne, there was definitely a resemblance in the look of scorn she was throwing his way.

"Did you miss my near decapitation out there?" he asked, nodding back out at the street.

Gwyn widened her eyes. "Wait, one of my dreams almost came true, and I didn't get to see it?"

"What dreams?"

Vivienne appeared from behind a star-spangled curtain in one corner of the store, a box of what appeared to be tiny skulls in her arms, her hair gathered up in a messy bun, and as she blew a strand out of her face, Rhys's heart kicked painfully against his chest.

If only she weren't so damned *pretty*. If only he hadn't been the biggest cock-up this side of the Atlantic nine years ago.

If only he didn't suspect, just the littlest bit, that she might be behind his sudden rush of ill-fortune.

He didn't want to think that, but for the past few minutes, ever since he'd looked up to see Gryffud's nose careening toward his, it had been there, muttering away in the back of his mind.

It seemed a little too much of a coincidence that the second he arrived back in Graves Glen after nine years away, everything went completely sideways, and while Vivienne had never struck him as all that vindictive, she *had* left him to be killed or eaten or run over yet again last night.

All of which he probably deserved, but that was not the point.

Now, he looked at her and asked, "Do you sell a scrying mirror in this store by any chance?"

From behind the counter, Gwyn snorted. "Yeah, right behind our jars of eye of newt. What are you, a thousand years old?"

Scrying mirrors *were* a little old-fashioned, even for witches, but so was Rhys's father, which meant that they were one of the better ways to communicate with him.

"I think there actually might be one in the back," Vivienne said, setting down her box of skulls. As she did, several of them opened their jaws, letting out a sort of creaking groan that made the girls over by the grimoires jump then burst into giggles.

"Seriously?" Gwyn asked, leaning on the counter. "We have a scrying mirror and I didn't even know it?"

"I found it in some antique store in Atlanta," Vivienne replied before glancing over at the customers, then back at Rhys.

Moving a little closer, she lowered her voice and said, "You can't use it in here."

Mimicking her whisper, Rhys replied, "Wasn't going to."

She frowned a little, a wrinkle appearing between her brows, and Rhys's fingers itched to reach out and touch it, smooth it away with his fingers.

As that was a terrible idea, he kept his hands firmly in his pockets.

"You good out here?" Vivienne asked Gwyn, who gave her a thumbs-up.

"Now that I have more noisy skulls to sell to noisy kids, I am set."

Folding her arms over her chest, Vivienne looked at him, and after a moment, jerked her head at the curtain in the corner. "Come on."

Rhys followed, and when she pulled back the curtain, he expected to step into a storeroom of some kind, some dusty shelving, a bunch of cardboard boxes, much like the back room at Llewellyn's pub.

Instead, he immediately found himself in a circular chamber, the walls a warm, honey-colored wood. Heavy iron chandeliers held fat candles that cast the entire place in a sort of cozy glow, as did a series of stained-glass globes affixed to the walls, spilling colored light onto the comfortably shabby rugs on the floor.

All around the room were a series of beautifully carved wardrobes, and Vivienne walked to the nearest one now, opening it and muttering to herself.

"This is . . . quite something," Rhys said, looking around, and when Vivienne looked back over her shoulder at him, her expression was a little softer, a little more familiar.

"Aunt Elaine likes things to feel homey," she said. "Why have a boring, depressing stockroom when you could have this?"

Then she looked around. "I mean, it does sometimes make me feel like I'm in a video game of *The Hobbit*, but still."

Rhys huffed out a laugh, and she smiled at him.

Just for a second.

One of her front teeth had the tiniest chip in it. He'd forgotten that. He'd *loved* that. That little imperfection in that sunny smile.

Then she turned back to the wardrobe and Rhys cleared his throat, moving back slightly.

"And if customers come back here?"

Vivienne reached farther into the wardrobe, digging in its contents. "They don't," she said. "Slight repelling spell on this part of the store. Elaine tweaked it so that they don't feel uncomfortable or scared, they just . . . don't want to walk in."

"That's rather genius, actually," Rhys said, impressed. It was one thing to cast a spell, but tailoring it to your specific needs took a fair amount of skill.

Turning back to him, mirror in hand, Vivienne raised her eyebrows. "Yeah, well, we don't all have to be fancy Welsh witches to know some kick-ass magic."

"Well, as this particular fancy Welsh witch is currently getting his ass kicked by magic, I cannot disagree with you there."

He reached for the mirror, but Vivienne didn't offer it, watching him with another one of those little frowns. "What do you mean?"

Sighing, Rhys dropped his hand and rocked back on his heels. "Just that when a man nearly meets his death twice in less than two days, he begins to think something *may* be afoot."

She was still frowning and had gone very still, and Rhys watched her carefully, looking for some sign . . . of what, guilt?

Did he really believe that Vivienne was out to get revenge after all this time? Over a relationship that hadn't even survived an entire summer?

He didn't. Not really.

Or maybe he just didn't want to.

"In any case, as soon as I have that," he went on, nodding at the mirror, "I can talk to my father, and make sure my charging the ley lines is a good idea given the fact that Gryffud Penhallow attempted to kill me."

When Vivienne just kept staring, Rhys filled her in quickly about the entire statue incident, finishing up with, "So see? If you'd stayed to watch my speech, you would've gotten quite the show."

"Are you all right?" she asked, looking him up and down, her lower lip caught between her teeth. The gas lamp nearest her cast red and blue patterns over her hair, picking up the little sparkles in her purple sweater, and Rhys stepped forward, holding out one hand.

"I'm fine. Or I will be once I use that."

He nodded at the mirror and Vivienne handed it over, the metal still warm from her hand.

"Why are you using this to talk to your father anyway?" she asked, her shoulders a little looser now, some of the tension leaving her face. "It's for telling the future, not communicating."

Rhys didn't even know exactly how to explain his father or this particular eccentricity of his, so he just shrugged and said, "More fancy Welsh witch stuff."

"Got it. So I'll just . . . you'll probably want some privacy," she said, reaching up to tuck one of those loose strands of hair behind her ear.

"I mean, if you'd *like* to stay and meet my father . . ."

Vivienne wrinkled her nose. "From what you've told me about him, I think it's best I pass on that. I'll be out front."

With a swish of the starry curtain, she was gone, leaving Rhys standing in the middle of the room, holding the mirror and dreading every bit of what came next.

Sighing, Rhys held up the scrying mirror and looked into it. He was scowling, an unfamiliar expression on his own face and one that, he realized with a bit of shock, made him look an awful lot like both Wells and their father.

If that's what this place was doing to him, he definitely needed to leave as soon as possible.

But first, this.

Muttering the words under his breath, Rhys pressed his free hand to the mirror's cool glass and felt it ripple under his fingertips.

It only took a few moments before his father's face appeared out of the swirling gray mist in the mirror, his library clearly visible behind him.

"Rhys?" he asked, his fearsome brows drawn together in a tight V. "What is it?"

"Lovely to see you, too, Da," Rhys muttered, and then his father's frown somehow deepened.

"Where in the bloody hell are you? Is that . . . some sort of theater? A fortune-teller's wagon?"

His father's face loomed closer in the mirror. "Rhys Maredudd Penhallow, if you are consorting with fortune-tellers—"

"Da, I only have you for a tick, can I tell you why I'm calling?"

Simon's expression cleared slightly and he leaned back, waiting.

As quickly as he could, Rhys told his father everything that had happened to him since arriving in Graves Glen, from the car trouble to the near-miss accident to the statue. He left out the bit about not having hot water for his shower this morning as he was fairly certain it didn't help his case, but by the time he was finished, his father looked almost . . . amused.

What a terrifying prospect.

"You're not cursed, lad," Simon assured him. "Penhallow men cannot be cursed. Not in over a thousand years has one of us fallen victim to any sort of hex."

Amusement gave way to smugness as he added, "All of this is no doubt a direct result of your decision to travel like a human rather than via the Traveling Stone, as I suggested."

"A head fell clean off a statue because I decided to fly commercial and rent a car? Is that what you're saying, Da? Because I'm not sure I see the correlation."

Now the scowl was back. That was actually a bit comforting.

"Have you charged the ley lines yet?"

"Not yet, no. But that's the thing, isn't it? What if I am cursed and that . . . I don't know, buggers up the ley lines or some such?"

"While I do not doubt your ability to, as you say, 'bugger up' most anything, Rhys, I am telling you, there is no possibility you are cursed, and even if there *were,* some girl who barely qualifies as a hedge witch could not have done such a thing. Not to you. Not to any of us."

"She's more than a hedge witch," Rhys said, his fingers tightening around the mirror's handle, but his father waved a hand.

"Whatever she is, I'm telling you there is no way she could've placed a hex on you. It's . . . ridiculous. Preposterous."

"Bit like talking to people through mirrors, really," Rhys replied, and his father's gaze sharpened.

"Do the job I sent you there to do, boy, come home and don't ever let me hear the word 'cursed' leave your lips again."

CHAPTER 8

"So I think maybe we cursed Rhys."

Vivi kept her voice low as she said it, glancing back over her shoulder toward the curtain in the corner of the room. He'd been back there for a while now, and she wondered what he and his dad were talking about. Could his dad do some kind of long-distance spell and find out that yes, Vivi and Gwyn *had* laid a curse on Rhys all those years ago? Would he declare Witchy War on them? Pull the magic from Graves Glen? Would he—

"Vivi, if we could actually place curses on people, that bitch who always gives me whole milk when I ask for soy at Coffee Cauldron would be a dead woman by now," Gwyn said, placing another one of the chattering plastic skulls on the display table in the middle of the store. They went through thousands of the things this time of year, parents happy to have something cheap and spooky to buy their kids, kids delighted to chase their siblings around downtown with a cackling head.

Vivi picked up a stray one from the counter now, tapping her fingernails against its teeth as she fretted. "Okay, but doesn't it seem like a lot? The car thing, that might be nothing, but the statue?"

"That thing has been there forever," Gwyn said, turning to face Vivi, her witch's hat slightly askew. "And maybe when they were setting up the stage, they bumped it or something. Look, if anyone should be freaked out about that statue, it's Jane. And trust me, she will be. It's gonna take, like, at *least* two bottles of wine to get her to chill out tonight."

"I didn't think you two were still a thing," Vivi said as the skull's mouth creaked open, eyes blinking, and Gwyn shrugged.

"We're thing-adjacent. Speaking of," she added, giving Vivi a look from the corner of her eye, "you and the Dickbag seemed a little sparky."

Setting the skull back on the counter with a thwack, Vivi straightened up. "Excuse me?"

Another shrug as Gwyn drifted around to the other side of the table. "Just saying. The chemistry seems like it's still there, and you *are* awfully worried about him."

"I'm worried that we might have accidentally hexed the son of a very powerful witch," Vivi argued, and Gwyn waved a hand.

"A likely story. *I* think you still like the Dickbag. Or at least want to have sex with him, which is understandable. I actually forgot how cute he is. Or did he get cuter over the past nine years?"

Moving to the counter, Gwyn faced Vivi, propping her chin in her hands. "What do you think?"

"I think that if you keep calling him 'the Dickbag,' you can't *also* act like you're a matchmaking tween in a Disney movie."

"I contain multitudes."

"Gwyn, I swear—" Vivi started, but before she could finish that threat, the curtain opened and Rhys appeared.

He looked irritated, an emotion Vivi had never associated with Rhys and one that, disturbingly, looked . . . really good on him. Something about the way frowning made the lines of his face even sharper, the blue of his eyes more intense.

She realized she was staring, and somehow sensing that Gwyn was looking at her with more smugness than any woman should, Vivi moved from behind the counter toward Rhys, holding her hand out for the mirror that he still held.

"Did it work?" she asked, and he blinked, like he was surprised to see her there.

"Hmm? Oh, yes. Yes, got through to him no problem, thank you," he said, handing her the mirror. "You said you found it at an antique store?"

Nodding, Vivi looked at her own reflection in the mirror, fighting the urge to stick her tongue out at her too-pink cheeks and too-bright eyes. *Get a grip, girl.*

"Yeah, just hanging out in the back. The owners had no idea what they had, and I decided to store it here rather than at my place."

"Why?"

Rhys was looking at her, really looking at her, and oh, shit, here was another thing she'd forgotten about him. He was a *champion* listener. And not for show. He genuinely cared what you had to say, always wanted to know more. It was like having a spotlight on you all the time, but not in a way that made you feel exposed or on display. It just made you feel . . . warm. Appreciated.

Until it was gone.

Vivi tore her gaze from his and looked back at the mirror. "I don't know," she said. "Too tempting, maybe. No one should look into the future too hard, right? Of course," she added, wiggling the mirror slightly, "I didn't know it could also be used for long-distance phone calls."

"Only if you're trying to contact a particularly pretentious prick," Rhys said, and Vivi raised her eyebrows.

"So it'll work to contact you, then?"

Rhys's smile spread across his face as slow and sweet as honey, and over his shoulder, Vivi saw Gwyn smirk, her fingers coming together to produce a quick shower of purple light as she mouthed, *Sparky.*

Had Rhys not been watching her, Vivi might have had a few choice words to mouth back to her cousin.

Instead, she lifted her head, holding the mirror against her chest. "Anyway. Everything's fine? With your father?"

I didn't curse you? This is just bad luck and has nothing to do with a drunk and brokenhearted teenage witch nearly a decade ago?

Rhys's smile faded, the moment lost, and Vivi told herself that was a good thing.

And then, to her immense relief, he nodded. "So it seems. Now just to charge the ley lines, and I'm back to Wales."

"Right, the lines. When?"

He pulled a delicate watch from the pocket of his vest, glancing at it. "The moon rises around seven tonight, so sometime around then?"

Gwyn was still watching them although, thank the goddess, at that moment the door chimed again, meaning customers. When Gwyn learned that Vivi was going to charge the lines with Rhys, she was never going to hear the end of it.

She still wanted to do it, though.

As Gwyn walked toward the door, Vivi nodded at Rhys. "Meet me here at six-thirty."

Just a few more hours. Then she could see the ley lines, Rhys could do what he needed to do and this could finally be over.

Which was what she wanted.

Absolutely.

OF ALL THE times Vivi had thought about Rhys over the years—and it had been more times than she wanted to admit—she'd never thought about something as basic and boring as having him in her car.

But here he was, leaning back in the passenger seat of her Kia, the seat moved back, his long legs stretched out in front of him, her travel mug, the one with the green sparkles and frogs on it, held in one of his hands as Graves Glen disappeared behind them and they climbed higher into the hills.

Twilight had just started to deepen, turning the sky a soft violet, the rest of the scenery blurring into blue, and Vivi's fingers flexed on her steering wheel as she tried very, very hard not to think of the night she'd met Rhys.

It hadn't been exactly like this, of course. It had been June, not mid-October, the air softer and warmer, the colors different, but it had been another magical night, a special one, and she wondered if he was thinking about it, too.

He was uncharacteristically quiet over there in her passenger seat, staring out the window, occasionally taking sips of coffee. Was that part of it? Did he have to center himself or something before he did magic this big?

For the first time, Vivi realized that she might be in a little bit over her head here. Not with Rhys, exactly, but with the magic she was about to witness. She kept her spells small, could go whole weeks without using her powers.

Was she ready for what she was about to see?

"It is truly amazing how much I can *hear* you thinking."

Vivi threw him a quick glance before turning her eyes back to the road. "What, literally? Like mind-reading?"

Rhys chuckled and took another sip of his coffee before shaking his head. "No, I don't have that power, and even if I did, I definitely wouldn't use it on you. Only so many times a man should hear himself called a bastard, really. I just mean that you get this look when it's clear you're concentrating. It's—"

"If you say 'cute,' I'll throw you out of this car."

"I would not dare. I was thinking more 'charming.'"

Vivi couldn't help but glance over at him again. He was smiling at her, that soft, fond smile she'd completely forgotten about until this moment, and this time it was a little harder to look back at the road.

"I'll allow that," she finally said. "And for your information, I wasn't really thinking about you being a bastard. I mean, that *is* a default thought in my brain at all times, but I wasn't actively thinking it."

"Good to know."

"I was thinking about the ley lines. What's actually involved in charging them."

Rhys shifted in his seat, putting the coffee in her cupholder. "Less than you'd think, really. A few magic words, a little razzle-dazzle"—he stretched out his hands, wiggling his fingers—"and it's done."

"Oh," Vivi said, sagging a little in her seat, and he grinned, leaning back.

"Were you expecting to be more impressed?"

"I don't know what I was expecting," she admitted, and Rhys looked over at her, folding his arms over his chest.

"You were the Full Potter, right?"

Vivi screwed up her face as she turned the car down the narrow lane right off the highway, the one most people would miss completely. "The what?"

"The Full Potter," he repeated. "Not finding out you're a witch until you're older, not growing up with it. 'Yer a witch, Vivi,' that sort of thing."

Now that she didn't have to watch for oncoming traffic, Vivi turned the full force of a glare on Rhys, knowing it was somewhat hampered by the smile she could feel tugging at the corners of her mouth.

"That is not a thing people say, 'the Full Potter.'"

"It is, too. You just don't know because you are, as stated, the Full Potter."

"Okay, so if you can hear me thinking again, know I'm back to the 'bastard' thoughts."

Still grinning, Rhys turned to look out the window as the car started its descent into the valley below. The night had gotten darker now, the sky more indigo than lavender, and the moon rose over the hills, bright and cold and white.

The perfect night for witching.

"Your mum was a witch, though, yes?" Rhys asked, turning back to her, and Vivi's fingers flexed a little on the steering wheel.

"She was, yeah. Apparently really good at it, but . . . I don't know. I guess that was her form of rebellion, rejecting all things magic." It didn't hurt to talk about her parents anymore. The loss still ached, but the pain was a weight rather than a sharp edge. Still, it had been forever since she'd mentioned them to anyone.

"Love a rebellious woman, me," Rhys mused, leaning back. He was still watching her. Even though Vivi's eyes were on the road, she could feel it.

"So you really didn't do any magic growing up?" he asked. "Not even accidentally?"

"Oh, I totally did," Vivi replied, smiling at the memory. "Did my first spell when I was five. I was in this tree house my dad had built for me, and I was making tea. By which I mean I was stirring dirt and water into an old teapot I'd found in the garage."

"My father makes tea that clearly uses the same recipe," Rhys quipped, and Vivi laughed.

"Anyway, there were these big azalea bushes under the tree house, and I thought it would be nice to add some of the petals, but I didn't want to go all the way back down the ladder, so I thought really hard. About them floating up through the window. And then they just . . ." She lifted her hands off the wheel for just a moment, fluttering her fingers. "Did."

She glanced back over at Rhys, who was still watching her with that fond smile, and it made something in her chest go so tight that she had to look away, concentrating on the road in front of her again.

"Anyway, my mom freaked, and had this big talk with me about how that kind of thing wasn't safe, and she was right, really. I'm sure if the neighbors had seen, I would've ended up on some kind of really lurid talk show or something."

Vivi hadn't thought about that moment for years, but now she could see it all over again, her mom sitting at the edge of the bed, her hair the same color as Vivi's, but shorter, brushing against her shoulders as she leaned in, smelling like smoke and spice.

I just want you to be safe, sweet girl.

Floating those petals hadn't *felt* dangerous. It had felt fun and . . . light. Easy.

But her mother's face had been so serious, and Vivi had never forgotten it, had never fully been able to detach the idea of *magic* from *danger.* She shivered now as the car descended, not from cold but just from the anticipation of what they were about to do.

Or maybe she could already sense the magic in the air.

"I see why ol' Gryffud picked this place," Rhys murmured to himself, sitting up to peer out the windshield.

"You can feel it, right?" she asked, and he nodded.

"Are we close?"

"Just around this bend."

The car came to a stop at the side of a stream, the water burbling and sighing over rocks as it flowed from the mouth of an open cave just in front of them, the entrance yawning and dark in the glow of Vivi's headlights.

She shut off the car, plunging them into deeper darkness, and in the gloom, Rhys turned to her, holding one hand out. "Well, Vivienne," he said, "shall we?"

CHAPTER 9

It really was unfortunate how much of magic took place in dark, dank places.

As Rhys helped Vivienne step over a particularly large rock just inside the entrance of the cave, he wondered why his ancestors couldn't have laid down ley lines somewhere warmer, somewhere a little less damp. Beaches needed magic, surely.

But no, his ancestor had apparently been the sort of grim fucker who preferred caves, so now Rhys was dodging dark puddles of water and slime-covered rocks.

Although, he admitted as Vivi once again placed her hand in his, the little ball of light she'd conjured hovering over them, the company certainly wasn't bad.

"How far into the cave are the lines?" she asked now, dropping his hand to reach up and push her hair back from her face.

"Not far," Rhys said, peering into the gloom in front of him. His father had drawn him a map, probably using ink made from raven's blood and five-hundred-year-old parchment, but Rhys had pointedly left the foul thing behind, fairly certain that he'd be able to find the lines on his own.

Now, however, as he walked farther into the cave, the walls becoming narrower around him, he wasn't sure that had been the best idea. He could feel the magic, of course, thrumming like a second heartbeat underneath his feet, making the hair on the back of his neck stand on end, but where exactly was it coming from?

Not quite as clear.

Pausing, Rhys looked around him. The main chamber of the cave came to a dead end a few yards away, and all he could see was solid rock on either side. Had his father's map mentioned a secret entrance? Or was this more of his bad luck mucking things up? His father may have sworn he wasn't cursed, but Rhys couldn't shake the uneasy feeling that something wasn't right. Maybe this was part of it.

"St. Bugi's balls," he muttered, and Vivienne paused, looking up at him.

"Are you lost?" she asked.

"No," he said, entirely too quickly, and she narrowed her eyes a little.

"Rhys."

"I am not," he insisted, and then turned in a circle, the light drunkenly trailing after him. "I just . . . need to get my bearings a bit."

"Mmmm," Vivienne said, crossing her arms. "And do your

bearings tell you there's a hidden opening just past your left shoulder?"

Rhys spun around, squinting into the darkness, at first seeing only more slick, wet rock.

And then . . . there it was. The slightest shadow in the midst of all that darkness, cleverly hidden against the rock.

Turning back to Vivienne, Rhys raised his eyebrows. "Have you been here before?"

She shook her head. "Never. I mean, I knew where the cave was, but Aunt Elaine was always really strict about this being a sacred space not to mess with."

Frowning, she shook her head. "But it's weird. It's like I knew where the opening was before I saw it. Like I knew if I looked in that spot, I'd see it."

Rhys wasn't sure what to make of that. It was possible she was just better at picking up the magic here than he was, family bloodline be damned, or maybe she'd caught a glimpse of it earlier that hadn't really registered. In any case, he no longer had to stand here looking like a complete tit, so he nodded toward the cleft. "Onward, then."

As soon as they stepped into the hidden entrance, the air around them seemed to change. It was immediately colder, so much so that Rhys shivered, wishing he'd brought a jacket.

Here, the passage was so narrow they had to walk single file, the damp rock brushing their shoulders, and the farther they walked, the more insistent the hum of magic became, Rhys's ears feeling like they were stuffed with cotton, his body covered in goose bumps.

From behind him, he could hear Vivienne's breathing getting faster and knew she must be feeling it, too.

But that was nothing compared to what he felt when the slim passage opened up into another chamber, and the ley lines glowed before him.

The whole cave was lit with a soft purple, flowing rivers of pure magic pulsing on the floor, and Rhys's mouth went dry, his knees feeling shaky.

That was, unfortunately, not the only thing he was feeling.

Turning behind him, he saw Vivienne standing just inside the entrance, her eyes wide, her chest rising and falling, and when she looked over at Rhys, he saw the same mix of surprise—and heat—in her face.

Thank sweet fuck, or this would've been truly embarrassing.

"Right," he started, clearing his throat, "so this is awkward and probably why this sort of thing is usually done alone."

He should've expected it, really, or maybe his father should've warned him, but then no, that conversation would have been excruciating enough to cause death, so maybe that was for the best.

Magic always had a physical effect. Some spells made you tired, some made you giddy. Some left you crying for reasons you didn't understand.

And some magic, for whatever reason, turned you on.

Apparently the ley lines were of that variety, and given the intensity of the magic in this cave, the effect was . . . similarly intense.

Probably magnified by the fact that he was currently sharing this cave with a woman he'd once had a lot of truly spectacular sex with, and he should not be thinking of that even a little bit right now, not the *slightest bit.*

But as he slammed his eyes shut, it was all there, unspooling in his brain in an X-rated highlight reel: Vivienne's legs wrapped around his waist, Vivienne's hair against his chest, the feel of her nipple under the lazy sway of his thumb, the hitch in her breath when his hand slid between her legs, the way she laughed when she came, which had always seemed *extraordinary* to him, that perfect, breathless laugh against his ear—

"Rhys."

He didn't *shriek* exactly as he opened his eyes to find her standing very, very close to him, but the sound wasn't far off, and then he made the mistake of putting his hands on her arms to steady himself.

Even through her sweater, her skin was warm, and as he looked in her eyes, he saw her pupils were huge, the black nearly swallowing the ring of hazel around it. "This is some kind of magic thing, isn't it?" she all but panted, and he nodded, his hands now moving up and down her arms when what he *needed* to be doing was stepping far the fuck away from her and possibly running back out into the main cave to stick his head in all that cold water.

Her fingers curled around the front of his shirt. "Rhys," she said again, her voice calm and steady even as her gaze moved to his mouth, her tongue darting out to wet her lips.

Rhys just barely managed to keep from groaning, his hands sliding from her arms to her waist. If he kissed her now, would that honestly be so bad? Couldn't they just look on it as a little formality, one last kiss before they parted forever?

That was romantic. Epic, even.

Didn't a man get to be epically romantic in a magic cave?

He ducked his head, moving in closer. God, she smelled good. Like something sweet. Vanilla, maybe. He was going to taste every bit of her until he found the source of that scent.

Vivi's eyes fluttered shut, her breath coming out in a shaky sigh.

And then she seemed to steel herself, her arms suddenly going rigid between them, shoving him back so hard that he actually staggered a little.

"Did you seriously bring me," she asked through clenched teeth, "to a magic sex cave?"

RHYS BLINKED AT her as Vivi made herself step back because right at this moment, it was taking all her willpower not to launch herself at his face. His stupid, handsome face, currently wearing an expression somewhere between confusion and outrage.

"Beg pardon?" he finally said, and Vivi moved even farther back, her arms crossed tightly over her chest. She was practically shaking with how much she wanted him, her head spinning, her heart pounding in her chest, her ears, between her legs.

She took another step away from him, and his eyes widened, his posture stiffening. "You don't think I knew this was going to happen, do you? Or that I brought you here on purpose? I mean . . . I *did* bring you here on purpose, but I had no idea—"

Vivi shook her head, which also seemed to help clear it a little. "Of course not, don't be gross. I'm just saying that maybe you should've, I don't know, asked your dad or your brothers or someone what exactly you'd be getting into in here."

"Ah, yes, the old 'Father, will this job you're sending me to do involve a magic sex cave?' talk. Truly, I was remiss not to have it."

"Don't be an asshole."

"Then don't be ridiculous. No, I didn't ask the exact specifics of this particular job. And for all I know, no one else has ever been in here with his ex-girlfriend, so this may just be a unique-to-us situation, Vivienne."

Some of the fog of desire was starting to lift now, and Vivi felt her breathing slowing down, her pulse not pounding nearly as hard. Had she just overcome the magic out of sheer irritation, or was it actually wearing off?

It must have been because Rhys was no longer looking at her like he wanted to eat her alive. He just looked pissed and more than a little offended, and Vivi told herself that was definitely the safer option right now.

"My point is," Vivi said, steadier now, "that you apparently had no idea what you were actually going to find in here, or you would've been warned about it. You didn't even ask, did you?"

Rhys didn't answer, his hands shoved in his pockets, a muscle ticking in his jaw. "What if there had been darker magic in here? Something that made us want to kill each other instead of . . ."

She wisely let that thought trail off, her face still hot, her skin still tingling.

"But there wasn't," Rhys said, and for the first time, Vivi noticed that the pendant at his throat was glowing a little, the same purple as the lines on the floor.

"But there might've been," she countered, and he sighed, tipping his head back to study the ceiling.

"You asked me here with no idea of what we'd actually be facing," Vivi went on, and he groaned, throwing up one hand.

"And you agreed to come with me!"

"Right, because apparently I didn't learn my lesson about trusting you nine years ago."

They stood there, staring at one another, and suddenly Vivi wanted nothing more than to be back in her own bed, sitting in her pajamas and catching up on grading, Rhys Penhallow nothing more than a faint memory of a misspent summer.

Then Rhys sniffed, shrugging his shoulders. "Fine," he said. "I am, as always, a feckless idiot who throws himself into things, so let me go ahead and finish throwing myself into this, shall I?"

"Rhys," she started, but he had already turned away, crouching down by the lines on the floor, his arms extended, and Vivi swallowed hard.

This was for the best. He might not exactly be a "feckless idiot," but he'd always be reckless, always leap without looking.

Vivi thought again of Gwyn's card of him. The Fool. The card of chances and risks.

And Gwyn had painted Vivi as The Star—peace, serenity. Steadfastness.

She and Rhys had been doomed from the start.

At least this time there wouldn't be any screaming or crying. They could go their separate ways, maybe not as friends, but at least as adults, people who knew who they were and what they wanted and where they belonged.

Which was definitely not together.

In front of her, Rhys flexed his fingers, and Vivi could feel a slight change in the air. Where it had been cold before, now it felt warmer, like someone had just opened an oven door nearby.

Vivi's hair blew back slightly from her face, and Rhys lowered his head, his hands still held out over the pulsing purple lines, his lips moving, but the hum of magic too loud for Vivi to make out any words.

Under her feet, the ground gave a slight tremor, and a flash of light shot out from Rhys's fingers.

Vivi shivered, wrapping her arms around herself, her own magic tingling in her veins as she watched the light race along the rivers of purple.

For a moment, the lines on the floor glowed even brighter, so bright it almost hurt to look at them, and Vivi lifted her hand to shield her eyes.

And then there was a sudden *crack*!, a shower of pebbles raining down as Rhys shot to his feet.

Vivi looked down.

The lines on the floor were still purple, but they were growing darker now, a black crust slowly oozing along the sides, blotting out the color.

The ground was still shaking.

She looked at Rhys, confused, as the temperature in the cave plummeted again, colder this time, so cold it almost hurt, and as the ley lines began to writhe on the floor like snakes, Rhys grabbed her hand.

"Run!"

She didn't have to be told twice.

They made their way through the narrow passage back to the main cave, the ground still trembling underneath her feet, and while Vivi watched lines of purple and black steam as they hit the pools of water.

When she and Rhys ran back out into the night, they both stood and watched as the magic raced past them.

Toward Graves Glen.

The shaking had stopped, and the night was suddenly very quiet in the wake of all that chaos, the only sound the occasional hooting of an owl and Rhys's and Vivi's rasping breath.

Stepping in front of her, Rhys stared off down the hill, shoving a hand through his hair. "The fuck *was* that?" he gasped, and then turned and looked at her. "You may have had a point about me not being all that clear as to what I was up to here, but I'm pretty sure that"—he jabbed a finger in the direction of the stream—"was a massive cock-up."

Vivi looked up the stream, then up at the sky, where the moon seemed even bigger and brighter now, remembering that night with Gwyn, the same moon, the candle flame shooting high, and a cold sort of weight settled in her chest.

Rhiannon's tits.

"So, um. Rhys."

He turned and faced her, his eyes still wide, his chest still heaving, and Vivi offered up a shaky smile.

"Funny story for you."

CHAPTER 10

She'd fucking cursed him.

As Vivi sped back toward Graves Glen, Rhys sat in the passenger seat, staring out into the dark, still trying to wrap his mind around it.

"So you took a bath," he said slowly, and next to him, Vivi made a frustrated sound.

"I told you," she said. "I took a bath, lit some candles, and then Gwyn and I said a whole bunch of silly stuff about your hair and clitorises that was obviously not a real curse—your hair looks really good, by the way, and I don't actually want to know about the rest of it—but at one point, there was, like, this whoosh of flame, and I might have said, 'I curse you, Rhys Penhallow,' but I didn't mean it."

Vivi's hands were gripped tight around the wheel, her eyes wide, and Rhys looked at her. "You . . . literally said, 'I curse you, Rhys Penhallow,' and now you're surprised that I, Rhys Penhallow, am cursed? Also, I'm sorry, what was that about clitorises?"

Vivi rolled her eyes as she turned back onto the highway. "The point is, we were just being drunk and stupid. No attempt at actual magic was being made."

"And yet actual magic has been done," Rhys muttered, settling back into his seat.

His skin still itched from the aftereffects of charging the lines, fingers tingling, and there was a strange cold sensation at the back of his neck. Was that normal, or was it part of whatever had just gone so spectacularly wrong back there?

Narrowing his eyes, Rhys peered into the darkness as though he might be able to see that racing spark of magic still making its way down the mountain. All he could see, though, was the ribbon of road unfurling in front of them, and for a second, just the barest of moments, Rhys let himself believe that nothing bad had actually happened. His father had seemed so confident he hadn't been cursed, after all, and when was Simon Penhallow ever wrong? Maybe this is what it was always like, charging the lines.

And then Vivi's phone rang.

Sang, actually. The Eagles' "Witchy Woman" wailed from Vivi's purse, shoved between the front seats, and Vivi barely glanced at it, her fingers tightening on the steering wheel.

"Gwyn," she said, but didn't reach for her bag. "It's probably nothing."

"No doubt," Rhys said, hoping more than he'd ever hoped for anything in his life that she was right.

"Wanting you to pick up pizza and cheeseburgers for dinner," he added, and Vivi looked over at him.

"What?" he asked to her look, shrugging. "America."

The phone went silent, and Rhys sensed that Vivi was holding her breath.

Fuck, he was holding *his*.

And then the song started up again.

Fumbling in her bag, Vivi pulled out her phone, sliding a thumb across the screen, and before she even had the phone up to her ear, Rhys could hear chaos. People shouting, someone screaming, and Gwyn yelling Vivi's name, and Rhys sank back in his seat, covering his eyes with one hand.

"Gwyn, calm down!" Vivi was saying. "I can't understand you—"

The phone was firmly pressed against her ear now, and Rhys watched her, actually saw the blood drain from her face as she said, "We'll be there in two minutes."

She let the phone slide from between her cheek and her shoulder, and gripped the wheel even tighter.

"What is it?" Rhys asked, but Vivi only shook her head and said, "Your seatbelt is buckled, right?"

"Obviously, I'm not an idiot, Vivienne," he said, sitting up slightly only to immediately be thrown back against his seat as Vivi pressed the gas pedal to the floor.

"That bad, then?" he asked grimly.

Vivi was equally grim as she answered, "Worse."

VIVIENNE HAD NOT exaggerated the speed with which they got back to Graves Glen. By Rhys's count, it was only ninety-something seconds after Gwyn's phone call that they were pulling up in front of Something Wicked.

Vivienne barely put the car in park before rushing out onto the sidewalk.

Rhys was a little slower, his hand resting on the top of the open car door as he tried to take in what was happening in the front window of the shop.

He spotted Gwyn easily enough, standing on top of the counter, a broom raised in her hands, and there in the back corner was a trio of girls, crouched down against the wall, their faces pale, their eyes huge.

And all over the floor between them and Gwyn were . . . skulls.

Small ones, about the size of a baseball.

Vivienne was already in the shop, and he saw her pull up short with a shriek as all the skulls turned toward her almost as one, their mouths opening and closing.

Rhys heard Gwyn shout something, but he was already moving into the shop, that absurd raven croaking at him as he threw the door open.

Magic lay heavily over the shop, so thick it made his teeth ache, his skin humming with its power, but there was something underneath all that power. Something dark and rank, a powerful sense of *wrongness* hanging over the whole shop.

Rhys had never felt anything like it before.

The skulls skittered across the floor, their jaws opening and closing and propelling them around the hardwood at a surprising speed. The eyes were lit up, too, but instead of the purple Rhys re-

membered from earlier, they were red now, bright red, and there
were so bloody many of them.

Something thumped against his ankle, and Rhys looked down
to see one of the plastic skulls grinning up at him.

"Steady on, mate," he muttered, wondering if he was talking to
the skull or to himself.

And then the skull's teeth closed around the leg of his pants.

Rhys was not proud of the sound that came out of his mouth
as he jerked his leg back, kicking out in an attempt at flinging the
thing off.

When that didn't work, he didn't even think. He pulled a
thread of magic up from the soles of his feet to the tips of his fingers and blasted the damn thing to little plastic confetti.

"Rhys!"

He looked over to see Vivienne still standing with her cousin,
armed now with one of the heavy crystal balls he'd spotted earlier.

She was glaring at him, and then gave a significant look to the
group of tourists huddled in the corner, now watching him with
wide eyes, and Rhys just barely kept from scoffing as he replied,
"What was I meant to do, Vivienne?"

There was a singed smell, the slightest hint of burning hair,
and Rhys saw he'd burned a hole in his trousers—and nearly his
leg—with that little spell. Cursing, he patted at the smoldering
hole even as he kicked another of the little plastic bastards away
from him.

"Fucking ridiculous," he muttered, stomping on one of the
skulls, then another, before holding out his hand to Gwyn.

"The broom," he called, and she tossed it to him.

Catching it easily, Rhys swung the broom back down toward the floor and, in what was perhaps one of the most satisfying moments of his life, swept the skulls directly in front of him in a wide arc toward the wall.

None of them broke, but they skittered drunkenly, bumping into each other, spinning around, and Rhys kept moving forward, sweeping the broom back and forth, clearing a path to the three girls in the corner.

"Ladies," he said with a smile when he reached them, "hopefully we've all learned a valuable lesson about ordering things off dodgy websites!"

He kept grinning at them even as they stared at him. He saw one glance down at the hole in his pants, and directing them to follow him said, "Lucky thing I had a lighter on me."

Given that he was currently cursed, Rhys knew using magic on them was dangerous, but charm, he'd found, was a sort of spell all its own. As he moved the girls toward the door, sweeping skulls all the while, he kept up a sort of inane chatter about checking the batteries in things before you put them out on the store floor, on the strongly worded email he was going to write to the manufacturer and on the discount Something Wicked would be sure to give them the next time they came in.

By the time he got them to the door, he was sick of his own voice, but the girls seemed less freaked out, one of them turning around to offer, "I once ordered an iPod off the Internet, but, like, some random website? Not Apple? And it, like, totally started smoking in my pocket."

"Even so," Rhys said, ushering them out onto the sidewalk. "Thank you for shopping at Something Wicked, please come again!"

The raven over the door shrieked as Rhys closed the door with a decisive bang and reached up to pull down the little shade over the window.

Once the door was firmly locked, he looked over at Gwyn and Vivienne.

Gwyn was still on the counter, her hands close together as a greenish light sparked back and forth between her fingers.

"Nicely done, dickbag," she said, and before Rhys could object to that—which he wanted to, vociferously—she nodded at Vivienne.

Nodding back, Vivienne moved to the front window, dodging the skulls with surprising grace.

Do not notice how nice her legs look as she's stepping over possessed pieces of plastic, you absolute pervert, Rhys thought to himself, but it was no use. Vivienne may have cursed him, may have been the cause of every bad thing that had happened to him since he set foot in this town, but his cock had clearly not gotten the message.

Stepping to the window, Vivi lifted one hand, white light glowing there. She was using magic to close the massive velvet drapes bracketing the shop's front window, Rhys realized, and before he could call out a warning, the light jumped from her hand to the curtain.

And promptly set it on fire.

Vivienne shrieked as one of the skulls snapped at the toe of her shoe, and Rhys crossed the store, kicking the skull even as he reached up with the broom in an attempt to bat out the flames.

The smell of burned plastic filled the room as the bristles kindled, and out of the corner of his eye Rhys could make out Gwyn directing her magic toward the window.

"Don't!" he shouted, and to his immense relief, he saw her drop her hands.

He was slightly less relieved to realize there was now a small crowd growing outside the window, which was very much open to reveal both the utter chaos inside and all the magic they were doing to try to stop it.

Wonderful.

All around them, the skulls were still moving, jaws opening and closing, and Rhys reached for Vivienne's hand. "The storeroom!" he shouted over all that chittering, and Vivienne nodded, taking his hand.

Up on the counter, Gwyn looked from the window to the pair of them, then back again. "So what?" she asked. "We just hide from Night of the Living Tchotchkes and hope for the best?"

"Do you have a better idea?" Vivienne asked, but before Gwyn could reply, the door to the shop blew open, slamming hard against the wall.

Rhys turned slightly to see who had managed to come in—he

was sure he'd locked the damn thing—but before he could, there was a nearly deafening blast and a flash of blue light that had him throwing his free hand up against the glare.

When he lowered it, he saw that there was nothing left of the skulls save for a few stray pits of smoking plastic and one red blinking eye that flashed off and on a few more times before slowly dying out.

In the silence that followed, Rhys was very aware of the smoky haze still lingering over the store, the scorch mark now scarring the floor in front of him and the fact that Vivienne was holding his hand.

He looked at their interlocked fingers, her palm almost hot against his, and then up at her face. Her cheeks were pink, eyes wide, and when she sensed him looking at her, her gaze shot to their hands.

Flustered, she dropped hers, stepping away from him as her aunt moved farther into the store.

"What," Vivienne's aunt said, her chest moving up and down with the force of her breathing, "have you two done now?"

CHAPTER 11

Maybe those toy skulls actually killed us and now we're in hell, Vivi thought as she sat in her favorite chair in the storage room, the golden velvet wingback that she'd spent so much time in, there was probably an impression of her butt in the cushion.

It seemed like a good explanation for why she was stuck in this night that wouldn't end. First the caves with Rhys, then that nightmare here at the store and now, despite being nearly thirty years old, she had to explain to Aunt Elaine that she'd broken one of the most sacred rules of witchcraft because a guy hurt her feelings.

And that guy was currently *here*.

"It was an accident," she said again for what felt like the twentieth time this evening. "We were just . . . being silly."

"There is no being silly with magic," Aunt Elaine said, as stern as Vivi had ever heard her. She was standing in front of one of the wardrobes, her arms folded over her chest, her hair pulled back from her face. Several earrings sparkled in her left ear, a long strand of silver dangling from the right, and she looked every inch the powerful witch she actually was. "As I told both of you, constantly," Elaine went on before walking over to the wardrobe and pulling out a T-shirt.

"What does this say?" she asked, shaking it, and Vivi saw Gwyn roll her eyes from her own spot, sitting crossed-legged on one of the trunks.

"Mom," Gwyn started, and Elaine raised a hand. "Oh, you will not be 'Mom-ing' me, young lady."

Rhys, who'd been uncharacteristically quiet since they'd all retired back here, walked up to Elaine and took the T-shirt from her.

"'Never mix witchcraft with vodka,'" he read, then nodded. "Solid advice, that."

"Okay, no," Gwyn said, standing up from the trunk. Her mascara was smudged and there was a run in her tights, but other than that, she didn't seem that much worse for wear, given what had happened tonight. "You don't get a say in any of this. This is all your fault."

"Because I did the curse?" Rhys asked, raising one eyebrow as he tossed the shirt back to Elaine. "Is that why it's my fault?"

Hands on her hips, Gwyn faced off with Rhys. "Because it's your fault we had to curse you in the first place. If you hadn't shattered Vivi's heart—"

"I didn't *shatter* anything," Rhys scoffed, and Vivi's heart sped up as she watched him pause, thinking it over.

Then he looked at her with those blue eyes and asked, "Vivienne . . . *did* I shatter your heart?"

Now not just the night that would never end, but possibly one of the *worst* nights of her life.

"You didn't," she said, desperate to save some kind of face here.

And maybe she could have had Gwyn not existed.

Gaping at Vivi, Gwyn said, "Um, he very much did. Remember all the crying? The bath? You kept conjuring up the smell of his cologne, for fuck's sake."

Vivi's face flamed red and she sunk farther into her chair. "I did not do that," she muttered even as Rhys stared at her in obvious shock.

"You called me a 'fuckerneck,' which is not even a word," he reminded her. "You threw my own pants at me. You weren't brokenhearted, you were angry."

"Right, because no woman has ever been both those things at the same time," Gwyn said, and Vivi finally stood, scrubbing her hands over her face.

"Would everyone stop acting like I was this tragic, lovelorn victim? I was a drunk teenager goofing around with my equally drunk cousin. This was not that big of a deal." She paused, then rolled her eyes. "Okay, so *this* part of it has turned out to be a big deal, but I mean the actual cursing bit. *That* was not meant to be a big deal, and you're all being ridiculous about it."

She pointed at Rhys. "Do you really want to tell me you didn't do something overly dramatic and stupid as a teenager?"

"'Overly dramatic and stupid' describes my entire teenage career, so no."

"Gwyn?" she asked, turning to face her cousin.

Screwing up her face, Gwyn said, "Girl, you lived with me when I was a teenager. You know."

Nodding, Vivi faced Aunt Elaine, who continued to frown at her for a beat only to finally throw up her hands and say, "I know you're just going to mention the whole thing with Led Zeppelin, so let's just skip it and admit we've all done stupid things in our pasts, and leave Vivi alone about her motivation."

"Thank you," Vivi said. "Now that we all agree that the *why* does not matter, the issue is the *what*. Namely, what this curse might mean for Graves Glen."

Sighing, Elaine reached up and tugged at her earring. "I assume the curse spread to the ley lines," she said, "and given that the ley lines fuel all the magic in town, that magic is now . . . corrupted."

Hence evil plastic skulls, and while Vivi prided herself on being optimistic, she wasn't naive enough to think that was going to be the limit of this disaster. Who knew what other things the cursed ley lines might unleash?

"I need to talk to my father," Rhys said as he leaned against the wardrobe, tossing one of the skulls that had survived Elaine's spell back and forth in his hands. Every time its teeth clacked together, Vivi felt her skin crawl. Too bad they'd never be able to sell those things again because they really had been popular. But revisiting a nightmare was not worth the occasional extra five bucks, in Vivi's opinion.

"Do you want me to get the mirror?" she asked Rhys, and he raised his head, startled.

"I said I *need* to talk to him, not that I'm actually going to do it." Rhys shuddered. "This night has been horrible enough already."

"Simon will need to be told," Aunt Elaine said on a sigh, sinking into the chair Vivi had just vacated. "And I don't look forward to his reaction."

"What can he do?" Gwyn asked. "I mean, other than be a dick about it."

Pushing off the wardrobe, Rhys gave a humorless laugh. "Ah, the times I've asked myself, 'What can my father do about something other than be a dick,' only to find out he can do plenty."

Vivi had already been worried—battling a bunch of toys come to life had that effect on a girl—but now she felt her heart plunge somewhere south of her knees.

Rhys's father.

"Is your dad going to come here," she asked Rhys, "and, like, smite us?"

The corner of Rhys's mouth lifted just the littlest bit. "Honestly, with most people, I'd make fun of the word 'smite' here, but in my father's case . . ."

The smile faded, and Vivi's hopes went with it. She thought of the tarot card Gwyn had drawn, Aunt Elaine's cabin as The Tower, cracked in two and sliding off the side of the mountain.

What if that had been some kind of prophecy?

"You're turning green," Gwyn said, crossing the room to stand in front of Vivi.

"We're gonna fix this," she said, laying her hands on Vivi's shoulders and giving a shake. "We're badass witches, remember?"

"You're a badass witch," Vivi reminded her. "Aunt Elaine is a badass witch. I'm a history teacher."

"You can be both." Gwyn's hands tightened. "And this isn't your fault. It was my idea to curse him, remember?"

"But it was my magic that did it," Vivi replied, remembering that candle flame, how the words coming out of her mouth had felt different. Heavier. Charged, somehow.

The one truly powerful spell she'd ever managed, and it was going to wreck everything for her.

Classic.

"If I, as the cursed party, might interject here," Rhys said, shoving his hands in his pockets, "isn't it possible we might all be overreacting a little? Yes, tonight was shit, no getting around that. Yes, we're all a bit freaked out and understandably so, but so far, these little buggers"—he nodded at the skull he'd tossed to the chair—"are the only thing we've dealt with."

"That and my simple 'hey, close the drapes' spell ending in fire," Vivi reminded him, and he shrugged.

"You said yourself, your magic has always been a bit . . . what was the word? Wonky?"

"Well, mine is very much unwonky," Aunt Elaine said, hands on her hips. "And that spell I used to clear the store was far more powerful than I intended."

Rhys nodded. "All valid points. But maybe not enough evidence to say things have gone completely tits up yet, begging your pardon, Ms. Jones."

"I have tits, so I think I can handle hearing the word spoken, Mr. Penhallow," Aunt Elaine said with a dismissive wave before sighing and steepling her fingers against her mouth.

Never a good sign. The last time Vivi had seen that gesture from Aunt Elaine had been the time Gwyn had briefly gotten engaged to the guy who read fortunes at the Ren Faire and called himself "Lord Falcon" despite his driver's license saying "Tim Davis."

But now Aunt Elaine only took another deep breath and said, "I think you may be right. Maybe this isn't as bad as it seems."

"It seems pretty bad, Mom," Gwyn said, frowning. "Speaking as someone nearly eaten by plastic."

"No, Rhys has a point," Vivi said, surprising herself. And Rhys, too, if his raised eyebrows were anything to go by.

"We don't know how bad this is, or if it was just some weird little spike. And whatever it is, we're not going to fix it tonight."

The more she talked, the better she felt. Of course, what they needed was a *plan*.

Vivi was really good at plans.

"Look, we'll all go home, get some sleep, and in the morning, we'll see what things look like. Rhys, you'll talk to your father."

He scowled, but didn't disagree, so Vivi went on, pointing at Elaine, "And you'll see what you can find about removing curses, and you"—she turned to Gwyn—"will . . . just keep running the store and assuring people that tonight's little show was all part of the Founder's Day fun."

"I like how my job is the only one with any real threat of danger," Gwyn said, but off Vivi's look, she lifted her hands in defeat. "Okay, okay, Operation Soothe the Muggles, I'm on it."

"Good," Vivi said. "So that's it. We have a plan. A . . . kind of half-ass one, but a plan nonetheless."

"Quarter-ass, if you ask me," Rhys muttered but then nodded at her. "But certainly better than nothing."

Glancing around him, he sighed. "And at least I'll get to reacquaint myself with Graves Glen after all this time."

When Vivi only stared at him, he added, "I mean . . . it's not as if I can go home until all this is over."

He was right. She knew that. Of course getting this sorted out meant that Rhys would stay here.

In her town.

Working with her.

He smiled at her then, winking, and despite all of it, the curse, the embarrassment, the freaking tiny plastic *skulls of death,* Vivi's heart did a neat little flip in her chest.

Yep, definitely in hell.

CHAPTER 12

Vivi woke up to find Sir Purrcival staring at her.

That wasn't all that unusual—he'd always liked to find whoever the last person in bed was in the mornings and snuggle in, and since Gwyn and Aunt Elaine were both early risers, that had almost always been Vivi back when she'd lived here.

What was unusual was that he blinked his yellow-green eyes at her, yawned and then said, "Treats."

Now it was Vivi's turn to blink.

"Dreaming," she muttered to herself. Last night had been awfully traumatic, after all. Made sense she'd have a really vivid, really bizarre dream that felt real but wasn't.

"Treats," Sir Purrcival said again, butting his head against Vivi's arm, and okay, no, this was real.

They had a talking cat.

"Gwyn!" Vivi called, scooting back a little bit in her bed, and Sir Purrcival continued to pace and turn in circles, a constant refrain of "Treats, treats, treats!" spilling from his whiskered lips.

Vivi heard footsteps on the stairs, and then Gwyn was there, still in her pajamas, her hair pushed back from her face with a brightly colored headband.

"What is it?" Gwyn asked, and Vivi nodded at Sir Purrcival.

"He talks now."

Gwyn blinked at her, then looked back to Sir Purrcival before giving a shriek of delight and clapping her hands. "He does?"

Rushing into the room, she scooped up her cat, holding him in front of her face. "What did he say?" she asked. "Because I've always wanted a talking cat, and I think if any cat is going to be a stimulating conversationalist, it's—"

"*Treeeeaaaaaats,*" Sir Purrcival croaked again, and then began wiggling in Gwyn's arms. "*Treatstreatstreatstreatsfoodtreats.*"

"He mostly says that," Vivi said, pushing back the covers, and Gwyn frowned at her cat.

"Okay, but maybe once he gets treats he'll have more to say." With that, she set him back on the bed and rushed out of the room, returning a few seconds later with the bag of cat treats. Shaking out a few in her hand, she offered them to Sir Purrcival, who gobbled them up. "Now say 'thank you,' buddy," Gwyn coached.

Purrcival licked his chops and headbutted her hand. "*Treats-treatstreats,*" he began again.

"I think maybe that's all he can say?" Vivi offered.

"*TreatstreatstreatsTREATSTREATSTREATS!*"

"I changed my mind," Gwyn said, scrambling to give Purrcival more treats. "Talking cats are bad. I see that now."

Then she looked up at Vivi, who was getting out of bed. "This is because of what Rhys did to the ley lines, isn't it? Like the skulls last night."

"It's because of what *I* did to Rhys," Vivi corrected on a sigh, her eyes falling on the duffel bag she'd hastily packed at her place last night. She couldn't quite say why she'd decided to spend the night at Elaine's, just that the idea of going to sleep in her apartment above the store had definitely not appealed. Now, as Gwyn muttered to Purrcival, Vivi took out the skirt and blouse she'd delicately folded into her bag last night.

"Which means that we were right—there's a lot more bad shit to come."

Gwyn shot her a look as she tucked Purrcival underneath her chin. "This is not bad shit," she argued, then, when Purrcival continued to ask for treats, shrugged. "Okay, it's not the *best* shit, but I still don't think it's evidence of a horrible curse."

She gave Vivi another smile before carrying Purrcival to the door. "I told you, Vivi. We're gonna fix this."

Vivi wished she felt that confident.

She also wished she didn't feel so damn . . . embarrassed about the whole thing. Because that's what had kept her awake last night, staring at the ceiling until well past two in the morning. There was guilt and fear and worry, of course, all that was mixed up in there, but overriding all of it was, *Rhys knows he broke my heart.*

Not only that, Rhys knew he'd broken it so badly that she'd done *magic* over it.

And clearly he hadn't felt the same way back then since it had never even occurred to him that she'd actually been that sad over it.

Which proved, as she'd always suspected, their fling had meant a lot more to her than it had to him. He'd probably barely thought of her over the past nine years, had certainly never googled her while kind of wine-drunk, and while there was no doubt they were still attracted to each other, Vivi was older now.

Wiser.

And the last thing she was going to do was fall for Rhys Penhallow all over again.

Fifteen minutes later, she was heading downstairs, her still-damp hair twisted up in a bun, her jacket hanging off her shoulders, and she was so focused on getting out the door that it took her a second to realize she heard voices in the kitchen.

And not just any voices.

Turning the corner, she looked at her aunt's cozy kitchen table, the table around which she'd made candles and plucked flower petals for bath salts and never, *ever* eaten breakfast, and there was Rhys, coffee mug at his elbow, sticky bun in hand, smiling at her aunt.

Who was smiling back almost . . . affectionately. Indulgently.

And then Vivi realized the kitchen didn't smell like its usual mix of herbs and smoke, but of sugar and cinnamon.

"Aunt Elaine," she asked, firmly ignoring Rhys, "did you . . . *bake?*"

Her aunt's cheeks actually turned a little pink. "You don't have to sound so scandalized, Vivi," she said, waving one hand as she got up from the table and crossed the kitchen to the coffeepot. "I *can* cook, you know. I've just usually chosen not to."

"Which is a crime and a sin," Rhys said, licking a stray bit of icing off his thumb, a gesture that made Vivi's own face suddenly feel a little pink. How did he look so good after the night they'd all had? Vivi felt like the circles under her eyes deserved their own zip code, and when she glanced down, she noticed that her blouse was misbuttoned. And there he sat, wearing dark jeans and a charcoal sweater, his hair still very much doing The Thing despite the curse that was evidently real, and for just a second, Vivi gave some serious thought to cursing him again.

Instead, she also made her way to the coffeepot, grabbing a mug from the shelf above it. It was one of the ones they sold in the shop, white with a purple silhouette of a witch zooming away on a broomstick, the words *Life's a Witch, Then You Fly!* in curling script below the rim.

"What are you doing here, Rhys?" she asked once she was a little more caffeinated. She wanted to resist the sticky buns on principle, but they smelled too good to pass up, so Vivi grabbed one still warm from the pan, careful not to let it drip on her skirt as she sat at the table.

Leaning back, Rhys folded his hands on his stomach and studied her. "Well, Vivienne, I don't know if you remember, but it turns out I was horribly cursed, so . . ."

Rolling her eyes, Vivi held up the hand still holding the sticky bun. "Yes, I know, we can skip the sarcasm. I mean, why are you in my aunt's kitchen right now?"

"We're looking into curses," Aunt Elaine said, rejoining them at the table. She nodded toward a yellow legal pad and a large open book Vivi had somehow missed, and now Vivi licked her own fingers before reaching over for it.

The book was heavy, the binding ancient and cracked, and Vivi could barely make out the letters stamped in gold foil on its spine. And even once she could, they didn't spell any words she recognized.

"I guess it's too much to hope that there was a really clear and easy-to-do anti-curse ritual in this, huh?" Vivi asked, carefully turning the pages. The paper was so thick that it crackled slightly, the illustrations painted and lurid.

Vivi paused on one that showed a man hanging from a tree branch by his ankles, all his insides on the outside.

"Ew," she muttered, and suddenly Rhys was there, leaning over her shoulder to look.

"Ah, yes, the 'Trial of Ghent,'" he said. "We had an ancestor that attempted that. Didn't end well. You basically take your own entrails out and then—"

"Do not want to know," Vivi said, quickly turning the page and also trying to ignore how good Rhys smelled.

You're not allowed to feel turned on when the word "entrails" was just bandied about, she told herself.

"So far, we haven't had much luck," Elaine said, "but one bright spot. Thanks to Rhys using his magic to fuel the ley lines, most of the curse has probably drained off of him."

She tapped the cover of another book. "The law of transmutation. Rhys was cursed, but in funneling his magic into another power source—"

"I passed on some of the curse to the ley lines instead," Rhys finished. "So still cursed, but diluted. Maybe. Half of that particular page was ripped out, so we're really just spitballing here."

"Great," Vivi replied weakly. And it was great that maybe Rhys could walk through town without being a disaster magnet, but she still felt guilt sitting like a rock in her stomach.

"One question," Gwyn said, coming into the kitchen. She was still in her pajamas, her long red hair in a braid over one shoulder.

"Only one?" Vivi asked, eyebrows raised.

"Okay, lots, but one for right now." She pointed at Rhys. "His hair. It's still doing The Thing. And it's been doing The Thing ever since he got into town."

Rhys frowned, reaching up to tug at his hair. "What thing?"

"Oh, like you don't know," Gwyn said, and Rhys's frown deepened.

"Seriously, what—"

Aunt Elaine stopped them both with a lifted hand. "I take it the two of you specified something about Rhys's hair during the curse?"

Now Rhys's hand dropped from his head and he stared at Gwyn and Vivi. "You tried to attack my *hair*?"

"Curse magic doesn't work like that," Aunt Elaine went on, ignoring him. "You'll get general bad luck or, if you go really dark, death. But nothing that small or specific."

"Good," Gwyn said. "Now we don't have to feel guilty about the clitoris thing anymore."

"Treeeeaaaaats."

Oh, thank the goddess.

Vivi looked up to where Sir Purrcival had just strolled into the kitchen, twining himself around Elaine's ankles as she stared at him.

"Oh, right," Vivi said, shutting the book. "Um. He talks now. But he mostly just says that."

Elaine and Rhys both took that in before Rhys nodded and said, "Right. Of course he does."

Reaching down to pet the cat, Elaine looked over at Vivi.

"Why are you all dressed up?" she asked, and Vivi looked down her body, frowning, too.

"I'm not," she said. "I'm just going to work."

"At the college?" Aunt Elaine's eyebrows disappeared beneath her shaggy bangs. "Today?"

"Yes, today," Vivi said, standing up and straightening her jacket. "Why wouldn't I?"

"We have important things to do today." Aunt Elaine placed one hand on her hip, the other holding a wooden spoon. "Witch business."

"And I have a nine A.M. class," Vivi countered. "Which I can't just cancel. We talked about this last night."

"We talked about Gwyn reopening the store as though every-thing were normal," Elaine countered, "not about you going to teach class. This"—she tapped the book in front of her—"is more important right now."

"I can do both," Vivi said, standing up. "Penhaven is also a witchy college, remember? I can teach class, then go to the li-brary, see if there are any more useful books there."

She only barely managed to keep from frowning as she said it. Vivi had worked hard to keep her work life and her witch life separate, which meant she very rarely dealt with anything involving Penhaven's more secretive classes. But when you had a witchy problem, it seemed stupid not to use that resource.

Even if that resource tended to smell like patchouli.

Rhys was already grabbing his own jacket from the back of his chair. "I'll come with."

Vivi stared. "To the college?"

He gave a shrug. "Why not? I am an alum, after all."

"You came for one summer course, which I don't think you actually attended more than, what? Five classes of?"

Rhys winked at her. "And whose fault was that?"

Okay, they were heading into dangerous territory now, and Vivi turned away to pull her keys out of her purse, breaking eye contact before she did something embarrassing like blush.

Again.

"Besides," Rhys said, "it's clearly not safe for me to be out on my own now, all cursed and what have you, so might as well stick close to the one that did the cursing."

"I am never living this down, am I?"

"It's certainly going to be the subject of conversation for a while, yes."

Vivi looked up at him then, scowling, and was about to remind him that there wouldn't even *be* a curse had he not been such an asshole nine years ago, but before she could, she noticed the shadows underneath his own eyes, the tension in his smile even as he attempted to give her his usual rakish grin. As horrible as it sounded, that was actually kind of comforting, knowing that Rhys was freaked out about this.

All this quippiness and pastry eating were just a cover.

Had he always done that?

She couldn't remember.

Of course, she'd only known him for a few months nearly a decade ago. Weird to think that someone who had loomed so large over her romantic life for so long was basically a stranger.

Shaking off that thought, Vivi stepped back from him. "Fine. Come with. I'll go teach, and you can go check out the Special Collections at the college library."

"Is that a euphemism?" Rhys asked. "I really hope it's a euphemism."

"Nope," Vivi replied, already pulling out her phone to send an email to the director of Penhaven's library. "It's exactly what it sounds like."

CHAPTER 13

Penhaven College was smaller than Rhys remembered.

And, as he and Vivi made their way across campus, it dawned on him that it was very strange a place named after his gloomy and depressing home could be this light, this cheerful, all redbrick buildings with white trim, bright lawns and autumn leaves in bold colors everywhere he looked.

"Nice place to work," he commented to Vivienne, who was about two steps ahead of him, her low heels clicking on the brick walkway.

"It is," she replied, but she was obviously distracted, looking around with these quick, darting glances, and Rhys jogged a little to catch up with her.

"What is it?" he asked in a low voice. "Something amiss?"

She shook her head. "No, nothing I can see right now, but . . ."

"But you're keeping an eye out."

"Exactly."

Rhys looked around, too, although he wasn't sure what he was looking for. There were no statues to fall on him, no cars to suddenly come careening his way. But who was to say a sudden sinkhole wouldn't open up in the ground or that a stray tree limb might not come winging down from the heavens?

The sooner they got this fixed, the better.

Besides, once he wasn't cursed anymore, maybe he would stop feeling like such an utter bastard.

He knew Vivienne had been angry with him, furious even, and he'd deserved every bit of it. But that he'd hurt her badly enough that she'd done this . . .

Fuck, that bothered him.

There was a set of concrete steps just ahead of them, leading down to a white building at the base of the small hill, and Vivienne stopped just on the top step, turning back to look at him.

"Be careful."

"With . . . five steps?"

She scowled, one hand on her hip. "Do I need to remind you of what's going on?"

"You don't," he assured her, "but you heard what Elaine said. The curse is almost certainly doing its thing on the town now, not me, and besides, do you really think these steps are going to take me out? Do you want to hold my hand as I walk down them?"

Vivienne muttered something under her breath, then turned and walked down the steps, leaving Rhys to follow.

Carefully.

Rhys didn't know what he'd expected Vivienne's office to look like, but as he followed her down the hall of the bright and airy building that housed the history department, it occurred to him that he hadn't exactly given a huge amount of thought to anything when it came to Adult Vivienne.

It was almost like she was frozen in his memory at nineteen, but now here she was, a grown woman with an office and a career, and he suddenly, desperately, wanted to know everything about her.

"Why history?" he asked as they stopped in front of a white door with a frosted window, *V. Jones* stenciled in neat black letters on the glass. "And why regular history, at that?"

She gave him a look as she unlocked the office door. "Why not witchy history, you mean?"

Shrugging, Rhys leaned against the wall. "It seems like a fair question."

Vivienne paused, her key still in the lock, and for a moment, Rhys thought she might not answer him at all.

And then she finally sighed and said, "Believe it or not, I actually like 'regular' history, and also . . . I don't know. I guess it's just that I spent most of my life being more or less a regular person, so that's where I'm more comfortable."

With that, she pushed open the door and after a beat, Rhys followed her inside.

The office was tiny, barely enough room for a desk, two chairs and a slightly crooked bookshelf, but it was homey and cozy, reminding him a little of the space at the back of Something Wicked. There were plants, and colorful posters of medieval tapestries, an electric kettle with big flowers painted on it, and on her desk, he spotted pictures of her with Gwyn and Elaine, plus a couple of shots with people he didn't recognize.

He would've liked to have said he didn't check for any guys, but that would have been the most blatant of lies. He was absolutely checking to see if there was some picture of Vivi in her polka dots, some absolute bastard's arm around her waist.

But no, nothing like that.

"So what sort of history do you teach?" he asked, turning his attention to the bookshelf. Christ, it even smelled like her in here, that warm, soft scent that either he hadn't remembered or was new. Another part of this new Vivienne he wanted to learn about.

"The basics," she replied, distracted as she dug through her desk for something. "Intro to Western Civilization."

"Ah, so you're stuck with the first-years."

"We say 'freshmen' here, and yes, although I actually like teaching them."

She looked up, smiling a little. "It's nice, getting to introduce kids to something you really love."

He could see it then, what she must be like when she taught. The way her cheeks would flush when she got on a topic she was passionate about, the light in her eyes. Her kids must love her.

"I get that," he said, nodding. "It's like when I arrange a trip for people to a place they've never been before. I love seeing their faces when they get back, love looking at the five million pictures they took on their phones. Okay, well, I don't actually *love* that, but it's still kind of fun."

Her smile widened a little. "I bet."

For just a moment, they could've been two strangers, Rhys

thought. Just two people chatting about their jobs, maybe lightly sussing each other out.

And then, once again, he had the unsettling feeling that that's what they were in a way.

Except that she could never be a stranger, never just be some woman he fancied, and he needed to stop being distracted by her pretty eyes and lovely hair, and remember that he was cursed now.

Clearing his throat, he turned back to the shelves. *Right. Curse. Problem to be solved. Focus on that.*

"You have a lot of books about Wales over here."

Bloody hell, mate.

When he glanced back over at her, he saw that Vivienne was no longer looking at him, had become very interested in something on her desk. "Yes, well. That, um. That was my focus. In grad school. Llewellyn the Great, Edward I, all of that."

She met his eyes. "Because of the town history."

"Obviously."

"Nothing to do with you."

"Wouldn't dare to think it."

He turned back to the shelves, thumbing through a book on the castles of the Marches when Vivienne suddenly asked, "Do you not like it there?"

Rhys put the book back, turning around. "Where, in Wales?"

She nodded, and he sighed, folding his arms over his chest as he leaned back against her bookshelf. St. Bugi's balls, how could he explain to Vivienne the way he felt about his home?

"I love it," he said at last. "The most beautiful place in the world, truly. Mountains, the sea, poetry, rugby. The national animal is a dragon, for fuck's sake. What's not to love?"

"But you created a job for yourself where you're always traveling," she said, straightening up. "And back . . . back when we were, um . . ." She tucked her hair behind one ear, cheeks coloring prettily. "When we were involved, you said you never liked to visit your hometown."

"Well, yes, but that's because of my father, not because of the town itself," he replied with what he hoped was a rakish grin. This conversation was beginning to skirt too close to things Rhys worked very hard not to think about, so a little rakishness was needed.

And it clearly did the trick because Vivienne narrowed her eyes, but didn't press further, and after a moment, she lifted something out from underneath a pile of papers. "Okay, found my library card, so let's get you over there. It's on the way to my first class."

Another trip across campus, this one shorter since the library was just up the hill from the history building, but this time, Rhys sensed something . . . different.

This part of campus looked the same as everything else—the brick, the ivy, all of that—but he could feel it in the air.

Magic.

Before he even asked, Vivienne nodded. "The other part of the college is here. In those buildings." She nodded at a cluster of four smaller classroom buildings, all grouped together underneath a copse of massive oak trees, shaded even on this bright sunny day.

"When I was here, they were just mixed in, in the regular class-rooms," Rhys said, and Vivienne rolled her eyes.

"Right. Well, that only worked until the first time a regular student bumbled past the wards and into a class on augury and tried to take a video of it with his cell phone. A couple of years ago, all magic classes were relocated to those buildings."

"Makes sense. And the bumbling students?" Rhys asked as he watched a couple of girls in jeans and sweaters jog up the steps of one of the magic buildings.

"Kept out by the same kind of repulsion spell that protects the back room of the store," Vivienne answered. "Easier to maintain and make stronger when it's over one central location, not a bunch of separate classrooms. Plus this arrangement keeps them out of everyone's hair."

They were at the library now, a building Rhys had decidedly never visited in all his time at Penhaven, and it was appropriately Gothic-looking with huge white columns and pointed windows.

Still, Rhys paused outside, jerking his head back toward the magical part of the college. "You never hang out with them? Even though they're witches, too?"

Vivienne followed his gaze and shook her head. "No, they're . . . look, you can meet them if you want. You'll see."

"Vivienne Jones, you snob."

She snorted at that, and then gestured for him to follow her. "Come on. We might not be talking to them, but we're definitely using some of their resources."

CHAPTER 14

Vivi had never liked Penhaven's library. Maybe it was too close to the witchy side of things, or maybe it was the fact that, unlike the rest of campus, it was dark and slightly foreboding, almost medieval with its narrow windows and dark stone, the towering shelves blocking out what little light did manage to make it in. Even with the banks of computers in the center of the first floor, Vivi still felt she was stepping into the twelfth century or something every time she came in here, and as she led Rhys toward the back, she actually shivered a little, pulling her jacket tighter around her.

"Bloody hell," Rhys muttered next to her. "Do they hang meat in here?"

"It's not usually this cold," she replied, frowning. Seriously, the library was not always her favorite place, but it usually wasn't quite *this* chilly and oppressive. And when she glanced around, she noticed that the few students in there at this time of the morning were clearly feeling it, too, huddled at the study carrels, their shoulders up around their ears.

"Heating must be out," she said before looking over at Rhys. "Good thing you brought a jacket."

"Also good thing I'm from a country for whom 'chilly' and 'dank' could be written on the flag or possibly in some sort of motto," Rhys said.

Viv opened her mouth, wanting to ask him more about Wales, but she shut it just as quickly, shaking her head as she continued to head for the Special Collections. Bad enough Rhys had found out that she'd studied Welsh history in college and grad school. She didn't need to make any more small talk with him that inadvertently revealed too much.

Not that she'd studied Wales because of Rhys—she definitely had not. Not even a little. Yes, him talking about it that summer had piqued her interest, but you didn't devote years of your life to study because a guy you went out with for three months talked about it one time.

Just like her never actually going to Wales had nothing to do with him, either. It was a small country, but she could've avoided him because what were the chances—

"Vivienne," Rhys whispered, leaning down so close that his breath wafted warm over her ear, and now her goose bumps were from more than the cold. "We're in a library."

She stopped, confused, and then Rhys put a finger over his lips. "You're thinking too loud."

Vivi wasn't sure if she wanted to laugh or flip him off, so she settled for ignoring him.

And if she smiled a little when her back was to him, that was her business.

THERE WAS SOMETHING wrong with this library.

Rhys hadn't been in all that many libraries over the course of his life, but he'd been in enough to know they usually didn't feel like this. Hell, even his family home, the scariest place on god's green earth, as far as Rhys was concerned, didn't feel like this.

It wasn't just the chill in the air, although as he and Vivienne walked through a pair of heavy wooden doors to access the back of the library, he was very glad he'd thrown on his leather jacket this morning.

It was something . . . unnatural. Something off.

And the feeling crawled over his skin in a way he didn't like.

Vivienne felt it, too. He could tell from the way her gaze kept darting around. But she wasn't saying anything, so he wasn't going to mention it either, even though he knew they were both wondering the same thing: Was this something to do with the curse and the ley lines?

They passed through long rows of shelves, the space between them getting narrower and narrower until they had to walk single file, Vivienne leading the way. She'd worn her hair up today in a messy knot caught at the back of her neck, and in spite of everything, Rhys's fingers itched to reach out and take it down.

What would she do if he did?

Kick you in the balls as you'd so rightly deserve, he reminded

himself, and shoving those feelings down, continued to follow
Vivi through the warren of shelves.

Finally, the shelves opened up, and they stood in a dim, circular room, a massive oak desk in the center of it, raised so high that
Rhys's chin barely came up to the edge. Vivienne, tall as she was,
had to stand on tiptoes to peer over.

"Dr. Fulke?" she called softly, and an ancient, wizened face
suddenly appeared.

"Ms. Jones?"

Smiling with relief, Vivienne rocked back on her heels and ad-
justed her bag on her shoulder. "Yes. This is my . . . research
assistant." She jerked a thumb at Rhys, and he looked up at the
ancient woman behind the desk, wondering if this would actually
work. If she was a witch and worked at Penhaven, there was a
good chance she might know who he was.

But the woman at the desk didn't seem to care much. She
barely gave Rhys a cursory glance before nodding and typing
something out on a computer in front of her.

"Two hours," she said, and there was a little whir as a machine
printed out a sticker, which she handed to Vivienne, who turned
and handed it to Rhys.

V. JONES GUEST, it read, a little time stamp underneath, and
Rhys frowned.

"This is . . . a lot more prosaic than I was expecting."

"We live in the twenty-first century," Dr. Fulke said from her
perch, folding her arms over her narrow chest. "Forgive us for not
scratching your name on vellum with a quill."

"Well, I don't need *vellum,* but the odd quill would be—"

"Thank you, Dr. Fulke," Vivienne said quickly, pulling Rhys away.

"Your research assistant?" he asked as they moved deeper into the stacks.

"It was the first thing I could think of," she whispered back. "And, I mean. It's not *completely* untrue."

She stopped as they reached the back of the room, nodding at a row of doors. "Take anything you find into one of those rooms, and I'll meet you back here in an hour or so, as soon as I get out of class. You can ask Dr. Fulke or any of the other librarians if you need help, but don't—"

"Vivienne." He stopped her by stepping closer, reaching out to put his hands on her shoulders before he thought better of it and stepped back again. "I am a grown, adult man," he said instead. "I think I can manage asking for help without giving away the whole plot."

Her pursed lips told him she might not actually believe that, but she gave a nod anyway. "Good. I'll help once I'm back."

With that, she was turning away in a swirl of golden hair and black skirt, leaving Rhys alone in her deeply creepy library.

Not just creepy, but *heavy.* Ancient magic, the truly old, deep stuff, hummed through the room like a current of electricity, the kind of magic that made you feel a little uncomfortable, skin suddenly too sensitive, teeth aching slightly.

Grimacing, Rhys rolled his shoulders and stepped farther into the breach.

Fifteen minutes later—and with no assistance at all, thank you very much, Vivienne Jones—Rhys had a stack of books and made his way to one of the doors in the back.

The study room was tiny, nearly claustrophobic with no windows, the only light from a heavy glass lamp overhead, and nothing more than a large wooden table in the middle, an ancient slab of oak that also seemed to hold some magical properties. When Rhys put his hand flat on the top, he could feel a slight vibration.

Sighing, he opened the first book from the stack.

It was mostly in Latin, and Rhys felt that part of his brain creak slowly into life as he read. Hadn't had much use for Latin since school, and had taken something of a perverse pleasure in not being as fluent in it as his father and brothers, insisting any magic that required this much work wasn't worth it.

He maybe regretted that now.

Just a smidgen.

And as he read, he couldn't stop thinking about his father, whom he definitely should be calling, right now, this minute, actually several hours ago.

Simon would know what to do. He always did. But that didn't mean Rhys was ready to talk to him about this yet.

Was that because he was afraid of his father's reaction when he learned he'd actually been wrong about something?

Or was it because of Vivienne?

Rhys groaned and closed the book in front of him, reaching up to rub his eyes with one hand.

What a fucking mess this all was.

How could he explain to Simon that this wasn't some act of war on Vivienne's part, but just a teenage girl who'd been hurt—hurt by *him* being a complete dickhead—and a spell that had gotten out of hand? Simon wouldn't understand that. Simon had not, to Rhys's knowledge, ever even been a teenager, probably. Seemed likely he'd just sprung fully formed and terrifying out of a cloud or something.

And then Rhys realized who he could call.

Simon was out, but there *was* the younger, slightly less terrifying version of Simon.

Pulling out his phone, Rhys quickly did the math on what time it was back home, and dialed.

Within about five minutes, he was deeply regretting that decision.

"You have to come home."

"Come home? All cursed and such? Wells, I know I'm not your favorite person in the world, but wishing me dead seems a bit much."

"I don't wish you dead, you git, but it's obvious that you can't stay there with a coven of witches who cursed you."

Sighing, Rhys closed his eyes and pinched the bridge of his nose between thumb and forefinger. This was what he'd been worried about.

"You're making it sound worse than it is. It wasn't like that, it was—"

"I don't care what it was like," Wells said, and Rhys could almost see him there behind the bar at the pub, glowering at his mobile. "You need to come home, and you need to talk to Father about this."

"Or," Rhys suggested, "secondary, also solid plan: I do neither of those things, and you help me think of some way to break this curse without having to involve Da."

On the other end of the line, Llewellyn blew out a breath that Rhys could practically feel.

"I can ask around."

"Discreetly."

Wells made a rude noise. "The day I need directions from you on how to be discreet is the day I fling myself off the top of Mount Snowdon."

"Something to look forward to, then," Rhys replied, cheerful, and there was a pause on the other end of the line before Wells said, "Seriously, mate. Be careful. It would . . . if something were to ever happen to you . . . I know we . . ."

Sitting up straighter, Rhys looked in horror at his phone. "Oh my god, Wells, please stop."

"Too right," Wells agreed, clearing his throat. "Anyway, try not to die. As your older brother, I get the first shot at taking you down, Bowen the second, so it would be very unfair if you perished there in the wilds of America without letting us have our chance."

Relieved to be back to taking the piss and not actually sharing feelings, Rhys nodded and tapped his pen on the desk. "Fair enough, old man."

He ended the call and slid his phone back into his pocket,

wishing he felt better about this whole thing. Having Wells on his side was definitely a boon, but it wasn't going to be enough. Rhys needed to figure out how to break this curse as fast as possible, and so far, the books weren't exactly helping.

Oh, there was information on curses, but mostly how to lay one. Apparently no witch ever wanted to *break* a curse.

Typical.

By the time Vivienne slid into the research room an hour or so later, Rhys's eyes ached from trying to parse out tiny script, his brain hurt from all the translating and his hand was cramped from writing down every little bit of information that might be useful.

And he still didn't feel like he had learned any more than he'd already known when he'd come in here.

"I don't suppose you brought coffee," he asked Vivienne, not looking up. He'd just come across an anecdote about a Scottish farmer who suspected his crops were cursed and had attempted to reverse the spell.

Going by the illustration, it seemed to have ended with him turning into a rather large cat, but it was still better than nothing.

"If I tried to bring coffee into this part of the library, Dr. Fulke would hang me up by my toenails, so no," Vivienne replied, coming to perch on the edge of the table.

As she did, Rhys caught that scent again, that sweet, almost sugary smell that clung to her skin, and his fingers tightened around his pen.

"How goes it?" she asked, leaning in to see what he was writing, and Rhys sat back in his chair, rolling his shoulders to alleviate some of the tension that had gathered there.

"Not well," he admitted. "But to be fair, I've only been at it for a little while. And of course, since I can't alert the other witches here as to what I'm doing, I'm stumbling in the dark a little bit."

Vivienne frowned, a wrinkle appearing over her nose, and Rhys wanted to reach out and smooth it away with his thumb.

Then she stood up. "Well, I'm here now, and I can help. What books haven't you looked at yet?"

Thirty minutes later, she sighed and closed the last book, its spine creaking ominously.

"So this one is useless." Leaning across the table, she reached for another from the stack, but even as her fingers closed over the cover, Rhys shook his head.

"Already tried that one."

"What about this one?" she asked, tapping her fingers on another book, and Rhys barely looked up before shaking his head again.

"Also a dud."

Vivienne sat up straighter in her chair. "Okay, so this entire endeavor has been a bust, then?"

Rhys finally looked up at her. "Did you think this was going to be easy?"

Rising from her seat, Vivienne rubbed the back of her neck. "No, but it just . . . it shouldn't be this hard to reverse a curse. Especially a curse this stupid." Throwing up her hands, she added, "I mean, we were barely even a thing."

Rhys was tired. He was cranky. And he was quite literally cursed, which is probably why those words . . . irked.

More than irked, really.

Infuriated.

"Enough of a thing that you cursed me when I left."

Vivienne frowned, her hand resting again on the back of her neck. "You didn't leave," she reminded him. "I left *you* after you suddenly remembered you were *engaged*."

Tilting his head back to look at the ceiling, Rhys groaned. "I was not *engaged,* I was *betrothed,* which is not—"

"I know," she said, standing up. "Not the same thing. So you tried to say at the time, but I gotta say, Rhys, I was not in the mood for a discussion about semantics then, and I definitely am not now."

Had he forgotten that she could be this frustrating, or was this a new trait, another facet of Adult Vivienne he hadn't learned?

Rising from his chair, Rhys stepped closer to her, suddenly aware of just how small the study room was, how close they were.

Christ, he should go home. To Wales. He should say "bugger it" to all this and leave.

Instead, he said, "That summer was important, Vivienne. It meant something."

Her lips were parted, her breath coming fast, and every cell in Rhys's body wanted to touch her even as his mind was screaming for him to back off.

Then Vivienne's eyes narrowed, and she stepped closer to him. "It was a three-month fling that I barely remember."

"Bollocks," he countered.

"Extremely not bollocks."

She was openly glaring at him now, her hands curled into fists at her sides as he moved in closer.

"So you don't remember the first time we kissed?"

Rhys did. He'd remember it until he died. They'd been sitting on top of a hill, the night a soft violet all around them, the smell of bonfires and summer in the air, and when he'd asked if he could kiss her, he'd nearly been holding his breath, wanting her to say yes more than he'd ever wanted anything in his life.

"I've kissed a lot of guys," Vivienne said, shrugging. "They all blend together after a while."

"Do they indeed," Rhys said, and somehow he and Vivienne were very close now, close enough for him to see how wide her pupils were, the flush climbing up her neck.

"Yup," she replied, and he saw her gaze flick to his mouth. "Guess you should've been more memorable."

"And if I were to kiss you now," Rhys said, his voice gone low as he looked down at her, "would that refresh your memory?"

She was going to tell him to fuck off. Or slap him. Possibly knee him in the balls. Those were all things he was ready for.

What Rhys had not expected was for her to step so close that their bodies aligned, chest to chest, hips to hips.

"Go for it."

CHAPTER 15

The moment his lips met hers, Vivi realized she'd made a terrible mistake.

It had probably been too much to hope that the intervening years had somehow made Rhys worse at kissing. Even with the curse.

And of course she'd lied to him when she said she couldn't remember his kiss. She'd remembered everything when it came to him. Every kiss, every touch.

Those months with Rhys Penhallow had been prime fantasy material over the years, her own personal X-rated scrapbook.

But maybe she hadn't been lying after all, because as he kissed her, she realized she hadn't remembered exactly how good it was. How good *he* was at this.

He kissed her like he'd been dying to kiss her every one of these past nine years, a low growl rumbling in his chest when his tongue met hers, and Vivi felt that sound all the way down to her toes.

Hands cupping her face, Rhys tilted her head, deepening the

kiss, and Vivi's own fingers clutched at his shoulders, wanting, needing to get as close to him as she could.

As he backed up, pulling her with him, his hip nudged the table. Vivi heard that one precarious stack of books hit the floor almost from a distance as she turned around, propping herself up on the edge of the table, never taking her hands off him, her eyes closed, her blood so hot in her veins she was surprised her skin wasn't steaming.

"Christ, I forgot," he was muttering against her neck, his mouth hot. "How did I forget?"

Vivi could only shake her head because she'd forgotten, too. Or maybe "forgotten" wasn't the right word. She'd driven the memory of this connection, this heat, from her mind along with all the rest of Rhys. She hadn't let herself remember how good it was between them because that would mean the summer fling she had at nineteen somehow trumped every other relationship in her adult life, and that was too depressing to contemplate.

Or maybe you were scared, a little voice in her mind reminded her. *Because if he was the best, you lost him too soon.*

His hands were skating over her hips now, gathering up the material of her skirt, and even as Vivi told herself she'd be completely out of her mind to have sex with her ex in a *freaking library,* she wasn't stopping him. In fact, she was helping him, her own hands going to shove his jacket off his broad shoulders even as she situated herself more firmly on the edge of the table.

Rhys was standing between her legs and she could feel him, hard and hot through the denim of his jeans, pushing against the cradle of her thighs as they just kept on kissing, and Vivi put one hand on the table behind her so that she could brace herself to press even closer.

The sound he made as she rolled her hips against him sent electricity racing down her spine, and Vivi tilted her head to give him better access to her neck, her eyes drifting shut as her fingers clutched the edge of his jacket.

Then he was kissing her mouth again, his tongue stroking hers, his hips moving against her in a way that made her feel more than a little crazy.

"Vivienne," he murmured against her neck, his hand stroking her thigh, and she nodded, needy and wanting.

"Touch me," she heard herself say. "Rhys, please . . ."

She was wearing tights, but she could still feel the press of his fingers along the seam there between her legs, and she tilted up into his touch, gasping.

"Okay, so that part of the curse definitely didn't work," she muttered, and Rhys lifted his head, gaze foggy with desire.

"What?"

"Nothing," she said, shaking her head. "Just do it again."

He did, and Vivi lowered her forehead to his shoulder, her grip on his shirt so tight she was surprised the fabric didn't tear.

This was insane. Irresponsible. Stupid.

And she was going to do it anyway.

When Vivi heard the first scream, the first thought her dazed, lust-addled mind could come up with was that someone had walked in on them.

But no, as the scream came again, it was clear that it wasn't that close.

Rhys had frozen, too, his head slightly tilted toward the door.

"I'm guessing that's not a normal sound in the library."

Still only half aware of what was going on, Vivi shook her head, blinking. "No, that's—"

The third scream was followed by a low rumble, and Vivi leapt to her feet, smoothing her skirt down back over her legs with one hand as Rhys took her other, pulling her toward the door.

"Come on."

As they came out of the study room, Dr. Fulke had already stepped down from her massive desk and was looking off through the stacks back toward the regular part of the library, her wrinkled face creased even further with worry.

"Something's wrong," she said, shaking her head, and Vivi had the sense Dr. Fulke wasn't even talking to them.

And then Rhys was pulling her back through the shelves in the direction they'd come this morning, closer and closer to that awful screaming.

The strange thing was, the closer they got to the source of the sound, the more Vivi's heart pounded, not just with fear but with that same overwhelming sense of magic she'd felt earlier, that cold sense of wrongness that had seeped in from the moment they'd entered the library.

She and Rhys burst out of the stacks, and the cold nearly sucked Vivi's breath from her lungs. Earlier, it had been chilly.

Now it was frigid, so cold it almost hurt, and she looked around her with wide eyes.

Students were cowered under study desks, huddled in corners, and in the center of the room . . .

"Is that . . . ?" Rhys asked, and Vivi could only nod, dumbfounded.

"It's a ghost."

RHYS STARED AT the apparition in front of them, wondering how someone who grew up where he had had never seen a ghost before.

Truth be told, he hadn't actually believed the damn things were real because if they were, there'd been no better place for them than Penhaven Manor.

This seemed very real.

The woman was a glowing greenish blue, her eyes wide in her pale face, feet dangling just a bit off the floor. But the weirdest thing about her was how she was dressed. She had on jeans, a flannel shirt over a T-shirt and a pair of Converse high-tops with Sharpie doodles on the toes, her dark hair pulled back in a messy ponytail as she glared at them.

Whenever she'd died, it hadn't been all that long ago, and Rhys found that more unsettling than he could explain.

The kid nearest him, a tall skinny guy in a Penhaven College hoodie and jeans, was sitting on the floor, his hands raised over his head like he was warding off a blow.

"What the hell is that thing?" he asked Rhys, and Rhys fought the urge to reply, *How in the name of sweet fuck would I know?*

Vivi stepped a little closer to the apparition. "What's she looking for?" she asked.

The ghost was still moving back and forth, her head swinging from side to side, and yes, she definitely seemed to be searching the shelves for something, her pale face contorted into a scowl.

And then she seemed to see him.

"Son of a bitch," Rhys muttered under his breath.

"I think she's looking at—" Vivienne started, but before she could finish the sentence, there was a banshee shriek, and the ghost was flying at him.

For a moment, the cold Rhys had felt earlier seemed to slip over him from head to toe, enveloping him as though he'd fallen into the sea.

And then he was flying.

Well, not flying so much as tumbling slightly above the floor, his back connecting painfully with a bookshelf. Dimly, he heard it creak and wobble, heard the shrieks of the students in the library, the pounding of running feet and Vivienne calling his name. But above all of that, he could still hear that shrill scream the ghost had uttered, like Satan's teakettle whistle, and as he tried to sit up, he winced, holding his ribs. None seemed broken, but they were definitely sore, and if that thing decided to take another shot at him . . .

The ghost had its back to him now, its attention focused on

the shelves in front of it, and as Rhys watched, spectral fingers reached out to take a book down, only for the ghost to howl in frustration as her hand passed right through whatever it was she was trying to hold. Still she tried again and again, her movements jerkier and more frantic, and Rhys swallowed hard as he attempted to come to his feet.

Vivienne was still standing there, frowning at the thing, and when she took a hesitant step even closer, Rhys lifted his hand.

"Vivienne!" he called, and the ghost's head whipped around, eyes narrowing.

He could feel it gathering up energy, the temperature in the room dropping even further, so cold now that he could see his breath, and every hair on his body seemed to be standing on end.

Bracing himself for another attack, Rhys gritted his teeth.

But then the ghost stopped, floating slightly to the right to glare at Vivienne, who still stood there, studying it like it was a puzzle she couldn't quite work out.

With a sound somewhere between a sigh and a wail, the ghost dropped her head, and, as suddenly as a soap bubble popping, was gone.

The room almost immediately became warmer, and Rhys looked around him.

The few students in the room had fled, leaving him and Vivienne alone among the overturned tables, the abandoned textbooks and pages of notebook paper that had fallen to the floor, the library suddenly very quiet after all that chaos.

Rhys moved over to Vivienne, taking both her hands in his. They were freezing, and he chafed her fingers between his palms. "Are you all right?" he asked in a low voice.

Moments ago, they'd been kissing. More than kissing, really. Rhys knew when a kiss was just a kiss, and when it was a prelude to more, and what they'd been doing in that study room had definitely been leading somewhere. He could still taste her on his tongue, still feel the damp heat he'd touched between her legs.

But now she was pulling her hands out of his and moving back, her eyes a little distant.

"Fine," she said. "You?"

Rhys gingerly touched his ribs again. "Nothing a hot bath and a nice whisky won't fix."

She nodded, then looked back to the shelf the ghost had been searching. "What was she looking for?"

"That's what you're concerned about?" Rhys asked, raising his eyebrows. "Not the fact that ghosts are real?"

"That part, too," she said, walking over to the shelf, frowning as she scanned the titles there. "Have you ever seen one before?"

"Most definitely not," Rhys said, shoving his hands in his pockets with a shudder. He could still feel the unnatural coldness of the spirit slipping over him, remembered how he'd felt suddenly not in control of his own body.

Fucking horrifying.

And it hadn't just been the cold he'd felt—that thing had been *angry* at him. But why?

"Ms. Jones."

A woman stood in the doorway between the regular library and Special Collections, Dr. Fulke hovering nervously behind her. She could've been anywhere between fifty and eighty, somehow ageless and ancient all at once, her hair a bright shock of white against her dark skin, and she was wearing, as far as Rhys could tell, about sixty-eight scarves.

Next to him, Vivi heaved a deep sigh.

"Dr. Arbuthnot," she said, and then looked at Rhys. "Head of Witchery."

CHAPTER 16

Vivi had never been in the witchery department before, and she was surprised to see it was a lot like the regular buildings on campus, just nicer. The floors were marble instead of linoleum, the walls wallpapered in a dark green damask pattern and the chairs in Dr. Arbuthnot's office were velvet instead of the hard plastic and polyester Vivi's office featured.

But the office was still small, there was still only one window, and as Dr. Arbuthnot passed Vivi a cup of tea, she noticed a stack of papers at the edge of the desk, waiting to be graded.

"Would you like to tell me what you were searching for in Special Collections?" Dr. Arbuthnot asked now, coming to sit on the other side of the desk from Vivi and Rhys.

Vivi didn't know about Rhys, but she felt like she'd been called to the principal's office, and she sipped her tea, trying to regain some composure. Between the kiss and the ghost, her brain felt like it had been scattered into a million pieces, and she knew she would need every shred of that brain to go toe-to-toe with the head of Witchery.

"We've had a magical mishap of sorts," Rhys said, smiling as he lifted his own teacup to his lips. "Something went wrong when I was charging the ley lines, as is my responsibility as a member of the founding family of this town."

Charm and authority, usually a winning combination, but Vivi saw Dr. Arbuthnot's expression harden. "A mishap," she repeated, her voice flat, then busied herself with collecting papers on her desk. "Well, this mishap has apparently released a ghost from a very powerful binding spell, so I suggest you fix it as soon as possible."

"A binding spell?" Vivi leaned forward. She'd heard of those before, but they were intense magic, far more serious than anything she'd ever attempted. "The ghost we saw today had been bound?"

The corners of Dr. Arbuthnot's mouth turned down, but she nodded. "Piper McBride, back in 1994. One of our best students. Unfortunately became too interested in the darker arts, and when she attempted contact beyond the veil, she ended up accidentally sacrificing herself. This is why we're so strict about certain types of magic being forbidden. Mess with the wrong thing, it kills you, as Piper learned, sadly."

Dr. Arbuthnot placed the papers back on her desk, her expression distant. "And when a witch dies as a result of shadow magic, we have no choice but to bind their spirit."

Vivi had never heard of that, but it made sense. Magic was energy, more or less. Do too much, it could drain your life force right out of you. And if you died doing something especially powerful, that energy had to go somewhere.

Like making a ghost.

"But now," Dr. Arbuthnot said, her tone brisk again, "the magic binding Piper's spirit is broken, so she's free to wreak havoc. Which is obviously of concern to us."

Linking her fingers, Dr. Arbuthnot placed her hands on her desk, studying Rhys and Vivi. "The normal parts of the college and the more . . . specialized parts live in harmony. Something I think you know very well, Ms. Jones. But ghosts in the library are obviously going to be very upsetting to the administration."

Vivi actually felt like a tiny piece of her soul was withering under Dr. Arbuthnot's gaze. "Absolutely," she agreed. "Which is why—"

"Which is why you will fix. This," Dr. Arbuthnot replied, biting off the words, and Vivi nodded so eagerly, she almost spilled her tea. "Yes. Yes, of course we will."

"Good." She stared at them for a moment, then waved one hand toward the door. "You can both go now."

Both Rhys and Vivi put their teacups back on her desk so quickly they rattled, and made for the door.

Once they were back across campus and safely ensconced in Vivi's office, Rhys took a deep breath, flopping into the chair opposite her desk. "All right, I see your point now."

"Thank you," she said, pressing one hand to her chest like that might stop her heart from galloping out of it. "They're intense, right?"

"Extremely. And how exactly are we meant to rebind a ghost?"

Shaking her head, Vivi walked around the desk and sat in her chair. "No clue. But we have to."

An idea occurred to her then, taking shape so fast she could almost see it. "Rhys," she said, laying both palms on her desk.

He eyed her suspiciously. "Yes?"

"This is what we have to do. It's going to take us a while to figure out how to break the curse, but while we do, we can at least solve all the issues the curse caused. Like how we fixed things at the store last night."

Rhys was looking at her like she'd grown another head. "We didn't fix that, though. Your aunt did."

Vivi just shook her head, some of that god-awful guilt finally abating. They could do this, between the two of them. Right the wrongs they'd inadvertently caused. "But you were able to convince those girls that nothing out of the ordinary was happening. That could've been an absolute shit show, but it wasn't."

"First of all, it was definitely shit show–adjacent," Rhys said, shrugging out of his jacket and hanging it from the back of his chair. "And secondly, Vivienne, we can't just put out fires left and right. Especially when we don't even know what those fires might look like."

"Maybe not," Vivi said, leaning back. "But we can try."

"I enjoy your optimism, Vivienne, I really do."

She pulled a face. "Don't be cynical, Rhys. Not about this."

"I'm not usually," he said. He blew out a breath, scrubbing a hand over his hair. It flopped perfectly back into place, absolutely doing The Thing, and Vivi groaned inwardly. It really wasn't fair. All the *bad* parts of the curse, and none of the silly bits? What kind of trade-off was that?

A complete bullshit one as far as Vivi was concerned.

Rhys's phone suddenly buzzed in his pocket, and he pulled it out, with a frown, muttering, "Ah, bugger it all."

"What is it?"

"Something's gone tits up at work," Rhys said, not taking his eyes off his phone as his thumbs moved frantically across the screen.

There was a cold sensation in the pit of Vivi's stomach all of a sudden. "Is it because of all this?" *Is it because of me?*

"'Course not," Rhys replied immediately, glancing up briefly to flash her a smile. "Shite happens in the travel business."

He was lying. Vivi knew that. For one, he wasn't very good at lying, his eyes somehow giving him away, and two, she knew that part of Rhys's magic involved luck. What better skill to have when you planned trips for people? If something was going wrong, it was because of the curse, which meant it was indeed because of her.

Rhys would be totally fair if he blamed her, but instead, he was trying to make her feel better.

That was also just deeply unfair.

"Mate!" he said brightly into the phone, posture tense even as his voice was all charm and ease. "Heard you've run into a sticky wicket."

Sticky wicket? she mouthed at him, and he rolled his eyes, shrugging as he shifted in his chair.

"No, no, not a problem at all," Rhys was saying even as he was frantically searching her desk for something.

Vivi handed him a pad and pen, and he gave her a thumbs-up as he leaned down to scribble across the pad.

"I can absolutely get that all sorted for you, not a problem."

For the next ten minutes, Vivi sat at her desk and watched as Rhys somehow transformed from the louche, carefree charmer she knew into the most competent man on the planet.

Phone calls were made. Notes were written out. More phone calls, and then several emails. At one point, he rolled up his sleeves and sat there across from her, phone pressed to his ear, elbows resting on his widely spread thighs, and Vivi nearly swooned.

When he was finally done with all his calls and emails and texts and who knew what else, Rhys flopped back against the chair, slouching so low that his head rested against the back of it, and Vivi did *not* take a flying leap from her chair to straddle his lap, which really showed a lot of restraint on her part, she thought.

Still, something must have shown in her face because he looked at her curiously.

"What?"

Shaking her head, Vivi cleared her throat and reached for the least sexy thing she could think of, a copy of her syllabus.

"Nothing."

CHAPTER 17

A ghost," Gwyn said, looking back over her shoulder at Vivi. They were at Something Wicked, but Gwyn had hung up the CLOSED sign as soon as Vivi walked in, and was now restocking the shelves of leather journals and grimoires.

Nodding, Vivi leaned her elbows on the counter. "A ghost."

"The Casper kind."

Vivi shook her head. "Way scarier than that, trust me."

As briefly as she could, she told Gwyn about what had happened at the library, adding, "But the bigger problem—"

"There's a bigger problem than a freaking ghost?"

"Mmm-hmm. The college witches are involved now."

Now it was Gwyn's turn to roll her eyes. "Those weirdos."

The witches who worked at Penhaven had always kept themselves apart from Vivi and her family, probably because most of them were transplants, and, Vivi suspected, because they didn't like the store. Lord knew they'd never set foot in it. They were too serious, too academic about magic for that sort of thing.

Their loss, Vivi thought as she studied a pile of crystals heaped on purple velvet there on the counter. "Anyway, they want us to 'fix this,' which, I mean, same."

Gwyn snorted. "Tell them about the curse. You'll have a fifty-page paper on curses by next week, but probably no actual solution."

"Rhys said we were being snobs."

Gwyn hooted at that. "Oh my god, a Penhallow Witch Boy calling *anyone* a snob is rich as fuck. And tell him they were rude to my mom first."

"I tried," Vivi said, "but I didn't want to actually get into all of it, you know? The less Rhys and I talk, the better."

She didn't add that when they weren't talking, they were kissing, which was a problem all its own.

Vivi honestly couldn't believe it had happened at all. Even now, it seemed like a dream, or like something that had happened to someone else. Surely she hadn't been so *completely stupid* as to make out with Rhys as . . . what? A dare? A bet?

This is why she'd ended up in this whole situation in the first place. She was normally a completely rational and calm person, and Rhys Penhallow made her totally lose her mind. Which is why they had to break the curse and send him on his way as soon as possible before she did something truly nuts like sleep with him.

Again.

Gwyn finished her arranging and turned around, brushing her hands off on her thighs. "Well," she started, "Mom is gonna be thrilled—"

She broke off suddenly, staring hard at Vivi.

"What?"

Narrowing her eyes, Gwyn leaned over the counter, getting closer. "Vivienne Jones. What happened with you and Rhys today?"

"Nothing," Vivi immediately said, but the fact that she could literally feel herself turn pink didn't exactly back her up.

And Gwyn knew it. Squealing, she clapped her hands. "Did you bang him in your office?"

"What? No!"

"In the library?"

"No," Vivi said, pushing off the counter and suddenly taking a lot of interest in the display of tarot cards. "There was zero banging."

Which was true. She and Rhys hadn't done anything more than kiss. Technically.

But if they hadn't been interrupted?

Vivi had never been one for sex in public, but she'd forgotten that Rhys could make her feel like that, like she'd die if she didn't have him right that second. Like her skin was too tight, and his was too far away, like she wanted to crawl inside him.

And that's why he was dangerous. She'd forgotten herself once with him, and look what had happened.

"Girl, if your kissing him can make you make that face, I have to say, I'm less surprised you were so devastated when the two of you broke up. The whole curse thing actually makes a lot more sense now."

"Ha-ha," Vivi replied before covering her face with her hands and groaning. "It was just . . . such an intensely stupid thing to do."

"Sweetie, again, you were nineteen and really upset, and—"

"Not that. I mean, yes that, that's way up there on the stupid meter, but I meant kissing him today. It just complicates things."

"How?"

When Vivi just looked at her, Gwyn lifted both her hands. "No, I'm serious. How? You're not nineteen anymore. You're not thinking he's gonna be the one and planning to marry him on a hillside covered with bunnies."

"Bunnies?"

"Stay with me here. You're an adult woman going through a stressful time in her life, and now your hot-as-hell ex is back in town and wants to kiss your face off. I say smoke 'em if you got 'em, babe."

Vivi couldn't help but smile, curling her fingers around one of the crystals on the counter. "That's always been your philosophy, Gwyn, but it's not mine."

"But it could be," Gwyn insisted. "And why not?"

Vivi realized she didn't really have an answer for that.

That kiss today had been good. Really good.

Why shouldn't she do it again if she wanted to?

The raven over the door squawked and Vivi and Gwyn both turned to see Rhys walk in. He'd changed since the morning, although he was still in his usual jeans and sweater, this one green, and Vivi had to bite back a sigh at the sight of him.

Gwyn caught it, though, shooting Vivi a look as she turned

to finish stocking the shelves. "Hi, dickbag," she called out, and Rhys lifted one hand.

"Lovely to see you, too, Gwyn. I assume Vivienne told you about our encounter this morning?"

Vivi dropped the crystal on the floor, the sound surprisingly loud in the quiet store, and Gwyn's smile when she looked over her shoulder was downright gleeful.

"Oh, she told me."

"*Gwyn,*" Vivi hissed, but Rhys seemed unbothered as he strolled over to the counter.

"Have to say, never thought I'd actually see a ghost," he continued, and Vivi rolled her eyes at herself.

Of course. He was talking about the ghost, not what had happened between the two of them.

But then, as he settled next to her, resting his elbows on the counter, she thought she saw the corner of his mouth kick up slightly.

"I can think of few things more depressing than haunting a library," Gwyn said. "At least if you're in a graveyard or something, there's stuff to do, you know? An aesthetic to maintain. But stuck in a library because you forgot to pay a fine in 1994 or something? That sucks."

"I think she was looking for something," Vivi said, trying to ignore how close Rhys was to her, how good he smelled. Had he showered after the library? He must have. Or maybe he just smelled good all the—

Okay, she was going to have to get a freaking grip.

Clearing her throat, Vivi pushed away from the counter. "Also weird that she just showed up now."

"That's because of the curse, right?" Gwyn asked, coming off her ladder.

Rhys nodded, turning his body slightly to face Vivi. "Or the ley lines, to be specific."

"What else could the cursed ley lines do?" Gwyn asked, frowning as she studied the two of them. "Demon toys, ghosts . . ."

"We don't know," Vivi admitted on a sigh. "And that's the issue. All magic in the town has gone haywire, and . . . random. So anything could happen."

She thought again about the frantic face of the library ghost, the way her eyes had moved restlessly over the shelves. She'd looked confused and scared, and that was . . . her fault.

Her curse had done that.

A curse she was no closer to being able to break.

CHAPTER 18

After the day he'd had, Rhys needed caffeine, and since the coffee shop was just down the way from Something Wicked, he'd suggested he and Vivienne go grab a cuppa.

As they made their way there, he had to admit that Graves Glen was a pretty place. The sun was setting behind the low mountains that surrounded the town, turning the sky a deep purple. The lights strung between the streetlamps twinkled, and in every store window, there was some charming display—a pile of pumpkins, cardboard witches on broomsticks, more fairy lights.

"It's like being in a souvenir postcard," Rhys said. "'Greetings from Halloweentown.'"

Vivienne chuckled at that, crossing her arms. "No arguments there."

"I see why you like it here."

"It's definitely a good place to be a witch. Even a secret one."

"Technically we're all secret witches," Rhys said, "but I understand your point."

The night had gone cool around them, but the sweet, soft sort of cool that comes on perfect autumn nights as opposed to the unnatural cold of the library. Wales got these nights, too, but earlier in the season and not usually quite this mild.

Still, as he wandered the cobblestone streets with Vivienne, Rhys felt an odd longing for home settle into his bones. Vivienne belonged in this setting, fitting as perfectly as a jewel.

Where did he belong?

Not wanting to follow that particularly maudlin train of thought, Rhys nudged Vivienne with his elbow and said, "So how exactly does it work here? The secret witch thing. Especially with the college. You can spot other witches, right?"

Shrugging, Vivienne tucked a stray lock of hair behind one ear. "Usually. And honestly, it's not as hard to keep a secret from people as you'd think. Lots of people dabble in witchcraft now, so it's not exactly weird to have an interest in that kind of thing."

"Or run a shop," Rhys said, and she nodded.

"Or that."

"But the other students at the college still don't know they're going to school with witches, right?"

"Right," Vivienne confirmed as they came to the coffee shop. Like every store or restaurant along this strip of main street, it was decorated for Halloween, little pumpkins stuck to the front window, and a garland of lights that looked like tiny cauldrons draping the door.

As they stepped inside, Rhys held the door open for a family with a baby swaddled up in a stroller, smiling down at the babbling infant as they passed, and when he looked back up, Vivienne was watching him with a strange look on her face.

"What?" he asked, but she only shook her head and gestured toward the counter.

"Tea?"

"Tea," he confirmed.

Once they had ordered—basic English breakfast for Rhys, something with honey and lavender for Vivienne—they made their way to a booth near the back, and Rhys was suddenly very aware of how cozy this setting was, how . . . intimate.

"So."

"So."

They sat there with their steaming mugs of tea on the table, but neither of them made a move to drink. Instead, Rhys looked at Vivienne, and Vivienne looked everywhere *but* at him, her fingers twisting the fingerless gloves she was wearing nervously, pulling at the edges until Rhys was afraid they might unravel.

He reached out and covered one of her hands with his own, and dammit all, even through the wool of her gloves, even with his palm only barely touching the bare skin of her *knuckles,* he felt the touch all the way down to the soles of his feet, his skin lighting up with awareness of her.

"I think we need to talk about the library."

She was already shaking her head, golden hair spilling over her shoulders. "No. No, no, no, no. We don't. That's a thing that in no way needs talking about."

"Vivienne."

"It was stupid, and it was just a kiss," she went on.

He raised his eyebrows. "Just a kiss? Really?"

A flush crept up Vivienne's neck, but she drew her hand out from underneath his and repeated, "Just a kiss."

Rhys had not known Vivienne all that long in the grand scheme of things, but he recognized the look on her face now. This was a closed subject, and pushing her on it wasn't going to get him anywhere.

So he slid his own hands back across the table, resting them on the edge and drumming his fingers as he looked around him.

"Busy place."

Clearly relieved at the change in subject, Vivienne nodded and picked up her mug of tea. "It's always packed. We're lucky we found a table."

Leaning forward, Rhys gave a subtle jerk of his head to the barista, a short girl with bright turquoise hair and a pair of heavy-rimmed glasses. "Witch?" he asked quietly, and Vivienne didn't even glance over to see who he was talking about.

"Yup. They only employ witches here. Usually students from the college. It's part of what keeps things running so smoothly in here. There's some kind of light enchantment, means orders never go wrong, no one ever drops a glass, that kind of thing."

Her words seemed to dawn on them both at the same time and, slowly, they both looked down at their teas.

"So. Magic helps run this place."

"Uh-huh."

"And magic is . . . bad now."

"Maybe it hasn't affected this place?"

He could see Vivienne steeling herself as she picked up her mug, and he already had a hand out, her name on his lips as she closed her eyes, jerkily lifted the mug to her lips and took a big gulp.

They both sat there, frozen, as she swallowed and then, to his massive relief, smiled, her hazel eyes bright. "It's fine," she said, setting the mug back down. "Totally normal tea, no disaster magic afoot."

Rhys took a sip of his own tea, and she was right—it tasted fine, and there was no hint of magic in it at all. "Right," he said, and then lightly tapped her mug with his own. "So maybe this place escaped the cur—"

The shattering of glassware cut him off, and Rhys had a horrible prickling sensation on the back of his neck as he slowly turned to look toward the source of the noise.

There, by the door, an entire table had been turned over, glasses and mugs lying in pieces on the floor, and amid all that broken glass was a body.

Rhys was on his feet almost without thinking, crossing over to where a man, an older guy in khakis and loafers, lay on the floor, the fingers of one hand still curled like he was holding a mug, his face locked in a rictus of surprise.

"He's breathing," Vivienne said, appearing by Rhys's side, her fingers pressed against the man's wrist. "And his pulse is fine. He's just . . ."

"Frozen," Rhys finished grimly as he took in the wide, staring eyes, the half-open mouth.

And then he noticed the mug the guy had been holding was lying on the floor next to him, its contents spreading slowly across the hardwood floor.

There might not have been any magic involved in Rhys or Vivienne's tea earlier, but there clearly was in whatever this man had been drinking. Rhys could practically see the spell, hovering like a miasma over the spilled liquid, and then he looked back toward the bar.

The woman Vivienne had pointed out as the owner was on the phone, looking back and forth between the man and the crowd of onlookers, but there was nothing in her face except concern. No guilt, no fear.

Then his eyes slid to the right, to where the girl with the turquoise hair stood, arms folded tightly around her body, her lower lip caught between her teeth.

And when she saw Rhys looking at her, she gave a little jump before opening the door behind the bar and disappearing into the storeroom.

"Vivienne," Rhys said in a low voice, nudging her, but she was already standing up, her eyes on the spot where the girl had vanished.

"I saw."

Outside, there was the distant wailing of sirens, but the man was already starting to stir a little, his eyelids fluttering, and Rhys assumed whatever the spell was, it wasn't strong enough to last long.

Small mercy, that.

As he stood up, Vivienne moved closer to him and the two of them were able to slip back into the crowd of people gathered around the guy. As the ambulance pulled up outside, the owner of the shop put her phone back in her pocket and hurried over, leaving the counter empty and no one paying attention to anything but the EMTs currently coming in.

Which made it easy for Rhys and Vivienne to slip into the storeroom.

Unlike the back room at Something Wicked, there was nothing magical about this space. It was like the back room you'd find in any coffee shop in any town. Tall metal shelves stocked with stacks of paper cups, big sacks of coffee beans on the floor and several plastic crates full of mugs.

Rhys was, honestly, a little disappointed.

The girl with the turquoise hair was sitting on one of those crates, empty and overturned, her knees drawn up against her chest, the toes of her boots turned in and pressed together.

As soon as she heard the door open, her head shot up, and her dark eyes looked huge in her pale face. A name tag pinned to her shirt read, SAM.

"Is he okay?" she asked, and Vivienne nodded.

"It's already wearing off," Sam said, and blew out a long breath, her shoulders sagging. "Okay, good."

"Do you maybe want to tell us what you did to his drink to make him like that?" Rhys asked, and when she looked up at him now, some of her sardonic cool had returned.

"It's a bespoke spell," Sam said, sitting up straighter. "You wouldn't know it."

"Hipster magic, excellent," Rhys muttered, rubbing a hand over the back of his neck. Had he been like this as a young witch? All arrogant and so sure of his abilities?

Stupid to even wonder it, really. He knew he had been.

Next to him, Vivienne drew herself up a little bit taller. "What was it supposed to do?"

"Are you two the Magic Police or something?" Sam asked, scowling, and Rhys shoved his hands into his pockets, rocking back on his heels.

"No, pretty sure that doesn't exist. If it had, I would surely have been arrested at some point. Just a fellow witch, trying to figure out what happened in there."

He jerked his thumb back toward the shop, and some of the girl's confidence faded, her eyes darting toward the door.

"It's stupid," she muttered, and Rhys shrugged.

"Lots of things in life are. So what was the spell?"

Sam tugged at the hem of her T-shirt, not meeting Rhys's eyes. "He wanted a potion to make him, uh. You know." She made a weird gesture with her hands, lifting her palms up and then flailing her hands in the general direction of Rhys's lap. "Like Viagra," she finally said. "But magic."

Rhys was very proud of himself for not betraying the slightest bit of surprise or amusement over this. Truly, he deserved a medal. Possibly a parade.

As it was, he just cleared his throat and said, "Right."

"I figured out how to make that kind of spell as a joke," she went on, "but then I gave it to someone who asked for it, and he told a friend, I guess, and he told someone else, and now I get these dudes coming in here a few times a week for it. But it's never done *that*."

"So wait," Vivienne said, stepping in front of Rhys and folding her arms over her chest. "You've been what? Dealing potions?"

Sam rolled her eyes. "Okay, that makes it sound super shady. It's not *dealing*, it's *giving*."

Vivienne's eyebrows rose. "You just give the potions away?"

Making a frustrated sound, Sam waved one hand. "Duh, no. I charge for them. A hundred bucks a pop, more if the potion is complicated or the ingredients were expensive to get."

Her smug expression wavered. "Oh, wait, I guess that *is* dealing. Huh." She shrugged. "Anyway, yes, I have a harmless side gig dealing potions here."

Then she glared at Vivienne. "Out-of-state tuition isn't cheap, lady."

"Point noted," Rhys replied, moving a little closer to Vivi's side, "but you realize that what you were doing was dangerous, right? Potions are not something to mess around with."

"Yeah, well, usually there aren't any issues, and I'd never make anything that would hurt someone. We're talking the lightest magic here. A potion to make your eyeliner last all day. One that makes sure you're always on time for twenty-four hours." She looked up at Rhys, pushing her glasses up the bridge of her nose. "That one is good for finals week. Makes sure you don't oversleep, but doesn't do anything scary like make you stay awake for days or something. Took some tweaking, but—"

"Sam, we're definitely impressed with your skills, but you can't make potions and sell them to people. It's dangerous and if the college found out, you'd be in serious trouble."

All of Sam's bravado popped like a soap bubble, and Rhys realized just how young she was. Nineteen, maybe twenty. Same age as he and Vivienne had been the summer they met.

Christ, he hadn't realized just how young they were until that age was sitting right in front of him, looking like she'd been sent to the bloody headmaster's office.

"You're not going to tell them, are you?" she asked, turning her beseeching gaze on Vivienne. "I know you work there. With the normies, not us, but—"

"I'm not," Vivienne said. "So long as you promise me you'll never do it again."

"I promise," Sam said quickly, holding up one hand, the silver rings stacked on her fingers flashing in the fluorescent lights. "Trust me, I don't want anything like this to ever happen again."

She got up then, dusting her hands on her apron before adjusting her beanie, only to pause, chewing on her lower lip again.

"It's just . . . I really don't think it was my potion. I didn't do anything different. Even the phase of the moon was the same when I brewed it." She flashed them a cheeky grin. "Always make that one on the waxing moon. Because of the whole 'growing'—"

"Right," Rhys said, cutting her off. "We've got that, thanks."

"Point is," Sam went on, "something went wrong, but it wasn't *my* magic." She shook her head. "It's like magic is off all over the place. Today some of the normie kids wandered into one of my classes on herb magic, and that's for sure not supposed to happen."

Rhys felt a headache building at the base of his skull. Curse, ghosts, now bad potions. He thought again about those lines of magic snaking out of the cave, racing toward the town, and wished he could go back in time and kick himself repeatedly in the head.

He'd known something was off. He'd felt it.

And, as usual, he'd ignored things like "self-preservation" and "common sense," and decided to just do it anyway.

And now look where they were.

"Maybe hold off on the magic for a little while," Vivienne suggested, coming forward to touch Sam's arm. She looked as tired as Rhys felt, and he had to fight the urge to rest his hand against her lower back, to pull her in closer to him and let her rest her head on his shoulder.

Sam scoffed at that. "'Hold off'?" she echoed. "That's like asking me to hold off on breathing. I know you don't get that since you're not a witch—"

"I am a witch," Vivienne said, stepping back, and Sam's face creased in confusion.

"Wait, seriously? But you teach the normal classes."

"Right, because—"

"And, like, obviously this dude is magic," Sam went on, pointing to Rhys, "you can tell, but you are? Seriously?"

Rhys saw Vivienne swallow hard, and for at least the thousandth time, Rhys wished that mind-reading were one of his abilities. Of course, the way things were going right now, he'd probably be able to hear every stray thought of a person within a hundred-mile radius and lose his bloody mind, but it might be worth the risk to know what was going on behind Vivienne's bright hazel eyes.

Her shoulders went back a little, chin lifting, and she said, "Anyway, still a witch, still think you need to be careful with your magic while things are out of sorts."

Sam was still looking at Vivienne like she couldn't believe what she was hearing, her eyes wide, her lips slightly parted. "I mean, I knew you were related to the people who run Something Wicked, but seriously, I thought you were just—"

"So you've said." Rhys cut her off as Vivienne's eyes began to narrow. He'd been on the receiving end of that look, and wanted to save Sam from herself.

"Ms. Jones here is right," Rhys went on. "Hold off on the magic until things have settled down a bit."

"But why are they all fucked up in the first place?" the girl asked, and Vivienne's face got that slightly murdery expression again that had Rhys stepping in front of her.

"They just are," he said. "But we're fixing them."

He wished that were actually true. So far, they'd been at this for nearly twenty-four hours, and all they had to show for it was eye strain and possibly stray bits of ectoplasm in his hair.

Sam scowled at that, but all the same she muttered, "Fine," before slipping past them and back out into the café.

Sighing, Rhys nearly flopped against a tall metal shelf, almost upsetting a stack of paper cups, and Vivienne moved across to lean next to him. For a moment, they were silent, both of their minds whirring.

"Hard," Vivienne murmured to herself, and Rhys blinked at her.

"Beg pardon?"

Startled, Vivienne glanced over at him. "Oh, um. I was just thinking. That's . . . that's where her potion went wrong. The spell was supposed to make him . . . you know, and it *did,* but it was . . . an all-over effect instead of . . . region-specific."

"Vivienne Jones, are you blushing?"

She pushed off of the shelf with a roll of her eyes, but he saw the way her hands fidgeted with the ends of her gloves again. "Definitely could've been worse," she said.

"Do you see now what I was saying?" Rhys asked, stepping closer to her, close enough that he could see the little constellation of freckles on her right cheek, close enough to touch her if he wanted to.

Which he did.

But he wouldn't.

"We can't keep putting out these little fires, Vivienne. We have to fix this."

"I know," she said, her head snapping up.

And then she lowered her voice, ducking her head. "Halloween is huge in this town. The biggest moneymaker, too. Some of the businesses in Graves Glen are set for the year after Halloween. And if we haven't fixed this by then, it might not be safe. We can't risk that."

"Also slightly concerned about *me* being safe," Rhys said, "but I see your point. Luckily, magic tends to be at its strongest around Samhain. And that means that if we work quickly, any kind of curse reversal might work stronger."

"I like where your head is at, Penhallow," Vivienne replied, pointing at him, and Rhys brightened, smiling at her.

"Did you just call me by my last name? Like we're on some kind of sports team together?"

To his surprise, she actually smiled a little at that. "In a way we are, right? Breaking a curse has definitely turned out to be a lot more . . . athletic than I'd anticipated."

"Hiking across campus," Rhys noted.

"Fighting ghosts," Vivienne added.

"Snogging in libraries . . ."

At that, her smile dimmed and she straightened up, moving back from him.

"That was a mistake," she said, and Rhys shoved his hands in his pockets.

"Was it, now?"

She turned back to him, meeting his eyes. No blush now, no fidgeting. "You know it was."

What Rhys knew was that kissing her had felt like waking up. Like he'd been drifting sleepily through everything for the past nine years until he tasted her mouth again and remembered what actually being alive felt like. Better than any magic, Vivienne's kiss.

And he didn't want to go without it for another nine years.

"We're adults," he reminded her. "Not kids furtively sneaking into dorm rooms anymore."

"Which is why we know better than to complicate things right now," Vivienne said, eminently sensible and, much as Rhys hated to admit it, completely right.

He was leaving when this was over.

She was staying.

What they had was not the kind of thing that worked in a long-distance sense, and hell, for all he knew, all they had was intense physical chemistry that would burn itself out.

It didn't burn itself out over nine years, the bastard part of his brain reminded him. *Do you really think it's going to now?*

CHAPTER 19

The next afternoon, Vivi sat in her office, pretending to make lecture notes.

In truth, she was staring at the blinking cursor on her computer and thinking about kissing Rhys while also wishing she'd never brought him to her office. This was *her* space, a very decidedly Rhys Penhallow–free space, and now every time she looked at her bookshelf, she saw him standing there, studying her books, asking her questions, actually seeming interested in her answers.

What a bastard.

But then every time she thought about kissing him, she remembered what had ended that kiss, the ghost in the library, and how she was so sure she'd seen that face somewhere before. How the ghost had so clearly been looking for something, and how it all had to be related to the curse somehow, but *how*?

So really, it was no wonder that her lecture on the function of the feudal system consisted of exactly two bullet points, one of which just said, "PEASANTS??"

Shaking her head, Vivi leaned over her desk and flipped the

switch on her electric kettle, hoping a strong cup of tea might get her head straight. Gwyn and Aunt Elaine had given her the hot-pink kettle last Yule, and she loved it, but loved the tea they'd wrapped with it even more. It was one of Aunt Elaine's own blends, and it tasted like mint and licorice and something a little smoky while also having enough caffeine to power her through even the most heinous grading sessions.

She'd just made herself a cup when there was a knock at her office door.

Brain still foggy with thoughts of Rhys, she almost expected to see him standing there—or leaning, really. Rhys never stood when he could lean.

But the woman in her doorway was definitely not Rhys, and also standing straighter than Vivi had ever seen someone stand, she was pretty sure.

The woman was young, probably Vivi's own age, and had dark hair caught back from her face with a pair of combs.

"Vivienne Jones?" the woman asked, her expression friendly, dimples appearing in her cheeks as she smiled.

"I'm Amanda Carter." She stepped into Vivi's office, shutting the door behind her. "From the witchery department."

Vivi's spoon clanged against the side of her mug. "Seriously?" she asked.

Amanda couldn't have been thirty, making her easily the youngest witch Vivi had ever heard of the witchery department hiring.

And she was wearing *jeans*.

Did they let them wear jeans on the Witchery side of things? Because if so, Vivi wondered if maybe she should transfer after all.

"Did Dr. Arbuthnot send you?" she asked, and Amanda nodded. "She did, yeah. About the whole ghost thing?"

Excellent.

Gesturing at the chair in front of her desk, Vivi said, "Please have a seat. Tea?"

Raising her chin ever so slightly, Amanda sniffed the air. "Is that one of your aunt's blends?"

Surprised, Vivi smiled a little, moving to the box of tea leaves on the corner of her desk. "It is. She sells it at the store, but this one is particularly good, I think."

"Awesome," Amanda enthused, and Vivi felt her mood lift. Someone from the Witch College who said "awesome" and wore jeans? Who knew?

She made Amanda a cup of tea, and handed it over as the other woman asked, "How long have you worked here?"

Vivi blew across the surface of her tea before answering. "Three years. You?"

"A few months." Amanda grinned at her. "Still finding my feet."

"I bet," Vivi said, and then Amanda reached down toward the bag that sat at her feet.

"So as you know, the ghost of Piper McBride is running loose."

"Right," Vivi said, remembering the ghost in her flannel and Converse, pacing the shelves. "Sorry about that."

Amanda gave her another easy smile, waving a hand. "Hey,

shit happens. And from what they've told me, Piper was a real mess back in the day. Obsessed with some history of the town, trying to summon spirits . . ."

Vivi frowned. Dr. Arbuthnot had told her Piper had been involved in dark magic, but she hadn't known it was a summoning. That was a whole different ball game. No wonder she'd ended up dead.

"Anyway, we bound her, but obviously, she's unbound now, so the trick is to capture her again," Amanda continued.

"How do we do that?"

Sitting back in her chair, Amanda pulled a candle from her bag.

"How do you feel about haunted houses?"

CHAPTER 20

Rhys hadn't had any really solid plans for his evening. Mostly he'd thought about sitting on the horribly uncomfortable couch his father had bought for this place and drinking a bottle of red wine. Somewhere in there, he'd planned on making time for both some half-hearted googling of "curse removal," and feeling sorry for himself, but he'd only just opened the bottle of Syrah he certainly hoped Simon had been saving for a special occasion when his phone buzzed.

Vivienne.

Many things went through his head when he saw that she was asking him to meet her near midnight, giving him just an address, and only 80 percent of them were filthy.

Clearly, he was growing as a human being.

So he grabbed his coat, plugged the address Vivienne had given him into his phone and hoped his rental car would hold up this time.

It did, but when he came to a stop on a dirt road barred by a metal gate, he kind of wished he'd blown a tire near the house and had just called it a night, gone back to his original plans.

Vivienne was standing by the gate, dressed all in black, her hair pulled back in a tight French braid, and as Rhys stepped out of the car, he took in her outfit, complete with black leather gloves.

"Have you brought me out here to murder me?" he called. "Because that probably *would* solve your problems, but I have to say, I object on both moral and personal grounds."

Shaking her head, she came closer, and Rhys caught another whiff of that damnable scent, sweet and heady against the crisp and smoky autumn evening. "We're going on a kind of . . . quest."

For the first time, Rhys noticed the satchel she had strapped across her chest, the torch—flashlight, he reminded himself—in her hand.

"A curse-breaking quest?" he asked, and she frowned.

"It's curse-related."

Well, that was promising at least.

Tapping the flashlight she held, Rhys asked, "Don't trust your little illumination spell?"

The flashlight blinked on, and he could finally see her face clearly. Her pupils were huge in those hazel eyes, and she looked a little pale. Nervous, too.

"Didn't think it was worth the risk."

Reaching into her satchel, she pulled another flashlight out, handing it to him. "Come on."

With that, she turned and headed back toward the gate, vaulting herself over with an ease that shouldn't have turned him on nearly so much, but then, he was becoming used to finding literally everything Vivienne did erotic. Walking, jumping over fences, liking polka dots . . . all of it was immensely appealing, and if Rhys took a bit of satisfaction when he noticed her own eyes glaze over a little as he placed one hand on the gate and easily hopped it, well . . . he was only human.

Which also meant that the second his feet crunched on the dry leaves littering the road, a shiver of apprehension raced up his spine.

They were in the middle of nowhere, in a forest, at—he checked his watch—11:47 P.M. The night was so black it felt like it was pressing in on him, and he stopped, catching her elbow with one hand.

"All right, I pride myself on being the sort of bloke who rolls with the punches, but seriously. Where are we going?"

Vivienne nodded up the road. "There's a house up there. Well, a cabin, really. Several of the witchy students at Penhaven have rented it in the past."

Pausing, Vivienne fiddled with her flashlight, and Rhys prodded her foot gently with his toe. "Go on."

She cleared her throat. "Including Piper McBride. The ghost we saw in the library, and now we have to catch her."

Vivienne went to continue walking back up the road, and Rhys caught her elbow again.

"I'm sorry, did you say we're going to catch a ghost?"

Blowing out a breath, Vivienne threw her hands up. "Not catch, exactly. We just have to—hold on."

She fished in her satchel again, and Rhys wondered if it was some sort of Mary Poppins bag. What was she going to pull out of that thing next? Sword? Houseplant?

"We just have to light this," she said, and Rhys squinted at the silver candle she held.

"A Eurydice Candle? Where did you even get that?" Rhys had only seen one once before, in a locked cabinet in his father's library, and Rhys was pretty sure Simon had threatened him with bodily harm if he ever touched the thing. They were rare to come by, and the magic they used was powerful stuff.

"Amanda," Vivienne said, and when Rhys just kept looking at her, she shoved the candle back in her bag. "She's one of the college witches. Dr. Arbuthnot sent her to my office with the candle. Apparently, all we need to do is go to Piper's house, find the spot where she kept her altar back in the day and light the candle. Then the candle will—"

"Pull her spirit into it, trapping it within the candle, which can then be lit somewhere else, releasing her more safely."

"Right," Vivienne said with a nod. "And then the college witches can rebind her."

Overhead, an owl hooted, and Rhys tilted his head back to study the night sky. The moon was nearly full, skeletal trees reaching up for the stars, the perfect night for summoning up evil ghosts, and Rhys knew deep in his gut this was a terrible idea.

"Why can't they come do it themselves?" he asked, and Vivienne sighed, pushing a stray bit of hair off her forehead.

"It has to be us. We're the ones who set her free, so we have to capture her. But the candle does all the work. We just have to light it, wait for her spirit to, you know, get"—she lifted a hand and made a kind of swooping motion—"sucked into it, and then, done!"

She smiled at him, possibly the fakest smile Rhys had ever seen in his life. "Easy as pie!"

"You mean one of those kinds of pies they used to stuff live birds in, I take it? Because nothing about this strikes me as particularly easy, Vivienne."

"Amanda said it would be."

"Oh, well, if Amanda said it would be, then no problem at all! Our old friend, Amanda."

Rolling her eyes, Vivienne turned away. "Maybe I should've come on my own."

"Maybe neither of us should have come, and you should have told that witch to bugger off. I thought you didn't like the college witches anyway."

"I don't," she agreed, her boots crunching over the dried leaves as they moved deeper into the forest, and Rhys raised his shoulders, tugging at the collar of his jacket. Wasn't this the South? Wasn't the South supposed to be warm?

"But Amanda was nice, and she wanted to help, and since it's my fault this ghost is out—"

"It's our fault," he said. "This entire thing is very much a disaster caused by two, Vivienne."

She stopped then, turning around again. "Well, if it's your fault, too, then maybe you should stop whining about helping."

"I'm not *whining*," he insisted, but then realized that it was almost impossible to say that sentence *without* sounding like you were whining, so he cleared his throat and said, "I just think that at a time when, as has been established, magic is on the fritz, maybe lighting a Eurydice Candle is a bad idea."

"Ah!" Vivienne pointed at him, but since she did it with the hand holding the flashlight, Rhys was momentarily blinded.

He threw a hand up against the glare, and Vivienne immediately lowered the flashlight.

"Sorry. But as I was saying, ah! I thought of that, too. But there are loopholes. One, we're not doing any magic ourselves. No spells, no rituals. The candle is doing all the work, and two . . ."

She crooked a finger at him, and Rhys was dismayed by how quickly he felt that gesture like a tug in his chest.

He felt it lower, too, his cock eager to follow wherever she wanted, and Rhys thought again of that kiss in the library, the feel of her under his hands, how quickly she lit up for him.

"Rhys," Vivienne said, and then dammit all, she crooked that finger again. "Come here."

He was truly an idiot, just the most besotted wanker in the entire world, because there was that tug again.

Keeping his hands in his pockets as he walked over to her, Rhys raised his eyebrows. "What?"

Placing one hand on his shoulder, she lightly pushed him a few steps to her right, and then looked up at him with that sunshine smile.

"I forgot to tell you. Aunt Elaine figured something out. The curse? It only exists within the town limits. Probably because the magic only fuels Graves Glen."

"Gryffud was a very specific bastard from all accounts, so that makes sense," he acknowledged.

"Right," Vivienne said. "And as of right now, we are officially two . . . no, *three* steps outside the town of Graves Glen."

With that, she lifted the hand on his shoulder and wiggled her fingers.

That little ball of light she'd conjured up his first night back in town sprung to life, and hovered there. It didn't immediately explode into a ball of flame that took his eyebrows off, so Rhys assumed she was right. The curse didn't extend this far.

That was a relief at least.

"Now, come on. We have a ghost to catch."

Aaaaand moment of relief over.

They continued up the road for a few more minutes, the trees getting thicker, the path narrower, and while Rhys didn't have the same sense of foreboding he'd felt in the library, he still wished he were anywhere but here.

And then, as the path narrowed even further, Vivienne's shoulder brushed his, and suddenly being on a road through the woods, headed to a haunted house, was not really that bad. Maybe he didn't want to be back on his sofa alone. Maybe he—

"Oh, fuck me running."

Rhys came to a sudden stop, staring up at the house that suddenly rose up in front of him.

If you looked up "haunted house" online, he thought, this was the picture you'd get. It looked like something out of every bad horror movie he'd ever seen, and he was less afraid of ghosts than he was catching tetanus as he took in the crooked steps, the shutter slumping from one window, the front door hanging drunkenly on its hinges.

"Maybe the library needs a ghost," Rhys said, studying the house. "Maybe we just leave it there. Bit of character, you know?"

Next to him, Vivienne sucked in a deep breath. "We just have to go in and light a candle. I bet we can be in and out in, like, three minutes."

"That is about four minutes longer than I want to be in that house," Rhys replied, but then he looked at her, saw her tug her lower lip between her teeth, and knew they weren't leaving until this was done.

So, taking a deep breath of his own, Rhys held out his hand to her. "Let's go catch a ghost."

CHAPTER 21

Vivi had told herself that the inside of the cabin could not possibly be any creepier than the outside. It was probably going to be one of those things where all the creep was there on the outside, and inside, it would just be an empty, old house. Nothing all that sinister.

In the few moments she had before Rhys pushed open the front door, Vivi let herself really believe that.

And then they stepped into the front room, and—

"I grew up in an actual haunted house, and this is worse," Rhys said.

"Way worse. I mean, I haven't seen your house, but I believe it."

The inside of the cabin had been wallpapered at one point in what had probably been a pretty charming damask, but now it was falling from the walls in sheets, revealing stained and warped boards beneath. Mildew and mold crept along the ceiling, and in the corner, there was a velvet settee that appeared to be rotting, one leg missing, a hole in the middle cushion.

The other furniture was in a similar state of disrepair, most of it covered in a thick coating of dust, but the floor was surprisingly clean, and Vivi glanced around, wondering if other people had been here before.

Rhys seemed to be noticing it, too, frowning as he looked around, shining his flashlight on a framed photograph tacked to the wall. Piper was in it with a couple of other teenagers, all rocking a very mid-nineties look, standing in front of one of the buildings at Penhaven College.

"Well, at least we know we're in the right place," he said, and then swung the beam around the room. "But why is the floor so clean?"

"Maybe she had a spell," Vivi suggested. "Some kind of cleaning spell that sort of hung on after she died?"

Rhys shrugged. "Possible. Stranger things have happened."

Avoiding glass from a broken window, Vivi moved farther into the room. One floorboard felt mushy as she stepped on it, creaking ominously.

"So," she said, swallowing hard. "We just need to figure out where she had her altar, light the candle—"

"And get the fuck out of here. With alacrity," Rhys finished, and Vivi nodded.

"Lots of alacrity, yes."

Luckily, the cabin was small. There was just the front room with a tiny closet, a small room that had probably been Piper's bedroom and a kitchen, the appliances old and rusting in places.

Vivi had thought the bedroom would be their best bet, but

the room was completely empty and, unlike the front room, covered in dust. Plus there was no hint of lingering magic there, no ancient wax stains or soot-marked walls, all the things Vivi would've expected to find.

She checked the kitchen next, but like the bedroom, it was empty except for an ancient table and chairs that had half rotted, the chair little more than a pile of wood.

Rhys was still checking the living room, squatting down by the fireplace and shining his flashlight over the cracked brick. "I'm not feeling anything," he said, and Vivi looked at him, his jeans taut over his thighs, his shoulders broad as he peered up into the chimney, the beam of her own flashlight highlighting the sharpness of his cheekbones, the line of his jaw.

"Um. Yeah. Me, neither," she said, then turned away before he caught her basically ogling him.

She was here to catch a ghost, pretty much the least sexy thing on the planet.

Of course, library study rooms were supposed to be unsexy, too, and they'd certainly proven that wrong.

She and Rhys plus dimly lit small spaces clearly equaled Bad Choices, so the sooner she got this over with, the better. "There has to be something we're missing," she said. "Maybe—"

They heard it at the same time.

Footsteps.

Vivi's mouth went dry, her knees suddenly feeling a little watery as her stomach pitched. Seeing a ghost in broad daylight in a building full of people had been terrifying enough. Having one appear here, in this, the setting for one of those cheesy ghost hunter shows Gwyn liked so much?

Vivi shuddered. No, thank you.

Rhys stood up, clicking his flashlight off, and Vivi did the same, also extinguishing her illumination spell, and they stood there in the dark room, only lit by the moon, listening.

The footsteps were closer, but now Vivi realized they were outside. She could hear the leaves and the pebbles crunching on the path outside, and as whoever it was moved closer, she heard the whispers of what sounded like more than one person.

Breathing a sigh of relief, Vivi looked over at Rhys. *No ghost,* she mouthed, and he nodded, but then gestured at the door.

But who is it? he mouthed back, and Vivi moved silently toward the cracked window, keeping in the shadows as she peered into the darkness.

There was just one flashlight, but it was clearly two people moving up to the house, leaning on each other, their heads close together. And then as the moon moved out from behind a cloud, Vivi got a good look at one of their faces.

You have got to be kidding me.

She whirled around, hurrying away from the window as fast and as quietly as she could.

"It's one of my students," she hissed at Rhys. "Hainsley. Who, by the way, is failing because he's a *cheater,* and—"

"Maybe fill me in on the specifics later?" Rhys whispered back.

He nodded at the front door. "That's the only way out. How do you want to play this?"

"Play this?" Vivi repeated. She could hear Hainsley and the girl he was with getting closer now, the girl laughing, Hainsley's voice a low murmur in response.

"Look, the clean floor makes sense now," Rhys said, his voice barely audible. "This is obviously a hookup spot, so do you want to pretend that's why we're here, just brazen it out?"

Vivi blinked at him even as she heard the front gate creak open. "The idea of my students thinking of me as a sexual being is worse than them finding out I'm a witch."

Rhys gave a firm nod. "Fine. Then we hide."

With that, he grabbed her hand and tugged her toward the little closet off the front room, closing the door behind them just as they heard footsteps on the front steps.

Vivi's heart was pounding hard, her hands shaking, and for a second, she was so busy focusing on the fact that they'd almost gotten caught skulking around a haunted cabin by *Hainsley Barnes* of all people that she didn't realize just how tiny the closet was.

And how close Rhys was to her.

There was hardly room for the two of them, Vivi's back against the wall, Rhys so close he'd had no choice but to put his hands on the wall behind her. It was either that or put them on her, and her own hands were pressed tight against her sides because she'd nearly grabbed his waist as the door closed behind him.

Rhys seemed to realize it at the same time. She could feel him suck in a breath, his body neatly pressed against hers, her breasts against his chest, their hips aligned, even their knees touching.

And his mouth . . .

Rhys turned his head, so close to her that Vivi's lips nearly brushed his cheek, and then she could feel his lips, there, near her temple.

"Sorry," he barely breathed, and she shook her head.

"It's fine." The words were little more than her mouth moving, but he seemed to get the message and relaxed a little, which somehow brought him even closer.

Even though Vivi couldn't see anything inside the closet, she shut her eyes.

Okay. Okay, she could do this. Maybe they wouldn't stay long. Maybe she wouldn't be put through the living hell of hearing Hainsley Barnes have sex with someone.

The front door opened with a groan, and Vivi heard both Hainsley and the girl laugh, then shush one another, their feet loud on the hardwood floor.

"This place is certifiably gross," the girl said.

So every sound from outside the closet was crystal clear.

Maybe the curse *did* work out here.

"If you think I'm getting naked in here, you're insane," the girl continued, and Vivi felt Rhys's lips quirk against her temple.

Yes, Vivi thought. *It's so gross. Don't get naked in here, please please please.*

But then Hainsley said, "You don't think it's a little hot? Doing it in a haunted house?"

Rhys dropped his forehead to the wall behind Vivi with what she was pretty sure was a silent groan.

"No," the girl said, but she was giggling again, and the silence that followed was thick.

When Hainsley spoke again, his voice was lower. "Come on, Sara. It'll be a good time, promise."

Vivi only barely managed to keep from snorting, and she could tell Rhys felt it because his smile against her temple widened.

"You promised that last time, and it lasted, like, two minutes," Sara replied, and Rhys moved his hand from behind Vivi to briefly press it against his chest, miming a fatal shot.

Vivi bit her lip to keep from laughing even as she was suddenly very aware of the back of Rhys's hand there between them, his knuckles brushing her collarbone. Even though she couldn't see his hand, his fingers, she could picture them perfectly, the elegant bones of them.

You have musician hands, she'd said to him once. They'd been lying in the tiny bed in her dorm room, Rhys's feet hanging off the end of the bed, the sheet sticking to their sweaty bodies. Vivi had been dreamy in her post-sex haze, playing with his fingers, tangling and untangling their fingers, scratching her nails along the back of his hand as he'd studied it in the candlelight.

Pardon you, madam, these are sorcerer's hands, he'd replied. *Can't play a single note.*

And then she'd taken that hand she'd been playing with and urged it under the sheet, between her legs, right where she'd wanted it, a move so bold it had made her blush, but she'd done it anyway.

In that case, she'd said, *I know a spell you could cast.*

He had. Over and over again.

For a hell of a lot longer than two minutes.

Hainsley and Sara were still talking, but Vivi wasn't listening anymore, and even though Rhys had made it very clear that he couldn't read her mind, she felt like he had to know what she was thinking about, what she was remembering. He'd gone so still against her, his breath slow and even, and when he ducked his head, just the slightest bit, his nose skimmed her jaw, making her shiver.

Just that. The littlest touch, and her nipples stiffened against his chest, her breath coming a little faster as every nerve in her body came to life.

Slowly, she let her hands unclench from her sides, resting them tentatively on his hips.

Rhys took it as the invitation she'd intended him to, pressing in even closer. No accident this time, no awkwardness. This was deliberate. He was hard against her, and she raised one foot off the floor, wrapping her calf around his, tilting her hips away from the wall as he lowered his head, lips drifting over the place where neck met shoulder and making her squeeze her eyes shut even tighter.

One hand was on her lower back, the other still flat against the wall next to her head, and they stayed that way for a long moment, the press of his lips not firm enough to be a kiss, and Vivi had to fight to keep from whimpering as his mouth slid up her neck, breath hot and damp.

Her hands had moved up from his hips to press against his back, the leather of his jacket cool against her palms, and his hand was cuffed around the back of her neck now, but he still hadn't kissed her, and she wondered if he, like her, was telling himself that as long as it was just this, these touches, this bare hint of lips on skin, it wasn't a mistake.

It was easy to think that in the darkness, not able to see him, not being able to speak. Easier to just touch and feel.

To want.

Then, from outside the closet, Vivi heard a thump.

She went still, felt Rhys lift his head from her neck as Hainsley said, "You're right. This place probably is too freaky to get freaky in. Wanna at least explore it or something? See what other creepy stuff is here?"

Vivi could suddenly see Hainsley's face as he threw open this closet door and found his history professor—the history professor whose class he was currently failing—wrapped around some random dude, her face flushed, her hair mussed.

No, that was not about to happen.

It was time for Hainsley and Sara to get out of here, and for her to get on with this ghost business.

Pushing at Rhys's chest slightly, Vivi indicated that he should move back as much as he could, and she was glad he could somehow understand her without seeing her.

Lifting her hand, Vivi pressed her fingertips against the side of the closet, her lips moving with a very simple spell.

She really hoped Amanda had been right about them being far enough from the town for the cursed magic not to fuck everything up.

There was another thump from outside, but this one was louder, and Vivi heard Sara's voice, sharp. "What was that?"

Still concentrating on the spell, Vivi envisioned that photograph on the wall, fixing her energy on it, and then she heard the crack of the frame hitting the floor, glass breaking, and Sara shrieked.

"I wanna go!" she cried, and Vivi prayed that Hainsley wasn't the kind of asshole to tell her it was no big deal, or, worse, to want to prove his manhood against a ghost.

Just to be safe, she sent another wave of magic out to the front door and heard it snap back on its hinge, slamming against the outside wall.

This time, Sara wasn't the only one who shrieked, and Vivi inwardly pumped her fist as she heard two sets of footsteps thundering out of the house and down the path back into the woods.

"Nicely done," Rhys said, his voice still low, and Vivi smiled in the darkness.

"I have my moments."

"You certainly do."

They were alone in the house now. There was no reason for them to still be in this closet, close together in the darkness, but neither of them was moving.

"Vivienne," Rhys said, and Vivi could feel him say her name, his breath moving over her lips. He was still so close. *They* were still so close.

Her other hand reached out for the opposite wall to steady herself a little as he lowered his head.

And then she yelped as her fingers tingled, almost like she'd touched a socket.

"What is it?" Rhys asked, immediately stepping back and turning on his flashlight, pointing it at the wall to their right.

"I think," Vivi said as she looked at the markings painted there, "we've found Piper's altar."

CHAPTER 22

Rhys knew he should be thrilled they'd found what they were looking for. He also knew it was probably stupid to feel slightly resentful that, years ago, a witch had made her altar in a small closet where, decades later, Rhys had come very close to kissing a gorgeous woman before being thoroughly cock-blocked by said altar, but it was very late, and he was not kissing Vivienne, so Piper McBride was now on his shit list for more than just throwing him across a library.

"Why would she keep her altar in here?" Rhys asked now, moving the beam of his flashlight over the runes Piper had painted all those years ago. Some of them he recognized, but others were unfamiliar.

"Guessing she had people in her life who didn't know she was a witch," Vivienne replied, kneeling down on the floor and pressing her fingers to the floorboard. "Or maybe it was because she was doing dark magic?"

Sitting back on her heels, she frowned. "Anyway, doesn't matter. Main thing is we light the candle, trap her, then get out of here."

"Hear, hear," Rhys muttered, still looking at the runes. There was something sinister about them, especially the ones at the bottom of the wall, all dark, slashing marks that hadn't faded after all this time.

Vivienne had pulled the candle out of her bag, and Rhys watched as she affixed it to a small silver holder before fishing out a pack of matches.

Rhys wasn't sure if she was holding her breath as she lit the candle, but he sure as fuck was. Why hadn't he tried to talk her out of this? He knew she felt guilty for the ghost in the first place, but it wasn't her job to do this. If the college witches wanted this ghost caught, they could bloody well do it themselves.

He was leaning forward to tell her that—and possibly blow out the damn candle—when the temperature in the closet seemed to drop by a good ten degrees.

Too late, then.

"She's here," Vivienne breathed, then looked up at him. "That sounded really creepy. Sorry."

"Yes, it was really you saying a two-word phrase that made this entire situation unsettling. Before? Pleasant as a day in the park."

Vivienne looked back to the candle, but he saw the corner of her mouth quirk in something close to a smile.

But then, as they waited and the air just kept getting colder, Rhys was aware of a sort of hissing sound, like someone had left the gas on, and as he turned to look back toward the front door, he saw what looked like mist snaking underneath it.

It glowed, casting the room in an eerie blue light as it gathered across the floor, undulating its way toward them.

The cold was almost unbearable now, and Rhys caught Vivi's elbow, helping her to her feet as they both stepped outside the closet, watching the mist gather and coalesce, spreading upward until the wavering form of Piper McBride floated in front of them.

She looked less substantial than she had in the library, and, goddess be praised, she also seemed a hell of a lot less pissed off.

Instead, she just seemed a little confused, her gaze moving restlessly over what had been her house.

As Rhys and Vivienne watched, little tendrils of the mist that made up the ghost of Piper McBride began to peel off, curling toward the candle like smoke, her form becoming even more transparent.

"I think it's working," Vivienne barely whispered, and Rhys nodded.

"Could work a bit faster, if you ask me."

"I'm sorry the ancient ghost-summoning candle magic is not impressing you enough, Rhys."

"I didn't say that, I just—"

"Penhaaaaalllllllow."

His last name was little more than a sort of garbled sigh, and real fear raced, icy and prickly hot all at once, down Rhys's spine.

The ghost continued to sway in place even as more and more

of her drifted off toward the candle. Her eyes were the same pale blue as the rest of her, the pupils so large they nearly absorbed the iris, and Rhys felt like she was looking through him, not at him.

"Cursed Penhallow," Piper added, her form becoming even wispier. *"Cursed for what was taken."*

"I thought I was cursed because I was a fuckerneck," Rhys muttered to Vivi, but she was frowning at the ghost.

"What does that mean?" she asked. "What did he take?"

"It was never yours, asshole," the ghost hissed. *"You took it."* She was coming apart now, her head floating far from her neck, hands drifting away into spirals of smoke that disappeared into the candle's flame.

It was one of the most frightening things Rhys had ever seen, and Vivienne was stepping *closer to it.*

"But he didn't take anything," she said, her chin lifted as the spirit's head floated ever higher. "Like, not even my V-card."

"That's true!" Rhys said to Piper. "And I'm not exactly a taker anyway, more of a giver, really."

"She's not interested in your sexual prowess, Rhys," Vivienne said, not taking her eyes off the ghost. "And I'm not sure she's actually talking about you."

It was hard to see where Piper was looking now, what with her head nearly brushing the ceiling, but the ghost opened her jaw, one of those banshee wails spiraling out even as more and more of her was sucked into the candle, and Rhys found himself moving closer to Vivienne.

"What was wrong must be righted, what was taken must be relinquished," Piper howled, and the air suddenly felt charged, like lightning was about to strike.

And then, with one more shriek and a sound disturbingly like something going down a drain, the rest of Piper was sucked into the Eurydice Candle.

The flame wavered once, twice, briefly glowing blue.

And then went out, leaving Rhys and Vivienne in the darkness.

Alone.

CHAPTER 23

It was nearly two in the morning by the time Vivi used her spare key to unlock Something Wicked. The Eurydice Candle was tucked in her satchel, and even though it just looked and felt like a regular candle, she didn't want to hold on to it any longer than she had to, and she definitely didn't want it in her apartment overnight.

The storage room at the store had seemed like the best place to keep it, and she made her way to that space now, Rhys close behind her.

They hadn't talked much on the drive over, and they definitely hadn't talked about that moment in the closet, much like how they weren't talking about the kiss in the library.

Vivi and Rhys were getting really good at Not Talking About Things, which, she thought, was how it needed to stay.

And, she thought as she pushed back the curtain leading to the storeroom, she needed to remember that whole thing about not being alone with him in dimly lit spaces anymore.

"Oh, for fuck's sake," she muttered to herself as she stepped into the storeroom.

She'd forgotten that Aunt Elaine's spell made the room shift depending on time of day, even depending on the weather. If it was raining outside, there'd be a fire in a fireplace, candles glowing cozily on the walls. If it was sunny, there were windows letting in soft pools of sunlight.

And if it was the middle of the night, you got the fire in the fireplace, the candles and a sky full of stars overhead.

"Is your aunt meeting someone in here later?" Rhys asked, looking around him, and Vivi kept her eyes on the wardrobe ahead of her as she said, "No, this is just . . . the vibe."

"The vibe," Rhys repeated, clearly pleased. "I like it."

Vivi didn't say anything to that, just opened the wardrobe and gingerly took the candle out of her bag. It was still a little cool to the touch, colder than a normal candle would be, and Vivi was careful as she set it among a pile of plain white candles and several jars of dried herbs.

In the morning, she'd text Gwyn and Elaine to tell them about this, but for now, she just wanted to go up to her apartment and take a very hot bath, followed by several hours of sleep.

"Christ, it's late," Rhys said on a sigh, and Vivi nodded as she finished settling the candle in its place.

"I know. I'm glad I don't have morning classes tomorrow."

From behind her, she heard Rhys give a low chuckle. "Scheduling teaching around witchcraft. Or witchcraft around teaching, I suppose."

"That's my life."

Except that Vivi hadn't done this much witchy stuff in ages. And even though tonight had not exactly been a joy, there had been something a little exhilarating about it all. Creeping through the woods to a haunted cabin, summoning up the spirit of a long-dead witch . . . It was the kind of thing Vivi had thought of when she'd first learned about who—about *what*—she was.

Maybe that's why she didn't feel all that tired or worn out or stressed about teaching her classes tomorrow.

She'd gone into a haunted house, lit a magical candle and captured a motherfucking *witch ghost*.

And that felt pretty awesome.

"Thank you for your help," she said to Rhys now, shutting the wardrobe and turning the key in the lock. "I'm sure being terrorized by a ghost wasn't high up on your list of things to do tonight."

Turning around, she leaned back against the wardrobe, crossing her arms over her chest. Rhys was still standing there across the room, the firelight playing across his handsome face, his hair definitely doing The Thing and his stubble really upping his whole rakish air.

Which is probably why Vivi said, "And let me add a retroactive thank-you for never trying to have sex with me in a haunted house back when we were in college."

"Young Hainsley does need to rethink his game," Rhys acknowledged, mimicking her posture against the cabinet just across from her. "But to be fair, had the option been available back then, I probably would've tried it. I would've attempted to shag you most anywhere. Haunted house, abandoned asylum, Department of Motor Vehicles . . ."

"If you'd done that last one, we could've also tried to have sex in jail," Vivi replied, ignoring the way her heart seemed to flutter in her chest at both his words and the half smile he was wearing, wishing Aunt Elaine weren't quite so committed to her aesthetics because this room with its warm wood and soft lighting and plenty of available soft surfaces was not helping matters.

"Would've been worth it," Rhys said, and then his smile faded even as the look in his eyes grew warmer. "I was mad about you, Vivienne," he said softly.

Sincerely.

"Utterly mad."

Vivi swallowed hard, her arms tightening around herself. She wanted to find a joke to throw at him, something that would puncture this moment like a balloon.

Instead, she told the truth. "The feeling was very mutual."

"Was?" Rhys pushed himself off the cabinet, moving closer to her. It was late, so late by now, and Vivi had been up for nearly twenty hours, but she felt like she had when she'd touched those runes in Piper's cabin.

Electrified. Alive.

"Because the more I consider it," he went on, still moving toward her, slowly, his hands in his pockets, "the less I think I should've used the past tense. Shall I try it out?"

He stopped, watching her, and Vivi knew if she told him not

to, if she said they should leave, he would, without question. It was one of the things she'd loved about him so much all those years ago, how easily he put the power in her hands. She could stop him in his tracks right now.

Or she could let him come closer and hear what he had to say.

Not sure if she trusted herself to speak, Vivi just nodded, and one corner of Rhys's mouth hooked up. "I *am* mad about you, Vivienne Jones. Again. Or maybe I should say *still,* because I'm gonna be real honest with you here, *cariad*. I don't think it ever went away."

Cariad. He'd called her that, that summer. She could still feel it, growled against her ear, whispered into her skin, murmured between her thighs.

He still stood a few feet away from her, still giving her the opportunity and the space to put an end to this if she wanted to.

She didn't.

Closing the space between them, Vivi rested her hands on Rhys's chest. His skin was warm through the material of his sweater, his heart thudding steadily against her palms, and as Vivi leaned in, she could smell the outside on his skin, the woodsmoke from the forest, the scent of night air clinging to him, and it suddenly seemed so stupid to have pretended she didn't want this.

Lifting her face, Vivi brought her lips to his.

The kiss in the library had been frantic, a match touched to gasoline, anger and frustration fueling it as much as lust.

This was different. Slower.

His hands came up to cup her face, thumbs rubbing soft circles against her jaw, and Vivi found her own hands resting low on his waist, opening her mouth under his, sighing as his tongue stroked along hers.

"The taste of you," he muttered when they parted, his mouth dropping to her neck as Vivi closed her eyes and tilted her head back. "Can't get enough of it. Never fucking well could."

Another memory. That first night at the Solstice Revel, tangled together in his tent. Vivi had never gone to bed with anyone so fast, had always gone through what felt like the appropriate number of dates for each stage. Kiss on the second, little further on the third and so on. She'd only had sex with one other guy before Rhys, and that had been after a solid year of dating.

But within two hours of meeting Rhys, he'd had his mouth on her, her thigh draped over one shoulder as he'd kissed and licked and sucked and driven her completely out of her mind, telling her over and over again how good she tasted, how gorgeous she was, and she'd *felt* gorgeous. Powerful, even, unashamed, uninhibited.

Sometimes she thought what she'd really fallen in love with that summer was the version of herself she was when she was with him.

But as lovely as that memory was, she didn't want to think about the past when the present was right here in front of her, hands skating over her sides, fingertips brushing the skin just above the waist of her jeans.

"Vivienne, if you'll allow me to make you come tonight, I'd consider myself the most fortunate of men."

The words were muttered against the place where her neck met her shoulder, and Vivi felt her entire body clench in response.

Suddenly, there was nothing more she wanted in the world than to let Rhys Penhallow make her come in the back room of this store, and she didn't want to look too closely at it, didn't want to think about all the reasons she shouldn't.

It had been a long night, she was feeling powerful and *good*, and a handsome man wanted to give her an orgasm.

Why shouldn't she have that?

Her hands clasped around the back of his neck, Vivi leaned in to kiss him again, letting her tongue stroke along his, loving the low sound that came from his throat as she did.

"Please," she whispered against his mouth, and then they were stumbling back against the ancient velvet settee by the fire. Some distant part of Vivi's brain reminded her that it had belonged to some famous witch, that Aunt Elaine was really fond of it as a result, but she couldn't think about that now, couldn't think about anything except Rhys and his hands on her.

They fell back onto the couch, Rhys reaching out to make sure the full weight of his body didn't land on her, and Vivi cuffed a hand around the back of his neck as he nuzzled her jaw, her neck.

Rhys was tugging her shirt out of her jeans, shoving it up over her breasts, and when his mouth closed over her nipple through the lace of her bra, Vivi gasped, fingers tightening in his hair.

His tongue made lazy circles, the drag of the fabric plus the wet heat of his mouth making her writhe underneath him, needing, pleading.

The rasp of her zipper sounded very loud in the quiet room, and Rhys looked at her again, his eyes meeting hers, pupils blown wide with desire. "All right?" he asked, and she nodded, almost frantically, as she clutched the back of his neck, bringing his mouth to hers.

"Better than all right," she panted, and then his hand was there, sliding over the cotton of her panties, and she was lifting her hips off the couch in a silent entreaty.

For a moment, he paused, rearing over her, his hair over his brow, his lips parted with the force of his breath, and it could've been that first night all over again. There in his tent at the Solstice Revel, looking down at her, that same pendant winking against his chest.

"Christ Jesus, you're lovely," he said, his voice a wreck, accent thicker, and Vivi almost could've come from that alone. From the look in his eyes, as fond as it was heated, and not for the first time, she thought how much easier it would've been if they hadn't liked each other so much. If it had just been sex and heat and desire, and not this warmth, too.

"Make me come, Rhys," she heard herself say, her voice faint against the crackle of the fire and the roaring of her own blood in her ears. "Now."

She needed the heat to blot out the warmth.

If she could tell herself this was just about sex, just about getting off, it would be easier to watch him walk away this time.

Or at least she hoped it would be.

For the space of a few breaths, Rhys just kept looking at her, his eyes nearly black, his chest rising and falling, and Vivi tensed, wondering if he'd put a stop to it, or try to make this more than it was.

And then his fingers found her again, pressing and circling, dipping into her wetness and using it to slick his touch, dragging his fingertips back over her, and Vivi was closing her eyes, incoherent cries coming from her lips as he touched her, and touched her and *touched* her.

The orgasm seemed to start somewhere deep inside her, radiating out to her toes, the tips of her fingers, her nipples, and she held him even tighter as sparks exploded behind her eyes, as she lost herself to everything except him, the same way she had that very first night.

It's different this time, she told herself even as she kissed his neck, his jaw, his mouth, anywhere she could reach.

It has to be.

CHAPTER 24

"So that's a Eurydice Candle."

Vivi hid a yawn behind her coffee mug as she nodded at Gwyn. "Mmm-hmm."

They were sitting around the big table in the back of the storage room at Something Wicked, the three of them taking in the silver candle lying among Elaine's piles of herbs and wicks for her own candles. In the daylight, in this cozy and comfy little room, it didn't seem like something that had a ghost lurking inside it.

But Vivi could still remember watching Piper McBride's ghost vanishing inside it, and shivered a little. The sooner Amanda picked this thing up and took it off her hands, the better. She was supposed to come by Vivi's office later that afternoon, but Vivi had wanted to show the candle to her aunt and cousin first, hence the impromptu meeting in the storage room.

As they studied the candle, Vivi focused very hard on not letting her gaze slide over to the sofa against the far wall. Even though it had just been hours ago, last night—well, early this morning—it almost felt like something out of a dream.

A really fantastic, really dirty dream.

But it had been all too real, and at some point today, she was going to have to deal with what had happened.

What it meant.

It meant that you'd had a rough night and deserved that orgasm, a part of her brain that sounded suspiciously like Gwyn said, and Vivi was inclined to agree. For all that she was exhausted and running on about three hours of sleep, she felt . . . good this morning. Better than good. Better than she'd felt in a long time, and even as she searched herself for that sinking sensation that she'd made a huge mistake, she knew she wouldn't find it.

Because it hadn't been a mistake. It had been *fun*. And wasn't that enough?

Frowning, Aunt Elaine leaned in even closer, pushing her glasses back up the bridge of her nose. "It's not like the college witches to use something like this," she murmured. One hand hovered over the candle like she might pick it up.

"The witch who came to talk to me was different," Vivi said with a shrug. "I think they might actually be modernizing over there a little bit."

Gwyn made a rude noise at that, drawing up one knee and wrapping an arm around it. "That'll be the day. I think they just wanted you to do their dirty work for them."

"Maybe," Vivi acknowledged. "But honestly, it wasn't that bad."

Off Elaine and Gwyn's look, she amended, "Okay, it was very scary and I never want to go back to that cabin again, but it could've been a lot worse."

"Ghosts can be dangerous," Elaine said, still frowning. "You should've come to me first."

"Rhys and I had it handled."

Gwyn's eyes sparked, and she opened her mouth, but before she could say anything, Vivi held up a finger. "No. No 'I'll *bet* Rhys handled it,' or whatever filthy thing you were gonna say."

"You're no fun at all," Gwyn replied. "And my joke was going to be a little more sophisticated than that, I promise."

"Sure it was."

Vivi reached across the table to pick up the candle, but before she could, Aunt Elaine laid a hand on hers.

"Is that all you wanted to tell us? You caught a ghost in a Eurydice Candle?"

For a moment, Vivi had the horrifying idea that Elaine knew what had happened back here last night, that there was, like, the magical equivalent of security cameras, and Elaine had gotten quite the show, in which case, Vivi hoped there was some kind of "disappearing into the floor" spell.

But Aunt Elaine wasn't giving her any kind of knowing look. She was genuinely asking, and Vivi realized there was something else she needed to tell them both.

"The ghost said some stuff before the candle got her," Vivi said, adjusting her bag on her shoulder. "About 'cursed Penhallow,' and taking something that didn't belong to him. But I don't think it was about Rhys specifically. I think it might have been about Gryffud, or some other ancestor."

"Could be worth looking into," Gwyn mused, resting her chin on her knee.

"I'll do a little research," Aunt Elaine said, then nodded at Vivi's bag.

"And you go give that foul thing to its rightful owner."

"Will do," Vivi said with a little salute.

And then Aunt Elaine smiled at her, her eyes bright behind her glasses. "I'm proud of you, Vivi. A Eurydice Candle is serious magic."

Vivi waved her off. "I didn't do much, really. I just lit it. Not exactly next-level sorcery."

"Still," Aunt Elaine insisted, covering Vivi's hand with her own. "You're a witch who won't even use magic to clean her apartment, and now look at you go!"

"Okay, that's just because I use that time to catch up on listening to podcasts, plus I watched that Mickey Mouse cartoon with the devil brooms as a kid and it freaked me out."

"I loved that cartoon," Gwyn said, propping her chin in her hand, her silver earrings winking.

"Of course you did."

"But Mom is right," Gwyn went on, nudging Vivi. "Very baller magic."

"I don't really know what that means," Aunt Elaine replied, "but I suspect it means 'impressive,' and it was. Your mother would have been proud, too."

Surprised, Vivi glanced at Elaine. "Except that Mom hated magic?"

Aunt Elaine shook her head, leaning back in her chair. "It scared her. She felt like being a witch was . . . I don't know, something that happened *to* her, not something she chose. But she was good. Really good when she wanted to be. She just chose another path."

Vivi had spent so long with this idea of her mom as firmly in camp Magic Is Bad that she didn't really know what to say to that.

Standing up, Vivi moved to the curtain sectioning off the storage room from the rest of the store, and came up short as she stared at the girl standing there, her eyes wide.

"Oh, wow," she breathed. "I've never seen this part of the store before."

Gwyn leapt up from the table as Aunt Elaine turned around.

"Hey, Ashley," Gwyn said, coming over and putting an arm around the girl's shoulders as she began leading her back into the store, and throwing a look back at Vivi and Elaine. "That's just the back room, nothing that interesting, but we *do* have some really cool wands in if you want to check those out . . ."

Gwyn's voice faded as she walked deeper into the store, and Aunt Elaine stood up, sighing, hands on her hips.

"Well, guess we know that spell isn't working as it should right now, either."

It wasn't exactly a surprise, but it was a reminder that this thing had to get sorted out, and fast. And that's where Vivi's focus needed to be.

Which is why she only glanced at the couch once before she hurried out of the storage room.

The drive to campus was uneventful, and Vivi was just locking her car when she heard someone calling her name.

It was Amanda, jogging over to her, a bright smile on her face. "How did it go?"

Relieved, Vivi reached into her bag for the candle. "Great! But now please take this because having a ghost in my purse is creeping me out."

Amanda's smile brightened as she wrapped her fingers around the Eurydice Candle. "Not a problem. I'll get this back to our side of campus, and you can go on about your day."

Since she had a class to teach in five minutes, Vivi was grateful to do just that, and with a wave, she turned toward Chalmers Hall, the building where her class met.

Clouds were thick in the sky today, leaves skittering across the brick walkways, and Vivi shivered a little, tugging her scarf a bit tighter around her neck. As she did, she glanced back over her shoulder and spotted Amanda walking across the parking lot. She turned left, disappearing behind a row of trees, and Vivi frowned as she turned back around.

That's not the way to get to the witch side of campus.

But maybe Amanda knew a shortcut, or was getting something out of her car.

That had to be it.

Vivi taught her first class, then her second, forgetting all about Amanda and the Eurydice Candle as she enlightened a hundred freshmen about the Magna Carta, even forgetting about Rhys for a little while, and by the time she got back to her office late that afternoon, she was actually starting to feel a bit . . . okay, "normal" would've been too strong a word, but at least more settled, more sure of herself.

Sure, they still had to deal with the curse, but they'd fixed the potion issue at the Coffee Cauldron, and now they no longer had an angry ghost roaming around campus.

She was actually on top of all this.

Smiling, pleased with herself, Vivi settled behind her desk and tugged a stack of grading to her, flipping on her kettle as she did.

She'd just gotten through the first three essays when there was a knock at her door. "Come in," she called without looking up.

As soon as the door opened, magic rippled over her skin, so thick and heavy she had to take a second to catch her breath, and when she looked up, Dr. Arbuthnot stood in the doorway.

"Ms. Jones?" she intoned, her voice like thunder. "I believe we need to speak."

RHYS HAD BEEN thinking about Vivienne all day, so in a way, he wasn't surprised when she turned up on his doorstep that evening. In fact, when he first opened the door, he wondered if he was having a particularly vivid hallucination.

But no, if he were conjuring up Vivienne, he definitely would not have made her look this sad.

Not just sad. Defeated. Her shoulders were slumped, hair

straggling out of her loose bun. Even the little cherries marching along the hem of her skirt seemed to be drooping.

"You were right," she said as soon as he ushered her inside, and as he locked the door behind them, he raised his eyebrows.

"First off, can I record you saying that? Secondly, right about what?"

Sighing, Vivienne threw her hands out to the sides. "We can't just keep putting out the fires this curse causes. Especially since it turns out that in trying to put them out, we might just be starting more, and . . . your house is weird."

She'd moved into the living room, and was looking around with a confused expression, no doubt taking in the heavy iron chandelier, the oxblood leather furniture, the genuine Gothic nightmare of the whole place. "How do you sleep here?" she asked, then pointed at a painting on the wall. "I mean, *I* may never sleep again just from seeing that."

"*That* is my great-great-aunt Agatha, but fair point."

Moving into the kitchen, Rhys called over his shoulder, "Is this a conversation that requires wine?"

He heard Vivienne sigh again, then the squeaking of the leather as she flopped onto the couch. "Yes."

When he emerged with a bottle and two glasses, she was leaning back, studying the ceiling, and it was the strangest thing, seeing her in this setting, her and her polka dots in his father's lair. And he didn't like the way it made him feel . . . better.

Happier.

Those are lingering sex hormones from last night, mate, he told himself, but he knew it was more than that.

Problem was, he didn't know what the fuck to actually *do* with any of that. What had happened at the store had been a one-off, *needed* to be a one-off, because all of this was entirely too mad to add shagging back into the equation.

Much as he'd like to.

Crossing the room, Rhys handed her a glass of wine, and she took it gratefully, taking a deep sip before sitting up a little and saying, "We fucked up."

Rhys perched against the arm of the wingback chair next to the couch, crossing one ankle over the other. "Is this about last night?"

"Obviously," she said with a little scowl, and then her expression cleared. "Oh. You're asking about the . . ."

Cheeks coloring, she took another sip of wine. "No, I didn't mean that. That's a whole other fuckup."

The words shouldn't sting. Lord knew, he'd just been thinking the exact same thing, so it was ridiculous to feel hurt.

But he'd made a habit of being ridiculous where Vivienne was concerned.

"Remember how one of the witches from the college gave us the Eurydice Candle to capture Piper McBride's spirit?"

"Given that that was literally yesterday, I *do* recall it. Fairly vividly, actually."

Vivienne rolled her eyes and drank more of her wine. "Well, turns out 'Amanda Carter' doesn't work for the college. In fact, she's not even a witch, which I should've been able to pick up on, but I was so relieved to have help with all of this that I ignored it."

Shaking her head, she looked darkly into her glass. "The jeans should've given it away."

Bracing one hand on the chair's arm, Rhys looked at her, sitting there nearly swallowed up by his father's insane couch. "What do you mean she wasn't a witch? How on earth did she have a Eurydice Candle, then?"

Vivienne raised her head, soft blue shadows under her pretty hazel eyes. "She's a con artist. A famous one, apparently. Her real name is Tamsyn Bligh. She deals in magical artifacts, and had been sniffing around Graves Glen for a while. The college witches were keeping an eye on her, but she somehow slipped past them and made a beeline straight for me."

Flattening her palm, Vivienne thrust her hand out in front of her, then shook her head. "Anyway, we captured the ghost of a very powerful, very scary witch, and then gave it to someone who'll sell it to the highest bidder all because I am a trusting dumbass."

"You're not," Rhys automatically objected, and when she only looked at him, he rolled his shoulders. "Well, you're trusting, but you're not a dumbass. Not by a mile."

Groaning, Vivienne set her glass on the coffee table and buried her head in her hands. "It's like it all just keeps getting worse. Just when I think I have a handle on it, or am actually doing something good, I do something like this."

Lifting her head again, she rested her hands on the back of

her neck and took a deep breath. "So now the college witches are pissed, plus they know about the curse, and they're *also* pissed off about this, and I just . . ."

Breaking off, she looked at him, beseeching. "Why am I such a goddamn disaster, Rhys? I've never done any serious magic in my life, but the one time I did, it cursed an entire town."

"I did that, Vivienne," Rhys said, standing up and setting his glass down on the table next to hers before sitting at the other end of the couch, slouching against the corner, his legs stretched out in front of him.

"Okay, but that's my point," she replied, turning so that she could face him. More of her hair had come down, framing her face, and Rhys's hands itched to push those strands behind her ears, to cup her face between his hands, rub his thumb over those soft pink lips. "*We* are a disaster. Apart, our lives run smoothly. Perfectly, even."

"That's a bit of an overstatement," Rhys objected, but Vivienne was clearly on a roll now.

"And then as soon as we're together, it all goes to shit. Even that summer. That really beautiful, perfect summer. Where did it end up? Demon plastic skulls." She ticked it off on one finger. "Poisoned potions." Another tick. "Library ghost." Tick. "And now this, which . . ."

Vivienne stared at the finger she'd held up to tick off and scowled. "I don't even know how to define this. Except *disaster*."

"So you've said. Repeatedly."

Picking up her wine, she drained the rest of the glass before setting it down and flopping back against the couch.

When Rhys didn't say anything, she raised her chin slightly. "What, not gonna try to argue with me?"

Rhys shrugged. "Why should I? You're right."

"I am?" Then she cleared her throat, sitting up. "I mean, I am, yes. I'm right, we're a disaster."

"Completely," Rhys said, lifting one hand off the back of the couch. "The proof is in the possessed candle, as the saying goes."

Vivienne smiled a little at that. "No one says that."

"Maybe they should."

They were both quiet for a moment, watching each other, and Rhys waited to see if she'd leave now. She probably should, but as he looked at her there, relaxed and rumpled, he very much hoped she'd stay.

Glancing around the living room again, Vivienne reached up to tuck her hair behind her ears. "I can't believe you live here."

"I don't *live* here," he said, tilting his head back to look at the chandelier. "I . . . am temporarily residing here, more or less against my will. Huge difference."

"Hmph," she sniffed, then picked up one of the pillows on the couch. It was black, embroidered with the family crest, and Rhys wasn't sure any literal cushion had ever looked less welcoming than that thing.

Vivienne turned the pillow over in her hands, and then looked up at him through her lashes.

"Okay, if this blows up in my face, know my intentions were good."

Holding her hands over the cushion, Vivienne closed her eyes and took a deep breath.

As golden light began to gather between her fingertips, Rhys's eyes widened. "Okay, Vivienne, maybe don't—"

But then the pillow sort of shimmered, the family crest bleeding out to be replaced with a red dragon.

Specifically the red dragon of Wales, but one that was grinning, claws extended in the air and painted the same bright purple as Vivienne's own nails.

Lifting the pillow triumphantly, she grinned. "Much better."

And fuck.

Fuck.

She might as well have hit him with a hammer. It was like that summer evening all over again, and Rhys set his glass down on the coffee table with a decisive thunk before sliding across the sofa to her.

The pillow hit the floor, and she reached out for him just as his fingers brushed over her jaw, tilting her face so that he could look at her.

"You bloody gorgeous girl." He sighed, and her own hands came up to his wrists, not to push him away, as she probably should have, but to pull him closer.

"I've run out of ways to say this is a bad idea," Vivienne murmured against his lips, and Rhys smiled, nudging her nose with his.

"We've made a lot of mistakes," he agreed. "But I don't think this is one of them."

And he didn't. For whatever else had gone wrong with them—and Christ, he could fill up a ledger book at this point—this, her, here in his arms, was not one of them. He knew that as well as he knew anything.

She leaned in closer, her nails lightly scratching the backs of his hands, and if Rhys hadn't already been so hard he ached, that would've done it. So would the way she just barely brushed her lips against his as she murmured, "Are you going to ask to kiss me?"

Rhys grinned. "I'm gonna ask to do a fuckload more than that if you'll let me."

CHAPTER 25

*M*ine, Rhys's blood hummed as he kissed Vivi, pulling her up the stairs, her mouth warm and soft and wet, her body pliant beneath his hands. *Finally, fucking* finally *mine.*

They tripped and stumbled, laughed against each other's mouths, until they were on the second floor.

Rhys stopped in front of the bedroom door, and Vivi, still twining around him like a vine, pushed even closer, her lips against his neck. "What is it?"

"Ah. Right."

Gently reaching up to pull her hand from his hair, he looked down at her, at those swollen, damp lips and hazy eyes. "Before we go in here, there's something you should know."

Some of the haze faded. "Kind of an alarming thing to hear right before you get naked with someone."

"It's nothing serious, I promise," he told her, leaning in to brush his lips against her forehead only to get distracted by how close her mouth was, and then he was kissing her again, turning so that she was up against the door, her thighs opening for his hips, a soft sound of need escaping her lips as he rocked against her.

"It's the bedroom," he murmured between kisses.

"What about it?"

"Well, you know how the rest of the house is—"

"A Gothic nightmare, yes."

Rhys huffed out a laugh that quickly turned into a groan as she wrapped a leg around his, pulling him in even closer. "Right, well . . . the bedroom is probably the pinnacle of that aesthetic, as it were. And as impressive as your skills were downstairs, I have no intention of waiting for you to magically redecorate the entire room before I shag you, so . . ."

Vivienne pulled back slightly, looking up at him with a sort of unholy light in her eyes that should've made him very, very afraid.

"Rhys," she said as a grin slowly spread across her face, "are you telling me we're going to have sex in Dracula's bedroom?"

"It is . . . a little *Dracula,* yes," he admitted, and she laughed, tipping her head back against the door. "Does it have a canopy bed? Please tell me it has a canopy bed."

It not only had a canopy bed, but said bed was up on a platform.

Not that Rhys was going to tell her that. She was just moments away from finding it out for herself, after all.

So reaching behind her, keeping a grip on her waist so she wouldn't stumble, he turned the doorknob.

RHYS'S KISSES WERE so drugging, so distracting, that for a minute, Vivi didn't even notice the room they were in. They could've been anywhere, in some blank space where only they existed. That's how he made her feel. How he'd always made her feel.

And then she saw all the red satin.

"Ohhhhhh my god," she breathed, and Rhys groaned, his knees bending so that his forehead was against her collarbone.

"You were supposed to say that because of me."

Giggling, Vivi pulled out of his embrace to fully explore the chamber in which she found herself.

And "chamber" really was the right word because this room was *bananas*.

There was a chandelier overhead that appeared to be made of some kind of black crystal, sparkling darkly in the low light, and the bed ...

"*Rhys,*" Vivi said, pressing one hand to her mouth. "Have you been sleeping in this every night?"

Sighing, Rhys stepped back, leaning against the wall. "I've spent a few nights on the couch just because I cannot deal with this room," he admitted, and Vivi could not blame him.

The carpet underfoot was thick and heavy, and there was a fireplace against the far wall, a fur rug slumped on the floor, plus more sconces than any one room should contain and a particularly graphic painting of Circe seducing Odysseus over the bed.

The bed in question was set high up on a platform, so high that the edge hit her right at her waist, and thick black-and-red curtains draped the massive mattress, which was covered in ...

Vivi peeked underneath the damask bedspread.

"Black satin?" she asked, her voice going high on the last syllable, and Rhys tipped his head back, his Adam's apple bobbing.

"I warned you."

Still smiling, Vivi turned to face him, her hands reaching up for the buttons of her blouse.

"Why didn't you bring me here before?"

"Why didn't I bring you to the terrifyingly creepy sex dungeon I sleep in?" he asked, his hands behind his back even as his eyes wandered over her in a way that made her blood feel hotter. "Can't imagine."

"Maybe I would've liked it," Vivi said, shucking her blouse and loving the way his gaze darkened as he took in her absolutely least sexy bra, the faded pink one with the sagging bow in the middle, the one she never would've worn if she'd thought she'd end up here, stripping down in front of him.

Rhys's gaze somehow got even more molten. "How did I ever give you up?" he murmured. Vivi took a deep breath unzipping her skirt and letting it fall to the floor, giving exactly zero fucks that her underwear was one of her older pairs, the one with lemons and oranges dancing across the fabric, not even remotely matching her bra.

He was across the room in a few strides, pulling her up hard against him, kissing her breathless. "Tell me what you want," he breathed against her lips, one of the most appealing offers Vivi had ever heard.

"You know what I like," she answered, desire pooling between her thighs, and he smiled at her, shaking his head.

"I know what you *liked*," he said. "I want to hear what you want now."

She felt almost dizzy with want, overwhelmed, and it made her brave. Made her bold.

"Taste me," she whispered, and his pupils somehow got even wider, even darker.

"Ah, *cariad*, there is nothing I want more."

She let him push her back against the mattress, hopping up because it was so high, and when she lifted her hips, he eased her panties down her legs, kissing her thigh, her knee, her ankle.

She fell back against the bed, eyes fixed on the canopy overhead, and suddenly it didn't seem so silly, so over-the-top. It seemed . . . romantic.

But maybe that's just because Rhys's lips were there, exactly where she wanted them, and her body was bowing up underneath him, fingers tight in his hair as he completely unraveled her with his mouth.

The orgasm snuck up on her, and she clutched his hair, her body curling up on itself as she panted his name, shaking and sweating.

He pulled back, his mouth wet, and then he fumbled in the nightstand.

"More?"

She knew what he was asking, and nodded as he gave a relieved sigh, pulling a condom out of the drawer.

There were spells, Vivi knew, that were supposed to act as protection, but Elaine had drilled it into both Vivi and Gwyn that when it came to their bodies, they should always trust science over magic, and she was grateful Rhys was prepared.

Sitting up a little, Vivi reached behind her, unhooking her bra, and Rhys groaned, surging up her body to cup one breast in his hand, his lips closing over her nipple as Vivi gasped, leaning back on her hands.

"I've dreamed about this," he murmured against her skin. "How soft you are. How beautiful." He muttered something else, something in Welsh, and even though Vivi didn't understand it, her body did. Whatever he'd said, it was filthy, and even though she'd just come, she found herself reaching for him, her hands greedy.

There was something decadent about being naked, splayed out before him while he was fully dressed, but now she needed more. Needed to see him, feel him.

Rhys clearly understood because he stood up, his hands pulling his sweater over his head, then falling to the button of his jeans.

Vivi propped herself up on her elbows, watching him with avid eyes. The hair on his chest wasn't thick, curling around his nipples, narrowing as it reached his waistband.

She sat up so that she could trace that line of hair with her fingernail, loving the way his eyes briefly closed, the shuddery breath he gave as she pulled his zipper down, sliding her hand inside to palm his cock.

He was hard, thick against her hand, and Vivi thought she might die if she didn't feel him inside her.

"Now, Rhys, *now,* please."

He didn't need to hear it twice. Vivi heard the foil wrapper tear, felt his hand between them, and then he was there, pushing inside her.

It had been a while, and she tensed briefly, but he took his time with shallow thrusts, his breath hot against her ear. "Make it good for you, Vivienne."

Rhys only needed the barest push to his shoulder to roll to his back, and Vivi went easily with him, bracing her hands on his chest as she rose above him, adjusting the angle, feeling him deep within her, her head falling back, hair brushing her back.

And then his hand was there, at the place where their bodies met, fingers working cleverly, and Vivi could feel herself coming again, her inner walls grasping him as he groaned and thrust up, meeting every roll of her hips.

She fell over the edge almost in an instant, her mouth opening in a silent cry, and Rhys sat up beneath her, clutching her back, fingers flexing on her skin, her name spilling from his lips as he came.

She collapsed against him as he fell back to the mattress, still holding her tight, still buried inside her, and as she tried to catch her breath, Vivi realized she hadn't compared this to the other times they'd had sex, not even once.

There had been no memories, no past. Just this. Just the present. Just him.

Groaning, Rhys tipped her to the side, sliding out of her even as his palm skimmed her thigh, like he couldn't stop touching her, and Vivi knew it was probably stupid to feel this happy when things were going this wrong, but that was the peril of multiple orgasms.

She laughed a little to herself, staring up at the canopy of Rhys's truly ridiculous bed, and next to her, he flopped onto his back, turning his head to look at her.

"That giggle had better not be about my prowess," he said, still out of breath.

"Never," she assured him with a solid headshake. "It's all for your furniture."

"Ah," he replied, turning his attention back to the canopy. "In that case, have at it. This is a profoundly silly bedroom for a grown man to have."

"Do all of the bedrooms in your dad's houses look like this?" Vivi asked, rolling on her side now, and Rhys looked over at her, narrowing his eyes slightly.

"Is this you trying to figure out if I grew up with a canopy bed?"

Vivi held her thumb and finger a tiny distance apart. "Little bit."

He smiled then, the expression, as always, making him look younger and softer, and Vivi wished she didn't like him so much, wished nineteen-year-old Vivi hadn't seen him standing there in that field and given her whole heart away with both hands.

But that wasn't true.

And she knew it.

CHAPTER 26

"Is it a little too obvious?"

Rhys twisted around from his spot on Vivienne's couch to see her standing in the doorway to her bedroom, one hand on her hip. No polka dots or cherries tonight; she was wearing a black dress that emphasized every curve, her purple-and-black-striped tights peeking out from tall black boots and a witch's hat perched on her hair, which fell loose to her shoulders.

In the past week, Rhys had seen her naked multiple times, had had her over him and under him, in his bed, in hers and, in one very memorable encounter, on the stairs at his house, but he still sucked in a breath looking at her there, so bloody beautiful and, even more deadly, *adorable* that he was very tempted to suggest they just stay in tonight and not go to the Fall Fair, whatever the fuck that was.

"I think you should wear that every day," he said now, rising from the couch to stand in front of her, bracing his hands on the doorframe above her head. "Or at least every night."

"I could maybe be talked into that," Vivienne replied, lifting her face to kiss him. "What would I get in return?"

"I could give you a preview," Rhys suggested, letting go of the door and moving his hands to her dress, slowly dragging it up her thighs as she laughed.

"If we're late to the fair, Gwyn will kill us," she said, but she was already unbuttoning the top few buttons of his shirt, her nails dragging along the chain he wore around his neck.

"Can you kindly explain yet again what this actually entails? Am I going to have to bob for apples or something?"

"That's certainly on the agenda," Vivienne said, "along with drinking cider and helping me and Gwyn sell witchy things at the booth. She and Aunt Elaine make a killing at this thing every year. *And* we get to eat Mrs. Michaelson's caramel-apple hand pies, which are so good, I think she might actually be a witch, even though Elaine swears she's not, and it's just all the butter she uses, and—*oh*!"

Rhys had slid her dress up high enough to dip his thumb between her legs, barely brushing against the damp silk of her underwear, and as he moved his hand, he brushed warm, bare skin.

Groaning, Rhys dropped his head to her shoulder.

"I would've been bobbing for apples without knowing these stockings weren't tights after all? You are a truly cruel woman, Vivienne."

"Nah, I was gonna let you feel me up on the hayride."

"I'm not even completely sure what a hayride is, but I think it might be my favorite part of this Fall Fair already."

Leaning in, Rhys kissed her again, capturing her lower lip between his own lips and sucking gently, making her sigh against his mouth and press closer.

The high neck of her dress prevented him from touching as much of her as he wanted to, but he settled on brushing the backs of his fingers against the curve of her breast, and dimly, he wondered how long he'd have to touch her to get his fill of it. He'd had her for three months that summer, and hadn't even begun to slake his thirst for her, had still felt as in her thrall that last day as he had the first.

And he knew that when he left this time, it would be the same. They could talk about "getting it out of their systems" all they wanted—this wasn't the kind of thing one got over.

You did it before, you'll figure it out again.

Because he would have to. They'd agreed there was no future for them, that they got to just enjoy the present for now, but every time he touched her, every time he kissed her, it was hard to remember that.

Vivienne drew back from the kiss now, and eyes bright, she urged him to his knees.

Rhys went more than willingly, pushing her dress higher, taking in the lacy borders of her stockings just there at the most bitable part of her thighs. And bite it he did, gently, loving the ragged sound of her breathing as she reached out to steady herself there in the doorway, the almost painful tug of her fingers in his hair.

He looked up her body at her, grinning as he pressed a kiss to the spot he'd just bitten. "Still care about being late?"

"Not even a little bit."

VIVIENNE MAY NOT have cared—and Rhys sure as fuck did not—but she was right about Gwyn. When they eventually arrived at the Fall Fair, nearly an hour later than they'd said they would, Vivienne's cousin was waiting for them in the parking lot, her arms folded over her chest. Like Vivienne, she was decked out in full witch regalia, although she was wearing a bright orange pair of ankle boots, and her tights were green.

"We're in trouble," Vivienne said, and Rhys shrugged as he unbuckled his seatbelt.

"I'm blaming it on you. Telling Gwyn you demanded I service you before we left."

"You are laaaaate!" Gwyn sang out when Vivienne stepped out of the car, and Vivienne waved her hand.

"Yes, I know, we—"

"Vivi, you're glowing brighter than a jack-o'-lantern, so I think I know what you were doing."

Rhys had to fight very hard not to look smug as Vivienne threw him an almost shy smile, but he clearly didn't succeed because Gwyn rolled her eyes at both of them, turning away.

"Y'all are gross," she grumbled, but Rhys saw the way she

grinned at Vivienne as she hooked her arm through her cousin's, tugging her close as they made their way toward the field where the festival was being held, their hips bumping.

Rhys watched them, their heads close together, and there it was again, that sort of tug in his chest, reminding him that this was Vivienne's place. She'd made a home in the small town her family had lived in for ages, made a life here, while his own hometown had nearly suffocated him.

Another reminder of how very different they were.

But when she looked back over her shoulder and smiled, that warm, sunshine smile that made his heart trip inside his chest, he wasn't sure he cared.

THE FALL FAIR had always been one of Vivi's favorite things in the days leading up to Halloween in Graves Glen. It was always held in the same field, nestled in a valley between the hills, the whole thing ringed in fairy lights and paper lanterns, the air smelling like fried food, popcorn and cinnamon. And while people definitely brought their kids, it didn't have quite the same family vibe as Founder's Day always did. There was something a little wild about it, something more than a little pagan.

Tonight, the sky was mostly clear, just a few clouds scuttering over the moon, and as Vivi wrapped a set of tarot cards in silk for a woman at Gwyn's booth, she hummed happily to herself.

"You have the annoyingly cheerful manner of a woman having an absurd amount of awesome sex," Gwyn said as the woman walked away. There was no one else in line, so she hopped up on the counter of the booth, long legs dangling.

"I am," Vivi said happily. "Both annoyingly cheerful *and* having the absurd amount of awesome sex."

"Yes, I'm aware," Gwyn replied, but she was smiling, and she reached out, kicking Vivi gently with one orange boot. "You deserve it."

"I kind of do, actually," Vivi agreed, her eyes already scanning the crowd for Rhys. And as soon as she saw him, making his way toward her with several wax paper bags in hand, grinning the second their eyes met . . .

Oh god, she felt that grin everywhere. She and Rhys had spent the last few days indulging in anything they could think of, anything they wanted, their bodies picking up right where they'd left off nine years ago.

But at moments like this, her stomach full of butterflies, her cheeks aching with her smile as she watched him amble his way toward her, she worried that maybe her heart had picked up right where *it* left, too.

"I hope this is what you wanted, *cariad*," he said, handing her one of the bags. "You would've thought they were made of solid gold from the line for them."

"Thank you," Vivi said, giving the bag the kind of look she usually reserved for Rhys. "I dream of these all year."

"And for you," Rhys said, handing one to Gwyn, who took it with only slightly narrowed eyes.

"You're making my cousin very happy *and* bringing me

caramel-apple pie? Clearly working hard at getting another nickname besides 'dickbag,' dickbag."

"I live in hope," Rhys said, leaning against the counter as he folded down the wax paper and bit into his own pie.

Vivi waited, watching him, and smiled smugly as his own expression went a little dreamy. "All right, I understand the line now," he said, then took another bite. "Vivienne, I'm so sorry, but I'm leaving you for the woman who makes these pies."

"She's ninety."

"Even so."

Giggling, Vivi finally took a bite herself, her eyes fluttering shut at the mix of salted caramel, butter pastry and cinnamon apples. "Okay, yes, marry Mrs. Michaelson. Just make sure you invite me to the wedding and serve these, okay?"

"A deal," he said, then reached out to shake her hand. When Vivi took it, he tugged, pulling her up to the counter so he could kiss her, and Vivi laughed against his mouth, tasting sugar and salt.

When she pulled back, Gwyn was watching them, a strange expression on her face, and suddenly a little self-conscious, Vivi wiped a stray crumb of pastry from the corner of her mouth. "What?"

"Nothing!" Gwyn said, raising both her hands, but she was smiling in a way that Vivi knew from experience meant they'd be talking later.

Finishing his pie, Rhys dusted off his hands, and tapped one of the sets of tarot cards sitting on the counter of the booth. "Are these your creation?"

Hopping down from her perch, Gwyn nodded and went to stand across from Rhys. "We sell lots of decks in the store, but my handmade ones are our biggest seller."

"She says modestly," Vivi teased, elbowing Gwyn, who elbowed her right back.

"Can you read the cards?" she asked Rhys.

He shook his head, both elbows on the counter. "I have a sort of rudimentary understanding of some of them, but no, not my magical strong suit."

Their area of the festival was still kind of dead, so when Gwyn glanced at Vivi and said, "Mind if I read for him? Might help with the whole," she lowered her voice, "curse thing."

"Go for it," Vivi said, looking up at Rhys. "If you want to?"

"Might as well," he said, cheerfully enough. "Vivienne and I haven't made any breakthroughs on that front."

Not that they hadn't been trying. It hadn't all been sex.

Okay, it had been a *lot* of sex, but in between, they'd been deep in research mode, mostly on Vivi's laptop since she didn't trust them in the study room at the library again. And given how pissed off Dr. Arbuthnot had been about the Eurydice Candle, they probably wouldn't have been allowed in anyway.

So far, Vivi knew more about curses than she'd ever thought possible. She knew the best moon phases for casting them, knew that wormwood made them stronger, knew that in 1509, a witch had managed to curse not just a town, but six different German principalities at once.

What she didn't know was how to lift a curse.

Typical that *that* was the bit witches wanted to be vague about.

Distracted, she moved to the other end of the booth, re-arranging the display of candles, making sure the SOMETHING WICKED—COME VISIT US IN TOWN! sign was straight, and only when Rhys called her name did she look back over at them.

He was holding The Star, her card, and smiling. "This seems like a good sign."

Vivi wandered back over, leaning against the counter as she plucked the card from Rhys's hand. "Depends on where it is in the spread," she said, and Gwyn tapped the spot where the card had been lying.

"We're going simple past, present, future. You're the present, obviously."

"Obviously," she echoed, and her eyes met Rhys's again. He was smiling at her in that way he had that was both sweet and fond, and also somehow let her know every filthy thing he was thinking of doing to her.

It was really one of her favorite smiles on the planet.

Gwyn was turning over the third card, the future spot, as Vivi looked at the past. Rhys had pulled The Lovers there, also not a surprise, but when Gwyn laid the third card down, she scowled at it.

"Ugh, The Emperor."

"He's not bad," Vivi objected, but as she looked at the version

Gwyn had drawn, she had to admit, he looked a little foreboding. It showed a man in a dark suit sitting on a wooden throne that looked like it had been carved out of an ancient tree. There was silver in his beard, and he was frowning out from the card, a heavy ebony cane in one hand.

"It's not *bad*," Gwyn agreed, tapping the card. "It's just, you know. Authority. Rules, structure . . ."

"My father," Rhys said, and Gwyn nodded, picking the card up.

"Exactly, he totally represents—"

"No," Rhys said, and something in his voice made Vivi look up at him.

He had turned around and was looking out into the crowd, his expression grim, as a dark-haired man in black made his way across the fairground to them, Aunt Elaine several steps behind.

Rhys turned to Vivi, his eyes serious. "It's my father. He's here."

CHAPTER 27

Rhys had thought it was odd seeing Vivi in his father's house, but that had been nothing compared to seeing his father in Vivi's house.

Well, her aunt's house, technically, but it might as well have been Vivi's for as much time she spent there, how natural she looked sitting at her aunt's kitchen table, a mug of steaming tea at her elbow.

Simon looked a little less natural, but then, to be fair, he was staring at a talking cat.

"Treats?" Sir Purrcival asked as he attempted to headbutt Simon's arm. "*Treeeaaats?*"

"What on earth is this abomination?" Simon asked, drawing his arm back even as Gwyn rose from her seat and heaved the cat up off the table.

"He's not an abomination, he is a precious baby. Although we do need to work on his table manners."

"Mama," Sir Purrcival purred, looking up adorably at Gwyn as she carried him out of the room, and Rhys saw his father give a shudder before reaching for the mug of tea Elaine had brought him. It got about halfway to his mouth before he seemed to think better of it, setting it back down so hard it sloshed over the side.

"It's not poisoned," Elaine said, coming to sit next to Vivi, briefly patting her niece's shoulder as she did.

Sniffing, Simon pulled a handkerchief out of his pocket and dabbed at the spilled tea. "Given this family's predilection for harming members of *my* family, you understand my concern."

"Da," Rhys said, his voice low, and Simon flashed him a look Rhys had seen a thousand times before: that mix of irritation and warning, plus just the slightest hint of bafflement, as if Simon could not believe this was his son.

"Am I wrong?" he asked Rhys now. "Do you or do you not find yourself under a curse placed by this very coven?"

"Oh, for heaven's sake," Elaine said, stirring a spoonful of honey into her tea. "We're not a coven. We're a family. And this curse is very much accidental, as both Vivi and Rhys have explained."

Simon sniffed at that, sitting up straighter in his chair. "There's no such thing as an accidental curse. And now, thanks to this foolishness, this entire town, my family's legacy, is apparently cursed as well. Now, from what I can gather, this has resulted in several accidents, plus a ghost being loosed, and also that living nightmare you call a cat."

Gwyn had just walked back into the room, and now she leaned against the doorframe between the kitchen and the hall, folding her arms over her chest. "Seriously, dude, don't care whose dad you are or how fancy a witch you are, keep talking shit about my cat, and I will personally kick you down this mountain."

Simon started to go a little purple in the face at that, so Rhys stepped forward from his own spot near the stove, hands lifted. "All right, let's all just calm down and focus on the matter at hand."

Oh Christ, he sounded like *Wells*. What a nightmare.

Clearing her throat, Vivienne tucked one leg underneath her and looked across the table at Simon. "We've been doing all we can to get the curse reversed, Mr. Penhallow. All of us, even Gwyn. We're trying to make this right."

"And what exactly have you been doing?" Simon asked. His tone was still frosty, but at least he wasn't shooting daggers from his eyes at Vivienne. Small mercies.

Vivienne pressed her lips together, tucking a strand of hair behind her ear before saying, "Well, we've been researching."

"Books?" Simon asked, his brows drawing together, and Rhys frowned.

"Why are you saying 'books' like that? You love books. If you could legally make books your children instead of me and Bowen, I think you would. You'd keep Wells, obviously—"

"Because the answer to this sort of magic cannot be found in *books*," Simon replied, shooting Rhys a glare. "Curses are complicated, complex magic. There is no universal solution. The cure is intimately wound up in the curse itself. The motivations behind casting it, the power used. All of which, I should add, I could have told you if you'd alerted me to what was happening here."

"I tried to, remember?" Rhys said, shoving his hands in his pockets. "And you told me it was ridiculous to even think I'd been cursed."

"Yes, well."

Simon looked down, flicked an imaginary piece of lint off his jacket, and Rhys wondered if he was always going to end up wanting to scream in these little tête-à-têtes with his father.

"The point remains, once you knew what was afoot, I should've been informed."

"How did you find out?" Vivienne asked, leaning forward a bit. "If you don't mind me asking."

"My brother," Rhys answered, then looked over at Simon with raised eyebrows. "I assume that's it, isn't it? I told Wells, so he told you?"

"Lewellyn was worried about you," Simon replied, and Rhys groaned, throwing up his hands, promising himself that the next time he saw his big brother, fratricide was on the menu.

"Should've called Bowen, I knew it."

"You were not kidding about the dysfunctional family stuff," he heard Gwyn mutter to Vivienne, who shushed her.

Rising from her seat, Elaine held her palms out, rings winking in the low light. "Who should've told who what when is not the issue right now. This is actually good to know about the curse magic. Gives us something to work off of."

"Something more than books, yes," Simon said, then looked up at Rhys, his expression grim. "You've been here for nearly two weeks, boy, what else have you been doing besides poring through useless tomes?"

Rhys kept his eyes off Vivienne because he knew if he even glanced her way, his father would understand immediately just what Rhys had been doing.

"We've also been working to reverse some of the effects of the curse," he said evenly, and even Gwyn managed not to snort at that. And it was true, he and Vivienne had spent some time putting out various curse-caused fires.

But he knew it wasn't enough. He knew they should've been taking this more seriously. It was just that it was so easy to get distracted by her, so easy to get caught up in how they were together, and Rhys has missed it too much to let it go now.

Even if he should.

Turning to Elaine, Simon leaned forward, bracing his hands on the table. "Is there any extra power source a member of your family could've drawn from? An ancestor buried here, something like that."

Elaine nodded, pushing her glasses up her nose. "One, yes. An Aelwyd Jones. She came over at the same time as your vaunted Gryffud Penhallow. But as far as we've always known, there was nothing special about her. Just another witch who emigrated here, and died of some random sickness, like so many of them did."

Something flickered in Simon's face, but it was there and gone too quickly for Rhys to know what it was.

"Very well," he said.

Simon stood then, pushing back his shoulders. "I need to return home and consult my own sources on this. Rhys, I think you should come with me."

Startled, Rhys rocked back on his heels. "What?"

"If you're home, I will be able to keep an eye on anything the curse might do to you. It will benefit my research."

The words were stony, detached, and he didn't even look at Rhys as he fished in his pocket for the Traveling Stone, and even though Rhys knew—he *knew*—what a fucking cold fish his father was, it still hurt, even now. Even after all this time. He wanted Rhys to come home because Rhys would be an intriguing experiment in curse work, not because he was his son; he cared about it because it fueled his interest in the real thing he loved—magic itself.

"I want to see this through here, Da," he replied, his voice surprisingly even, and when his father only gave a "So be it," in response, Rhys told himself he'd gotten off lightly. After all, Simon had come all the way from Wales more or less just to chide him, and now he'd done that and was leaving. It had certainly been worse in the past.

But then Simon paused, his fingertips lightly resting on the table. "Hopefully my son's presence will not distract you ladies from the important business of selling crystals and novelty T-shirts."

"Da," Rhys started, but Vivienne was already rising to her feet.

"We do sell an awful lot of crystals and novelty T-shirts," she said, her own hands braced on the table. "We also sell fake grimoires and plastic pumpkins and pointy hats. The whole shebang, really."

The lines around Simon's mouth deepened, but he didn't say anything, not even when Vivienne smiled and said, "And yet we're still the witches who managed to curse your son, and you had no idea it had even happened. So maybe back off a little."

She kept smiling, her eyes hard, her cheeks a little flushed, and truly, how could any man not be wildly in love with her?

Vivienne glanced over at him, and since Rhys was fairly certain he had cartoon hearts literally pouring out of his eyes, he stood up, nodding at his father.

"I'll see you on your way, shall I?"

Simon was still looking at Vivienne, but after a moment, he nodded, heading for the door. Walking his father out, Rhys paused at the top of the porch steps. "Sorry for the wasted trip."

Simon turned and looked at him, and Rhys saw the lines around his mouth, carved deep, the hollows beneath his cheekbones. "Rhys," Simon said, and then he shook his head, the Traveling Stone already in his hand. "Take care of yourself."

"I always have," he replied, but the words were barely out of his mouth before his father was gone, blinking out like a light, leaving Rhys alone on the porch.

"Want me to follow you home?"

Ah. Not alone.

Vivienne stood in the doorway, still in her witch's dress, the hat long since discarded, and Rhys nodded. "I'd like that, yeah."

It took them only about three minutes to make the drive from her aunt's house to his, and Rhys told himself he should be nothing but relieved that his father had come and gone so quickly. That he wasn't staying here in the house tonight.

He dropped his keys on the table by the door, Vivienne just behind him.

"Thank you," he said, turning to look at her. "Both for seeing me home like a lady, and also for putting up with my father."

"He really wasn't so bad," she said with a shrug. "Way less scary than I'd thought he'd be."

"Vivienne, you gorgeous girl, you are a woman of many talents, but lying is not one of them."

She smiled a little at that, and then crossed the room to stand in front of him. "Do you want me to go?" she asked, reaching up to brush his hair back from his face. "Get some time to yourself?"

"Stay," he said, taking her hand and kissing her palm, then her wrist. And then he was kissing her mouth, suddenly, desperately needing her, wanting her, and her hands were already at the button on his jeans.

"Stay," Rhys murmured again, and he knew he didn't just mean tonight, but rather than say that, he pulled her down onto the sofa with him.

"YOU KNOW, THE one place where this decorating scheme really works is in here," Vivi said, leaning back against Rhys's chest in the giant claw-foot tub that dominated the master bathroom. Like the rest of the house, it was done in shades of black and deep burgundy, but Rhys had to agree with her: in here, the mood was definitely more romantic than terrifying. Of course, that might have been all the candles they'd lit and the fact that he currently had Vivi, naked and wet, pressed up against him, but in any case, Rhys was suddenly very fond of this spot in the house.

"Thank you," he murmured against her temple, kissing the damp hair there, and she tilted her head back to look at him.

"For complimenting your bathroom?"

"For all of it. For holding your own against my father."

"He loves you," she said softly, reaching down to tangle her fingers with his under the water. "Yes, he's overbearing and kind of a lot, but he's scared. Worried. And you can't blame him for that."

Rhys didn't want to think about his father right now, and he didn't want to explain to Vivienne that family didn't necessarily mean people who cared about you. She had Elaine and Gwyn, she had warmth and love and home and all the things Rhys had always hoped Simon might be, but never had been.

She was lucky.

And he was lucky to have her, even if it wasn't for much longer.

CHAPTER 28

Vivi woke up the next morning and had the brief, disorienting sensation of not knowing where she was.

Rolling over, she pushed her hair out of her face and took in the heavy velvet drapes and flocked wallpaper.

Rhys's house.

Rhys's father's house.

Rhys's father.

Sighing, Vivi flopped onto her back as last night came rushing back. Simon hadn't been wrong about them ignoring the curse, or at least not paying it as much attention as they should have. They'd cursed her entire town, and what had they spent the last week doing?

She glanced at Rhys's side of the bed, already empty, and her body went warm with the memories of this past week. It felt silly to call it magic, but it had been. Just spending time with Rhys again, showing him around Graves Glen, having dinner with him in her apartment, or here in this bizarre mausoleum of a house that had, somehow, started to feel a little homier.

She even kind of liked the canopy if she was honest.

But Simon had been right—Halloween was just a day away, and they needed to get serious about this.

Easier said than done when it comes to Rhys, she thought, pushing the sheets back.

Which is why it was something of a shock to come downstairs and see Rhys fully dressed in the kitchen, a pair of sunglasses caught in the deep V of his shirt, two travel mugs of coffee in his hands.

"Morning, my darling," he said, entirely too chipper for—Vivi checked the grandfather clock in the hallway—barely seven in the morning.

"Who are you, and what have you done with Rhys Penhallow?" she asked, narrowing her eyes at him even as she took one of the mugs from him.

"I do run a business, you know. I occasionally get up early, and have even been known to make a spreadsheet or two."

"Entirely too early for dirty talk."

Rhys smirked at that, leaning over to kiss the tip of her nose. "Go get dressed, and in the car, I'll tell you all about my spreadsheets and the color-coded folders I keep in my office."

"The car?" Vivi asked, wishing the coffee would make its way to her brain already.

"We have an errand to run," Rhys replied, and something about the suddenly firm line of his mouth, the set of his shoulders, told her this was about the curse.

Twenty minutes and a phone call to Gwyn later, Vivi was

showered, dressed in a pair of jeans she'd left at Elaine's and a striped sweater that actually belonged to Gwyn, plus her own black boots from the night before, and she and Rhys were in his rental car, heading north out of Graves Glen.

"I guess about now would be a fabulous time to tell me what this errand actually entails," Vivi said, reaching up to twist her hair into a messy bun.

Rhys glanced over at her. He had his sunglasses on, the sleeves of his dark gray button-down rolled up, and Vivi wondered why it was that she could've had so much sex with this man, and still be so turned on by something as basic as his forearms while driving. Was that some kind of heretofore unknown fetish of hers, or was it just that everything about Rhys turned her on?

Then he said, "We're going to let that ghost out of the candle," and her libido got a healthy splash of cold water.

"I'm sorry, what?" she asked, her hands still frozen on top of her head, the ponytail holder stretched between two fingers as she stared at him.

"Piper McBride," he answered, as calm and collected as ever, and Vivi scowled at him as she let her hands drop, her hair falling back to her shoulders.

"That would be the *who,* Rhys. What I meant was, 'What the hell do you mean, we're letting her out of that candle?' We don't even know where that candle is right now."

"Actually," Rhys said, reaching over to pick up his travel mug, "we do."

He casually sipped his coffee and Vivi grumbled as she went back to fixing her hair.

"This is punishment for not telling you about the ghost in the first place, isn't it?"

"Little bit, yes," he said, then gave her that half smile that always hit her somewhere squarely in the chest. "All right, cards on the table. I couldn't sleep last night, and while staring at you while *you* sleep is a treasured pastime—"

"Creeper."

That grin again, and a quick squeeze to her thigh. "I decided to put my insomnia to use. My father was right, much as saying that makes me want to die. It's almost Samhain, and we need to be focused on the curse. So I thought to myself, 'Rhys, you devilishly handsome bastard, what was the last truly solid lead you got on the curse?' And then I remembered ol' Piper with her 'cursed Penhallow' bit, and it struck me that she might know more than we let her reveal before the candle sucked her in."

Vivi nodded slowly even as her stomach went icy at the thought of dealing with Piper again. "Okay, I can see all that," she agreed. "But Tamsyn Bligh has the candle if she hasn't already sold it. And god knows where she is."

"She's two towns over," Rhys said, turning left off the highway. "In a place called Cade's Hollow."

Vivi blinked at him. "How do you know that?"

Rhys tapped the side of his nose with one long finger. "Can't trust doing magic in Graves Glen, but that doesn't mean I can't get other people to do magic for me. Specifically, in this case, my brother Llewellyn. Wanker owes me one. So I called him, had him run a little tracking spell for me. Now, had Miss Bligh already been on the other side of the country, we might have needed a plan B, but turns out, she didn't go far."

"But she might not still have the candle," Vivi said, not wanting to get her hopes up, and Rhys nodded.

"She might not," he agreed. "But we'll burn that bridge when we come to it."

"Cross. The saying is 'cross that bridge when we come to it.'"

"Huh," was Rhys's only reply, and Vivi settled back into her seat, watching the early morning sun play over the purplish-blue mountains, watched as the fields slowly became houses, and as the houses gave way to a town even smaller than Graves Glen.

Once the downtown was behind them, Rhys took another series of turns, eventually pulling up in front of a Victorian mansion that looked like a wedding cake, all gingerbread trim and peaked roofs, a wreath of autumn leaves adorning the front door.

Shutting off the car, Rhys ducked his head down to study the building through the windshield.

"She's at a B-and-B?" Vivi asked.

"This was definitely the address Wells gave me," Rhys said, then, after a pause, added, "You know, when we're done here, we *could* get a room, and—"

"Rhys." Vivi gave him a look. "Focus, please."

"Sorry, you're right. Curse work now, sex later."

They got out of the car, the morning chilly and still a little damp, dew sparkling on the thick bushes outside the bed-and-breakfast as they made their way up the steps, and Vivi smiled at the little jack-o'-lantern sitting on a wicker table just outside the front door.

Bells chimed overhead as they opened the front door, and a cheerful blond woman behind a large oak counter beamed at the two of them. "Good morning! How can I help you?"

Vivi realized she hadn't asked Rhys if he had a plan for how they were going to talk to Tamsyn. Any hotel worth its salt wasn't just going to offer up the room number of a guest, and Vivi wasn't sure how long they could just hang out in the lobby, hoping Tamsyn came down.

Rhys smiled at the woman behind the counter. "We're actually hoping to say hello to a friend," he said, his accent thicker than usual, and Vivi fought the urge to elbow him in the ribs.

Charm. That was his entire plan. Smile, drop a few Welsh words in, do that Leaning Thing against the counter while his hair did that Other Thing, and hope for the best, aka the Rhys Penhallow Special.

But before Rhys could even do the Leaning Thing, footsteps were pounding down the massive staircase to their right, and Amanda—no, Tamsyn Bligh—was suddenly there, practically leaning over the bannister. "Hi, you two!" she said, her voice so bright and cheery that Vivi was surprised cartoon birds didn't appear by her head.

And then Vivi noticed how pale she was, the deep shadows under her eyes and that her smile had a kind of rictus quality to it.

She waved at both Rhys and Vivi. "Come on upstairs! So glad you're here!"

Rhys shot Vivi the most eloquent *What the fuck?* look she'd ever seen, and then the smile was back, the easy charm, and he slipped an arm around Vivi's waist, pulling her toward the stairs as the blond woman behind the counter went back to her computer.

"Good to see you, too," Rhys said as they climbed the steps, following Tamsyn, who nearly sprinted to her room.

This B-and-B still used big old-fashioned keys, and Vivi saw Tamsyn's hands tremble a little as she unlocked the door.

Rhys and Vivi followed her inside, and Vivi immediately gasped at the cold in the room despite the fire crackling in the fireplace, tugging the sleeves of her sweater down over her hands as she glanced around. The room was dark, curtains drawn, and there, in the middle of the floor, was the Eurydice Candle.

Tamsyn closed the door, and whirled around to face them.

"You guys have got to help me."

CHAPTER 29

"And why exactly would we do that?" Vivi asked, folding her arms over her chest. "You lied to me."

"I did," Tamsyn replied, not sounding all that sorry about it. Then she schooled her expression into something a little more contrite. "And that was wrong of me, but I had a very good reason."

"Which was?" Rhys asked, walking over to the fireplace to brace a hand against the mantel.

Tamsyn looked between him and Vivi, and then sighed. "Okay, I was gonna say something about how I needed a trapped ghost to save my grandma or something, but really, I just wanted to make a whole bunch of money. People will pay thousands for a Eurydice Candle that has a ghost in it, and one with a *witch ghost*? Please. I was going to spend the summer in Portugal from this one sale alone. But"—she glared at the candle where it sat—"turns out, I can't off-load that thing after all. Something's wrong with it."

She gestured around the room. "See how cold it is? How dark?

It's been doing that every day since I got here, and it's just getting worse."

Vivi slowly made her way over to the candle, and immediately saw what Tamsyn meant. The whole thing was radiating a kind of dark energy that let her know Piper's ghost might still be trapped, but it was very unhappy about it.

"Eurydice Candles aren't supposed to do that," Rhys said in a low voice, coming to stand beside Vivi.

"Yeah, no shit," Tamsyn replied, placing one hand on her hip. "I've bought and sold tons of the things but that one? It's completely busted. And I can't just dump it somewhere, and I definitely did not want to take it to the witches at your college, so I've been stuck here, trying to figure out what to do, and then you two showed up like some kind of witchy angels."

"You're not a witch, then?" Vivi asked, looking back over her shoulder at Tamsyn.

"Definitely not," she replied with a little shudder. "Just make money off their stuff."

"And lie to people to obtain said stuff," Rhys said, to which Tamsyn shrugged.

"No one got hurt."

"Yet," Vivi said, reaching down to pick up the candle. It was so cold to the touch, it almost burned, and she winced as she tugged at her sweater, covering her hand so she could carry it.

"Why are you still so close to Graves Glen?" Vivi asked as she turned around, the candle still freezing in her hand. "I would've thought you would've gotten as far from there as you could've."

"That was the plan," she said on a sigh, then nodded at the candle. "But do you wanna take that thing on a plane?"

"Fair point," Rhys muttered, glancing around the obviously haunted room.

"I guess we can do you the favor of taking this off your hands," Vivi said, making herself sound irritated and not relieved.

"At great personal cost to ourselves," Rhys added, his voice solemn, expression so serious Vivi had to bite back a grin.

"Oh god, thank you," Tamsyn said, her shoulders sagging. "And seriously, I'm sorry about tricking you into trapping the ghost for me. Really. You seem nice. And I liked your office."

"Thanks?" Vivi replied, and then Rhys had his hand on her lower back, steering her toward the door.

"Christ, that was easy," he muttered once they were out in the hall, and then he looked around at the heavy wooden doors. "You know, we have some extra time now. I expected this to take up much more of the day. So if you *wanted* . . ."

"No," Vivi replied, poking him in the chest. "We're not getting a room. We're taking this thing straight to Aunt Elaine."

Giving a heavy sigh, Rhys cupped her face with one hand, leaning in to brush a kiss against her mouth. "I both love and hate when you're sensible, Vivienne."

OKAY, WE PROBABLY should've gotten a room, Vivi thought several hours later as she sat shivering in the woods beyond Elaine's cabin. They'd gotten back to Graves Glen before noon, but Elaine was insistent that this kind of magic needed to be done at night, under the moon, although now, as Vivi huddled a little closer to Rhys, she wondered if this was more of Aunt Elaine just leaning into aesthetics.

Across from her, Gwyn sat with her knees drawn up to her chest, watching Aunt Elaine pour a salt circle on the forest floor, the Eurydice Candle in the middle, still radiating cold. "This is extremely metal of us," Gwyn observed, then glanced down at herself. "Probably would be more metal if I weren't wearing my pumpkin jammies, but what can you do?"

Snorting, Rhys wrapped an arm around Vivi's shoulders, tugging her closer. "Trust me, having seen this ghost in the . . . well, in the flesh isn't appropriate, but having seen it . . . in person isn't good either, is it? In any case," he finally said, shrugging. "The ghost is metal enough for all of us."

"And this ghost hates you, yes?" Aunt Elaine asked, the bells on her skirt jingling softly as she completed the circle.

"Seems to, yes."

"Hmmm." She pushed her glasses up the bridge of her nose. "Then maybe move a little farther back."

Rhys looked down at Vivi, and she nodded, remembering him flying through the air at the library, the anger in the ghost's eyes when it had seen him. Elaine's theory was that because Piper McBride had been a witch, she might be a little more receptive to talking to fellow witches, especially ones who were setting her free. Vivi had reminded Elaine that she had *also* been the one to capture Piper, but Elaine was hoping Piper wouldn't remember that bit.

"Ghosts don't always have a good sense of what's going on," she'd said. "Time doesn't exactly have any meaning for them."

Vivi hoped she was right.

Rhys had stood up and moved back into the darkness, leaning against a tree as Vivi and Gwyn both rose to their feet, standing on opposite sides of the salt circle.

"Vivi?" Aunt Elaine asked, handing her a cardboard tube of long matches. "Would you like to do the honors?"

And so, for the second time in her life, Vivi lit a Eurydice Candle.

It was different this time. There was no slow creeping feeling as a spirit was drawn in. Instead, the candle sparked, flamed, and suddenly Piper McBride was there, in all her floaty, seriously pissed off glory.

She was emitting enough light to cast them all in a blue-green glow, and across the circle, Gwyn's eyes went huge in her face. "Oh, shit, a ghost," she breathed, then fluttered her hands. "I mean, I knew we were gonna see one, but there's knowing and then there's actually seeing it."

Piper floated around to face her, and even in the dim light, Vivi could see Gwyn swallow hard. "Um. Nice shirt, by the way. I like Nirvana, too."

The ghost turned slowly, taking in Vivi and Elaine, and while her expression didn't change all that much, Vivi didn't get the sense she was as angry this time.

Maybe Elaine had been right.

"Are you a coven?" Piper asked, her voice sounding like it was

coming from far away, an eerie effect given how close she was to them.

"Yes," Vivi said, even though it wasn't technically true, and the ghost turned back to her.

"*You,*" she said, upper lip curling slightly. "*I've seen you.*"

Her mouth suddenly dry, Vivi licked her lips. "Right. In the library."

Piper was fully snarling now. "*With a Penhallow.*"

"Right. Which is what we want to talk to you about, actually. You knew Rhys, the Penhallow, was cursed. And you were right. I'm the one who cursed him, so—"

"*It wasn't you.*"

The words were flat, almost bored, and Vivi wondered if she'd misheard.

"*What?*"

"*I know the magic surrounding that Penhallow,*" Piper said, still hovering over the ground, but starting to seem more like a teenage girl, less like a terrifying supernatural being. "*And it was not yours. Or not only yours.*"

"Whose was it, then?" Elaine asked, and Piper twisted again to face her.

"*There is other magic running in the blood of this town,*" Piper said, "*magic that was stolen by the Penhallows. Hidden. Aelwyd Jones deserves her revenge.*"

Aelwyd Jones.

Vivi's ancestor, the one buried here in the town cemetery.

She looked at Elaine, whose face was creased in confusion.

"Our ancestor didn't have powerful magic," she told Piper. "She was a regular witch, like all the women in our family."

"She was more powerful than anyone knew," Piper retorted, *"but Gryffud Penhallow stole from her, used her, erased her name."*

"How?"

Vivi whirled around to see Rhys step forward just as Piper's gaze fixed on him, and any trace of the regular girl vanished. Her eyes went black, hair streaming back, and with that same unearthly howl Vivi had heard in the library, she launched herself at Rhys.

Without thinking, Vivi stepped forward, putting herself between Piper and Rhys, her foot stepping into the salt circle, breaking it, and felt something icy cold wash over her, pushing into her, her vision whiting out as suddenly Piper's own thoughts, own memories, swirled through her mind.

Piper in the library researching Graves Glen's history, her black hair hanging down over a notebook, Aelwyd Jones *written in purple ink, Piper in the cabin at her altar, candles lit, runes glowing and a spell, a spell to raise Aelwyd's spirit, but it's too much, the magic is too much and Piper can feel it pulling at her, sucking her down, and then it's dark, it's so dark, and it's* cold . . .

Vivi gasped, leaves crunching under her fingers as the cold rushed out of her, her heart racing, her vision still blurry as she tried to make sense of what she'd just seen.

"Vivienne."

Rhys was kneeling down next to her—how had she ended up on the ground?—his hands on her shoulders, his face pale, and

Vivi looked beyond him to see Piper still hovering over the candle, the salt circle repaired, Elaine looking frazzled.

"I'm fine," she managed to croak, even though she wasn't sure she was. "Really."

She let Rhys help her to her feet, leaning heavily against him as she stared up at Piper.

"Trying to contact Aelwyd killed you," she said, her voice still raspy, and Piper nodded even as she continued to glare at Rhys.

"It wasn't her fault. It was mine. My magic wasn't strong enough to break the bonds that held her."

Her gaze swung to Vivi. *"But yours was. You called her forth with your curse, and she gave you power because you're her blood."*

"A blood curse," Elaine said, frowning. "I didn't even think of that."

"Is that bad?" Gwyn asked, and then shook her head. "Okay, stupid question, anything called a 'blood curse' is clearly bad."

"So how do we lift it?" Vivi asked Piper now, and Piper smiled. *"You can't. Only Aelwyd can do that."*

"But she's dead," Gwyn said, hands on her hips. "Because she got an ear infection or whatever it was that killed people back then."

"*Gryffud killed her,*" Piper retorted. *"When he drained her magic from her to fuel this town. He covered it up, said she'd died from influenza."*

Gwyn blinked at that, and Vivi thought again of that cave, the magic pulsing through the ley lines. Not just magic, but Aelwyd's very life force, taken from her.

"Still," Gwyn went on. "You died trying to contact her, so it seems like asking her to lift this curse is kind of out of the question."

"*She wouldn't lift it even if she could,*" Piper replied. "*I've seen what it's done to this town. This town, Gryffud Penhallow's legacy, suffers. So does Gryffud Penhallow's heir.*"

Those malevolent eyes fixed on Rhys again, who stared back at her, nonplussed.

"Me?" he said, laying a hand on his chest. "I'm not really his 'heir.' There are loads of us."

"*But you're the one who's here.*" Piper smirked. "*And tomorrow is Samhain, when the veil is the thinnest, and Aelwyd's magic will be at its most powerful.*"

Halloween. Tomorrow.

Vivi looked at the ghost, her blood suddenly ice cold, her stomach clenched. "So you're saying—"

"*The curse reaches its zenith tomorrow night at midnight,*" Piper said, and that smile turned poisonous. "*Tomorrow night, both this town and the Penhallow die.*"

CHAPTER 30

Vivi's whole body ached as she and Rhys made the drive up to his house, and she was more tired than she'd ever been in her life. A kind of bone-deep tired that made things like unbuckling her seatbelt and opening the car door seem impossible.

Rhys must've seen it because he reached over and pushed the button for her, then walked around to her side of the car and opened the door, helping her out.

"Want me to carry you?" he asked, and she looked up at his house.

"No offense, but getting bridal-carried into this house might make me feel like the swooning heroine in a horror movie."

"Understood," Rhys said with a little smile, but he still put his arm around her as they made their way up the porch steps.

"Who knew getting momentarily possessed was so draining?" she asked, and as Rhys unlocked the door, he looked over at her again, eyes searching her face.

"You're sure you're all right?"

She was, technically. Okay in body at least, just tired.

It was her heart that ached.

Tomorrow night, both this town and the Penhallow die.

Piper's voice was so clear in her mind, the way her eyes had burned as she'd glared at Rhys.

Rhys, who was . . . whistling as they walked into the house.

Vivi followed him, watching as he tossed his keys onto the table, then went into the kitchen, emerging with a couple of bottles of water.

"At least now that Piper has said her piece, she can stop haunting the library," Rhys said, and that was one good thing that had come out of this night. Once she'd delivered her pronouncement, she'd vanished, the Eurydice Candle crumbling into dust, and Vivi had the sense she was gone for good this time, no binding spells necessary. But it still made her sad, the thought of that bright, talented witch feeling her power slowly drain away as she attempted magic that was entirely too much for her. It felt like such a waste.

Rhys handed Vivi a bottle of water, flipping his own in his hand a couple of times before opening it. "Still, mission accomplished and all that." He moved toward her, but Vivi stepped back from him, suddenly not quite as exhausted.

"Rhys, did you miss the part where if we don't fix this tomorrow night, you're going to *die*?"

He stood there in the living room, nonchalant, sipping his water. "So she says."

Vivi gaped at him. "No, not *so she says*. Seriously. You'll die unless we can raise Aelwyd's spirit and somehow convince her to forgive you for the sins of your family. Which, let me remind you, is a very tall order."

"Never know until we try, so don't really see much point worrying about it," he said, and then set his bottle on the table, walking over to take her hands.

"Now, should I die, I was thinking some kind of Viking funeral. Launch me in a fiery boat, you know? Do they have lakes around here?"

Jerking her hands out of his, Vivi stared into those blue eyes, that handsome face, and once again, she could see Gwyn's card for him clear as day. The Fool, cheerfully walking off mountains.

"Can you not make jokes about this?" she snapped, and Rhys rocked back on his heels, a trio of creases appearing on his forehead.

"Sorry," he said. "I forgot what a night you've had. Not a good time for quips, you're right."

"Don't do that."

"Do what?"

Crossing her arms, Vivi faced him there by the front door, her head pounding, her mouth dry.

"Act like I don't think it's funny just because I'm tired. I don't think it's funny because there's nothing amusing to me about you possibly dying, especially since it's my fault."

Her voice cracked on the last word, and she felt tears sting her eyes.

Please don't let me cry in front of him, please don't let me cry in front of him . . .

But it was too late, and he made a pained sound as he reached for her again.

Backing away, Vivi lifted her hands. "No. I'm . . . okay, I'm not fine, but I just . . ."

She looked at him and said the words in her heart, the words that were scaring her so much. "What if we can't fix it, Rhys?"

"But what if we *can*?"

He reached for her again, and this time, Vivi let him, let him pull her against him, his arms wrapped tight around her as she rested her head on his shoulder, closing her eyes, and feeling her heart sink somewhere south of her navel.

This was Rhys. This was who he was. And she loved that about him, the kind of cheerful optimism that it would all go his way because, honestly, it always kind of had.

He would always be like this.

And he would always break her heart. He wouldn't mean to, he definitely wouldn't want to, but he would.

And who knew what would happen then? Vivi hadn't meant for any of this to happen, but it had, all because she'd loved him too much, felt too many big feelings for him. And maybe a woman who didn't have witchcraft running through her veins could risk that kind of thing, but Vivi couldn't.

Not again.

Swallowing hard, she pulled away. "I'm going to go back to Elaine's tonight," she said, and he frowned.

"Vivienne—"

"I'll see you tomorrow," she said, making herself smile even as she wiped her tears away with the flat of her hand. "And you're right, we'll fix this, and it'll be fine, and you can go back to Wales without me calling you a fuckerneck again."

He still wasn't smiling, but he nodded and let her go. "I can drive you back," he said, hands in his pockets, eyes serious.

"I'll walk," she said. "It's not far."

And it wasn't, the fresh evening air doing her some good as she made her way back to Elaine's. She wasn't even crying anymore as she walked in the front door.

"Vivi," Sir Purrcival said from his basket, and she smiled as she crouched down to pet him.

"Learning new words every day! Look at you go."

"Treats?" he asked, blinking those big green eyes, and from the kitchen, Gwyn called, "Don't give him any! He's eaten his weight in them already."

Vivi followed the sound of her cousin's voice, propping a hip against the kitchen table while Gwyn stirred something on the stove.

"Not staying with Rhys tonight?"

"Nope. Needed a breather."

Gwyn didn't reply to that for a long time, and then she turned away from whatever it was she was boiling and said, "You can say you're in love with him, you know."

"I'm not," Vivi argued, but she turned away so that she didn't actually have to lie to Gwyn's face. "It's just . . . like it was before. An infatuation. Really good sex. A distraction."

"Vivi."

Gwyn had crossed the kitchen and had her hands on Vivi's shoulders as she gently turned her around. "I love good sex and distractions more than just about anything. But I also can recognize when something is the real deal. And this is, isn't it?"

Vivi could've withstood a lot of things. Sarcasm, prying, possibly even torture. Had Gwyn attempted any of those, she would've been able to breezily insist that she was not in love with Rhys Penhallow, and that she was just a twenty-first-century woman having a good time in the midst of what was otherwise a total mess.

But Gwyn was looking at her so sincerely with those big blue eyes that had always seen right into her soul, and oh, goddammit, now she was *crying*. Again.

Just a little, but that was enough for Gwyn.

Her face creasing in exaggerated sympathy, Gwyn pulled Vivi in, smothering her in orange wool and the scent of lavender.

"Baby girl." Gwyn sighed, and Vivi hugged her back, letting herself cry.

"It's so stupid!"

"So is love, to be honest."

"We're completely wrong for each other!"

"Which is why it's hot."

"I *cursed him*, Gwynnevere."

"Who among us hasn't."

Pulling back, Vivi stared at Gwyn before swiping at her wet cheeks. "Even you have to admit this is very bad timing."

But Gwyn only shrugged. "There's no really good timing for

this kind of thing, is there? Finding your person? It just kind of happens when it happens. Or so they say."

With that, she turned back to the stove, and for the first time, Vivi noticed what she was making—the particularly sweet and, in Vivi's opinion, gross hot tea that Gwyn had always loved, a mix of truly obscene amounts of sugar, black tea, a bunch of spices and orange-flavored Kool-Aid.

It was Gwyn's go-to comfort drink, even above vodka, and it always signaled something bad.

"Jane?" Vivi ventured, and Gwyn didn't turn around.

"Talk about people who were completely wrong for each other."

Without saying anything else, Vivi walked over and put her arms around Gwyn's waist, resting her cheek against Gwyn's back. Then, after a pause, she asked, "Wanna curse her?"

Gwyn burst into laughter, dropping her hands to cover Vivi's, and squeezed. "You know, let's wait to see how your sitch turns out before we attempt cursing again, okay?"

"Fair," Vivi answered, giving Gwyn one more hug before going over to the cabinet to get them both mugs.

Tonight, she'd sit at the kitchen table and drink Gwyn's Breakup Tea.

And tomorrow, she'd make a deal with the devil.

Maybe literally.

CHAPTER 31

Rhys woke up on what might be the last day of his life in an unsurprisingly bad mood.

For one, he was alone.

He'd slept on one side of the massive bed last night, like some kind of heartsick idiot, and now, as he rolled over and stretched his hand out to the place where Vivienne should be, he *felt* very much like some kind of heartsick idiot.

He'd fucked up last night. Badly.

And he wasn't sure exactly where. He knew she'd been upset about the curse and what it meant, but he believed in her. Believed in *them,* that they could fix this, and it had stung that she clearly didn't have the same faith.

But then, she never had had a huge amount of faith in him. Rhys might have bungled that summer pretty badly, but she hadn't even given him a chance to explain, had immediately assumed the absolute worst interpretation of what he'd said, and until this moment, he hadn't realized that that had stung, too.

Vivienne had loved him, but she didn't trust him.

She didn't trust him now.

And now he was lying in black satin sheets and brooding, which was frankly humiliating.

Rhys sighed and heaved himself up in the bed just as his phone went off on the nightstand, and his stupid, treacherous heart immediately leapt, thinking it might be Vivienne.

But no, it was Bowen on a video call, and as Rhys answered, they both stared at each other in horror.

"What's happened to your face?" Rhys asked just as Bowen scowled and said, "You're naked."

Sitting up higher in the bed, Rhys dug the heel of his free hand into one eye. "No, I'm not, I just woke up, and—"

"Why would you answer a video call naked?"

"Why would you attach a badger to your face?"

For a moment, the two brothers glared at each other through their respective phones, and then a smile cracked through all that beard. "It is kind of out of control, isn't it?" he asked, rubbing his jaw.

"It needs its own post code, mate," Rhys replied, but he was smiling, too. Bowen, was, like Wells, a right pain in the arse a lot of the time, but it was also good to see him, even if he had grown the world's most terrifying beard.

"Wells told me you fucked up," Bowen said, to the point as always. "Got yourself cursed."

"It's a long story," Rhys warned, but Bowen only grunted, pulling the phone back to show Rhys the desolate mountainside he was sitting on.

"I could use the entertainment."

So Rhys told him, all of it, starting with the summer nine years ago, ending with Vivienne walking out of his house in tears last night.

When he was done, Bowen was frowning, but since that was one of Bowen's default expressions, Rhys wasn't that concerned.

"She's right," he finally said. "About you never taking shite seriously."

"That's not true," Rhys objected. "I take lots of shite seriously. My business. Her. I would take you seriously, but I can't because of that beard."

"See, that's what I mean," Bowen said, pointing at the phone with one finger. "Always taking the piss, making jokes. You say she doesn't trust you, but how can she when you act like nothing matters to you? Like it's all a big fucking lark?"

Rhys blinked. "Have you started giving free therapy to sheep up there, Bowen?"

Bowen's scowl deepened, and Rhys held up a hand in surrender. "Right, right, I get it, I'm doing it again."

He didn't know how to explain to Bowen, a man who had always said exactly what he was thinking in the bluntest way possible, that it was easier for him to dodge and weave, not to let anyone know things ever got to him. To live life right on the surface and not worry about getting too deep.

But the thing was, he was already in too deep. He was in love with Vivienne. Had, he was beginning to realize, never stopped loving her. That summer hadn't just been a fling—it had been the real deal.

And he'd fucked it up. Just like he was fucking it up now.

"Tell her how you feel," Bowen said now. "Be honest. Oh, and also don't die tonight."

"Thanks," Rhys said with a rueful smile. "Take care of yourself up there. And shave."

Bowen flipped him off, but he was grinning as they hung up, and Rhys got out of bed feeling a little bit better.

He just needed to see Vivienne and tell her the truth. Tell her he was head over heels for her, and that yes, tonight scared him shitless, but he trusted her.

The issue was how to tell her. It wasn't exactly the sort of thing one declared over text. He'd go to her aunt's, tell her there.

But when he drove down the mountain and knocked on Elaine's door, she was the only one there.

Well, her and the cat.

As soon as Elaine opened the door, the little furry bastard looked up at Rhys and very succinctly said, *"Dickbag."*

"I defended you the other night, mate," Rhys said, shaking a finger at Sir Purrcival. "Don't make me regret it."

Elaine chuckled at that, leaning down to scoop up the cat, but she didn't invite Rhys in, and when she looked him over, he felt like she could see into his soul.

"You're here to tell Vivi you love her," she finally said, and he nodded.

"Along with some other things, yes, but that's the main one. But since she doesn't appear to be here, I'll just pop over to—"

"Rhys."

Elaine laid a hand on his arm, and for the first time, he noticed that she had the same hazel eyes as Vivienne. Those eyes were kind now, but Rhys knew he wasn't going to like what she was about to say.

"She's already home, getting ready for tonight. The magic she needs to do is . . . it's more than she's ever done before. Honestly, it's more than I've ever done before, and it takes preparation. You can't disturb that."

Rhys felt like someone had just punched him in the stomach.

He was too late.

It seemed like he was always too fucking late.

"Right," he said, making himself smile at Elaine. "Definitely not."

Elaine squeezed his arm. "Tell her after."

"I will," he replied, even as unease crawled along his spine.

Assuming I'm still around after, I will.

THE BATH WASN'T helping.

Again.

At least this time, as Vivi sat in the tub, up to her chin in hot water, surrounded by candles, there was no vodka in sight. And she wasn't conjuring up Rhys's face or the scent of his cologne. She wasn't even sniffling.

Really, a big improvement over her last Heartbreak Bath.

So why did she feel so much worse?

She knew the answer to that—because this time, the heartbreak felt so much bigger, and the task that loomed ahead of her was terrifying. Aunt Elaine was the best, strongest witch Vivi knew, and even she had never attempted something like this. And now Vivi, whose most-used spell was reheating her tea without a microwave, was going to summon up a long-dead spirit and demand it reverse a curse.

Somehow.

The water sloshed as she stood up and reached for a towel, dimly wondering what kind of thing she should wear to a ritual summoning on a graveyard on Halloween night. Probably something suitably impressive, all black, maybe, some silver jewelry.

But as Vivi looked through her closet, her eye fell on the dress she'd been wearing the night Rhys had first come back into town, the black one with the little orange polka dots and the orange patent leather belt.

She fucking loved that dress. But it didn't exactly scream *Powerful Sorceress.*

She reached past it, going for the black dress she'd worn to the Fall Fair, but then she paused.

This was her spell. No matter that her ancestor had given it the necessary boost, she was the one who'd cast the original curse, and she would be the one trying to remove it tonight. She *was* a powerful sorceress, polka dots or no, and if wearing her favorite dress would make her feel better, why not?

And she did feel a little bit better as she made the walk from her apartment to the cemetery. The sun had just set, and the town was in full swing, Halloween-wise. All the streetlamps were illuminated, creepy music blaring from the speakers placed all along the main drag, and Vivi smiled as she passed Coffee Cauldron. They'd placed a real cauldron outside full of dry ice, and a couple of kids dressed as witches were laughing and shrieking as they ran through the fog.

Graves Glen was a good place. A happy place.

And she was going to save it.

The sounds of the Halloween revelry got more distant the closer Vivi got to the cemetery, and by the time she opened the creaking iron gate, all she could hear was the wind in the leaves overhead and the occasional cry of a bird.

Aelwyd's grave was at the very back corner, and as Vivi walked toward it, she could already see Gwyn and Elaine standing there, waiting for her.

They both held candles, and the warmth in both their faces had Vivi's throat suddenly feeling tight.

"We're almost ready," Elaine said, handing Vivi a black candle. "As soon as Rhys gets here."

"And here Rhys is," Vivi heard him say behind her. She turned to see him sauntering down the path like he was strolling toward a date in the park, not potentially his own death, and her heart thumped painfully in her chest.

He was dressed all in black, the pendant winking against his throat, and as he took the candle from Elaine, he threw Vivi a wink. "Ready to get me uncursed, *cariad*?"

Vivi took a deep breath, and there was a sharp sound and the sudden scent of sulfur in the air as Gwyn lit a match, touching it to the wick of Vivi's candle.

"As I'll ever be."

CHAPTER 32

Rhys wasn't sure he'd ever been so nervous in his life as he watched Vivienne situate herself at the foot of Aelwyd's grave, her blond hair pulled back from her face, standing there in her polka dots, clutching her candle.

She was so beautiful, so brave, and even though he knew he should probably be a little worried for himself, it was the idea of anything happening to her that had his stomach in knots, his hands clenched into fists at his sides.

I should have told her before, he thought, but it was too late now. She was already murmuring under her breath, kneeling down at the foot of Aelwyd's grave. Rhys wasn't sure exactly what went into this ritual, but he knew it was more than summoning a ghost. Ghosts were entirely separate beings, made of energy that couldn't get free.

A spirit, still trapped in its grave, was a much harder beast to summon.

Piper McBride had learned that the hard way, and now, watching Vivienne, Rhys had to fight the urge to rush forward and pull her out of here. To hell with the town, to hell with *him,* just don't let Vivienne risk her own life to save either, he thought.

But she wanted to do this. Believed she could do this.

And he had to believe in her.

Gwyn and Elaine knelt down as well, and when Elaine pulled a small silver knife from her belt, Rhys gritted his teeth. It was a blood curse, and Vivi was Aelwyd's blood relative, so it shouldn't surprise him that blood was involved, but he still winced as that blade flashed over the meaty part of Vivienne's palm, a quick, tiny cut, but a cut nonetheless.

Vivienne didn't flinch, though, pressing her palm against the earth, lowering her head.

Gwyn and Elaine were whispering along with Vivienne, the flames of their candles flickering in the night wind, and Rhys felt cold race up his spine as the ground trembled slightly underfoot.

He couldn't pinpoint exactly when he felt it happen. There was nothing dramatic like there had been with Piper, no sudden form leaping up from the grave.

But when Vivienne turned her head and looked at him, he knew it was not her behind those eyes.

"Penhallow," she said, and it was her voice, but another one underneath it, Welsh accent lilting, and it was in Welsh that Rhys answered.

"That's me."

Vivienne's lips tilted upward at the corners. "You look like him. Like Gryffud."

Touching the bridge of his nose, Rhys frowned. "Dammit all."

"Are you as feckless as he was? As cruel?" she went on, rising to her feet. It was the strangest thing, seeing Vivienne's body, a body he knew as well as his own now, but without her familiar gestures, her posture completely different. And she was watching him so coldly. He'd never seen that look on Vivienne's face before, not even when she hated him.

"Feckless, possibly," he answered now. "Cruel? I certainly hope not."

Moving toward him, Vivienne spread her arms wide as behind her, Gwyn and Elaine watched, ashen.

"Gryffud wanted his magic to build this town," she said. "Wanted it to be his legacy. His own private kingdom."

"That does sound like the men in my family."

"But there wasn't enough. *He* was not enough," Vivienne went on, so close now that he caught a whiff of ozone and earth, nothing like Vivienne's own sugary sweet scent. "And so he asked for my help."

The eyes fixed somewhere over Rhys's shoulder, and he somehow knew she was seeing the caves, the ley lines. "I meant to blend my magic with his, but he took all of it."

Her gaze fastened on him. "All of me. He drained me dry to build his town, and then erased my name from it. Built shrines in his own image. No thanks for my sacrifice, not even acknowledgment. It was as if I never was."

Rhys could hear the hurt underneath all of that, and even

though he knew it wasn't Vivienne speaking to him, the words still lodged somewhere in his chest like a stone. "If it's any consolation," he said, "Gryffud did die of smallpox which I hear is pretty awful, so—"

"There can be no consolation!" Her voice rose, the wind whipping higher, Vivienne's hair blowing back from her face as overhead, the trees swayed and groaned.

"My descendant called on me to curse you, and so I did. And you in turn have cursed this town. My revenge would be complete, watching you both turn to ash."

She tilted her head, watching him, and Rhys braced himself for . . . he wasn't sure what, exactly. A smiting? That seemed likely.

But then, she said, "Except that this woman, this sister of my blood, asks me to spare both. To lift this curse from you and the town."

Rhys took a slow, deep breath. "She does."

"And why should I?"

Rhys thought for some reason, some completely unimpeachable argument to save both his life and Graves Glen, but all he could say was, "I love her."

Those eyes didn't blink. "You love her," Vivienne/Aelwyd repeated, and Rhys nodded.

"I love her, and I hurt her, and I deserved to be cursed. But Graves Glen is her home. Her family's home. I can't let it be destroyed because of me."

The moonlight spilled down into the graveyard, and for the

first time, Rhys noticed a sort of shimmering veil around Vivienne, could see her heart pounding in her throat. Was she still in there, his Vivienne? Could she hear him?

"And if I were to spare the town but take you, what then?"

Gaze dark, the witch pressed even closer, and Rhys made himself stand his ground. "Then take me," he said. "It's a fair price for what was done to you."

"Rhys," he heard Gwyn cry, but Elaine stilled her with a hand on her wrist, and Rhys gave her a wobbly grin.

"Ah, finally, I'm not 'dickbag' anymore."

Aelwyd was still studying him through Vivienne's eyes, and Rhys was very, very aware that his life was hanging in the balance.

And then she backed away from him, some of the wind dying down, that smell like lightning striking the earth fading.

"You must love her, then," she said.

"I do," he answered. "Madly."

She gave a sigh, Vivienne's chest rising and falling, and then she closed her eyes. "I can see her heart," Aelwyd said. "Feel it inside her chest. She loves you, too, and would not see you harmed, and as she is of my blood, I've decided to grant her request."

Rhys tried not to actually fall to the ground with relief, but it was a struggle. "Thank you," he breathed, and he saw Gwyn and Elaine clutch hands.

"Thank you," Rhys repeated. "And I promise, I'll set this right about that bastard Gryffud. No more statue, definitely no Founder's Day. I might even see if I can get my brother Wells to change his middle name."

Aelwyd frowned, and for a second, Rhys wondered if mentioning the family connection had been a bad idea, but it wasn't that. She wasn't even looking at him, but back up toward the grave, her hands opening and closing at her sides.

"It's . . . the curse. I cannot lift it."

"Beg pardon?"

She went to her knees, head tilting back to look up at the sky. "I'm not strong enough." And her voice was sounding weaker, fainter, Vivienne's voice stronger.

Her eyes found his again, and this time, it felt more like Vivienne was looking back at him. "I'm sorry, Rhys Penhallow," Aelwyd said. "It's too late."

And then there was a sound like the crack of thunder and Vivienne slumped to the ground.

CHAPTER 33

Vivi was getting a little tired of doing magic and somehow end-ing up on the ground.

She opened her eyes to see Gwyn, Rhys and Elaine all stand-ing over her, and from the expressions on their faces, she was guessing the ritual hadn't worked. Or had she even managed to do it? The last thing she remembered was her hand on Aelwyd's grave, asking her ancestor to lift the curse, and then it was all a big blank until now.

"Is it over?" she asked Rhys, and he tried to smile at her as he helped her to her feet.

"You were magnificent. Honestly."

"That's not an answer," she replied as she dusted off her skirt, looking over at Gwyn and Elaine, both of whom were as grave as she'd ever seen them.

"You did it, Vivs," Gwyn said, coming forward to take Vivi's hand. "You pulled Aelwyd's spirit right into you, it was the cool-est magic I've ever seen. You were all goddess-y, and your hair was blowing in the wind like Beyoncé . . ."

Vivi stared at her. "And it didn't work," she said. "I can see it in your face."

Gwyn's bravado collapsed, and she pressed a hand to Vivi's cheek. "It wasn't your fault."

Panicked, Vivi looked to Rhys, standing there so handsome, so casual, hands in his pockets, but there were lines around his mouth, his shoulders tense. "Apparently Aelwyd didn't have the juice, Samhain or no." He shrugged. "Win some, lose some."

"No," Vivi said, shaking her head. She still felt wobbly from the spell she'd just done, could still taste a strange metallic flavor in her mouth, and she was shivering, but she was also really, really fucking sure she wasn't about to let anything happen to Rhys.

Or Graves Glen.

"No, this isn't over," she said, and Elaine stepped forward, taking Vivi's hand.

"My love, we've done our best. Do you know how many witches could survive what you just did? Even on Samhain, calling up a spirit is work. The magic involved can kill, and look at you. I'm so proud of you."

"Thank you, Aunt Elaine," Vivi said, and she meant it. "But I'm serious. We can't just quit."

"Vivienne," Rhys said softly. "There's nothing else to do."

Closing her eyes, Vivi shook her head. "No, there has to be. If we just think . . ."

Thinking might have been easier had she not just had a three-hundred-year-old spirit inside her, and were her mind not chanting, *Rhys will die, Rhys will die, Rhys will die,* over and over again, but she tried to still her thoughts a little, tried to take a deep breath and will herself to calm down, to find the solution.

Rhys was cursed, so the town was cursed. Rhys and the town, bound up together, because of the ley lines. The magical lines that Rhys's ancestor had laid.

But no.

Her eyes flew open.

It hadn't been Rhys's ancestor. Not *just* his ancestor. Aelwyd had been there, too. Aelwyd's magic was in those ley lines, and Aelwyd's magic was in Vivi's blood. In Gwyn's, in Elaine's.

It might not work. It probably wouldn't work.

But she had to try.

"The ley lines," she said to Rhys now, already heading for the cemetery gate. "We have to get to the ley lines."

And Rhys, goddess love him, didn't even question it. "I have my car, and we have," he checked his watch, "about an hour until midnight."

"You two, too," she said to Gwyn and Elaine. "I need both of you."

"We'll be right behind you," Elaine said, and again, Vivi felt a rush of gratitude for these people, these people who loved her and trusted her.

The drive to the cave was a blur, neither Rhys nor Vivi saying much, and when they arrived, Gwyn and Elaine had actually beaten them there.

"Rhys," Vivi said as they stepped into the first cave, the larger chamber leading to the rest of the system, "I need you to wait here, okay? This has to be just the three of us."

He didn't question it, just nodded. "Of course."

As Vivi made her way to the opening leading to the ley lines, though, he couldn't help but call out, "Good luck making me not dead!"

This time, when Vivi walked into the chamber where the ley lines were, she didn't feel that rush of heat she'd felt with Rhys. If anything, she just felt a little nauseous, disoriented, like she'd spun in a circle too many times. The magic was still in here, still just as powerful, but now it was also powerfully, horribly *wrong*.

"Holy shit," she heard Gwyn whisper, and the three of them looked at the magic, pulsing on the floor of the cave. What had once been clean purple light was murky with corruption, thick and sluggish, sparks of reddish light occasionally flashing off it.

"It's gotten worse," Vivi said. "It looked bad that first night, but this . . ."

For the first time since she'd come up with this plan, she started to worry that maybe it was a stupid idea after all. Maybe she wasn't going to be able to pull this off.

But she had to try. For Graves Glen. For Rhys. Even for Aelwyd, who deserved so much better than what had happened to her.

"Hold hands," Vivi said, and she, Elaine and Gwyn formed a circle, clasping their palms together.

"We made this magic," Vivi said, closing her eyes. "Our family did. Maybe nobody built a statue to her, or named a college after her, but she was real, and she was here and she helped make this town what it is. She gave her life for it. And we're her descendants."

She felt both Gwyn and Elaine squeeze her hands, and it gave her the courage to take a deep breath and say, "So fuck Gryffud Penhallow. The Jones Witches are taking this back."

Vivi could feel the power surge beneath her feet and both Gwyn's and Elaine's hands were suddenly so hot they almost burned, but Vivi kept holding tight, kept sending every bit of magic she could muster into the circle made of the three of them, and then down into the ley lines themselves.

It was like trying to push a boulder uphill, and there was something pushing back. Whether it was the remains of the Penhallow magic or the curse itself, Vivi didn't know, but she pushed just as hard right back, feeling sweat break out on her brow as she concentrated.

And then she heard Gwyn cry, "It's working!"

Opening her eyes, Vivi looked down at the ley lines, watching as purple light sparked, strengthened, the black sludge receding, and she held on tighter to her aunt and her cousin, thinking of Aelwyd, thinking of Piper McBride, even thinking of the college witches, all of whom had power and just as much of a claim to the magic of Graves Glen as anyone.

There was a sudden flash of light, so bright that Vivi gasped, dropping Gwyn's and Elaine's hands to cover her eyes, and then, just as quickly as it had appeared, it was gone, leaving her vision a little distorted and dazzled.

But in front of her on the cave floor, the lines ran straight and clear and purple, humming now.

"Rhiannon's tits," Gwyn breathed, and then turned to Vivi with a blinding smile. "You did it!"

"We did it," Vivi corrected, and then threw her arms around both Gwyn and Elaine, laughing even as tears sprang to her eyes.

"I love you girls," Elaine said, dabbing at her own eyes. "And now promise me you will never, ever mix vodka with witchcraft again."

"Solemnly swear," Gwyn said immediately, and Vivi nodded.

"Lesson more than learned, trust me."

"So . . . it seems like I won't die?"

They turned to see Rhys poking his head in the cave, and Gwyn pointed at him.

"Hair still does The Thing."

"It does," Vivi agreed, earning her a wink from Rhys before he jerked his thumb at the entrance of the cave.

"In that case, can we get out of here? Uncursed or not, this is not where I'd like to spend what's left of Halloween."

CHAPTER 34

Vivienne was glowing as they drove back into town, and Rhys had trouble keeping his eyes on the road and not on her.

"It was just like . . . like there was a river inside me, only the river was *magic,* and I could feel it, actually *feel it* as it left my hands, like *whoosh,*" she enthused, gesturing with both hands, her cheeks pink, her eyes bright, and Rhys laughed.

"So you've said, *cariad,* so you've said."

Dropping her hands, Vivienne grinned at him. "Sorry. I'm getting a little overexcited, aren't I?"

"I mean, you saved an entire town and my life with your magic," he reminded her. "You're allowed."

Tipping her head back against the seat, Vivienne laughed again. "I did. I did that. I am a certified badass witch."

"The baddest of asses," Rhys agreed, drumming his fingers on the steering wheel, "and also possibly a little Magic Drunk."

"That is a distinct possibility, yes," she agreed, and then smiled at him again, a smile Rhys felt warm every inch of him.

He was more than a little euphoric himself. Cheating death

had that effect on a man, and even though he wasn't sure how his father was going to take the news that Graves Glen was no longer Penhallow territory, he didn't really care right now. That was a problem for Future Rhys, and surely that cheeky bugger would be able to work it out.

Vivi suddenly reached over, grabbing his arm.

"Pull over."

Rhys eyed her suspiciously. "You're not going to vomit, are you?"

"Ew, no," she said, pulling a face, then pointing out the windshield. "Right there."

Rhys followed her instructions, bringing the car to a stop on a dirt pull-in at the edge of a hillside, looking down into a valley. The moon was bright enough that he could just make out the field below them, the surrounding hills dark shapes against the navy-blue sky.

"This is where we met," she said softly. "The summer solstice. Right down there in that field."

Rhys had known that from the moment he'd parked the car. He remembered those hills, remembered sitting with her and looking up at them, remembered that flower crown that sat crooked on her hair, and her sweet smile.

"Can I tell you a secret?" she asked, her voice quiet, her mood a little more subdued.

"It's not that you didn't actually reverse the curse, and you've brought me here to kick me off this hillside, is it?"

She laughed, lower this time, her hair brushing her shoulders as she shook her head. "I loved that summer," she said. "I held it up as this perfect, wonderful moment, and told myself it's only because it was a first, you know? First magical rite I ever went to, first summer of college, first boy I ever fell in love with."

When she turned to him, her eyes were filled with something Rhys couldn't name, but whatever it was, it warmed his chest, his heart.

God, he loved her.

"But this time was even better," she said, leaning in close. And then she smiled.

"May I kiss you?"

Rhys's heart jerked almost painfully against his ribs. "Now?"

"I'm open to whatever your schedule allows."

"Well, lucky for you, I am currently free as fuck," he replied, and she laughed as he pulled her in, clambering over the seat so that she could straddle his lap.

It had been a while since Rhys had shagged someone in a car, but somehow, they managed, her dress pushed up to her waist, his fly undone, and they only hit the car horn twice.

And when he was inside her, her arms around him, her hair in his face, this gorgeous, magical woman he'd fallen in love with twice now, he knew he had to tell her how he felt.

After, he'd promised himself, and this was after.

But first, he wanted to feel her come apart around him, wanted to hear her make those soft little cries and feel her teeth nip his earlobe.

He did all of that and more, and when she lay panting against his chest, he pushed her hair back, kissing the sweaty skin of her neck.

"Vivienne," he started, and she sighed, sinking even deeper against him.

"I'm going to miss you, Rhys," she said, her voice soft and dreamy.

That's when he understood what this was. Bringing him here to this place where they met, making love to him.

She was saying good-bye.

IT WAS PAST midnight by the time they made it back up the mountain to Elaine's, and as she and Rhys walked up the porch steps, fingers loosely clasped, Vivi nodded up at the sky. "Samhain is over. Officially All Souls Day now."

"And I am officially uncursed, and you are officially the most impressive witch I know."

Giggling, Vivi gave a little curtsy, still slightly high from magic and sex and some mystical combination of the two.

In fact, she thought, as they stopped in front of Elaine's door, she could maybe go for a little more of both.

"Come inside?" she asked. "I don't have much practice sneaking boys into my room here, but honestly, I don't think Elaine would mind."

Rhys smiled at that, but it was a brief one, and when he reached up to smooth her hair back from her face, Vivi felt like she knew what he was about to say.

"Much as I would love that, *cariad,* I'm afraid I need to get back tomorrow."

Vivi rocked back slightly, her hands falling from his waist. "Back as in . . . to Wales?"

"The very place," he said. "My father needs to be told about all this, and that's really a conversation best had in person. And work will get busier with the holidays . . ."

Vivi felt like someone had dunked her in cold water, all that silly, magical happiness draining off her as she stood there on the porch, looking up into Rhys's blue eyes.

"Right, of course," she said, and made herself smile. "I mean, we both knew this was temporary. Your life there, mine here."

"Exactly," he said, and his smile seemed a little forced, too. "Of course," he added, pulling her in, "I could beg you to come with me. Down on my knees, the whole bit, very dramatic, quite a scene."

She laughed a little at that even as she closed her eyes against the sudden stinging of tears. "I would really like to see that." And she would, was the thing. Wanted Rhys to seriously ask her to come, wanted to know what this meant to him.

But he'd showed her, hadn't he? He cared about her, he always would. But he wasn't exactly the kind of guy who could stay in one place. He'd built a whole life around that.

And now that her magic was inextricably bound up in Graves Glen, she didn't want to leave. This was her home.

"You do enjoy me down on my knees."

Vivi closed the space between them, wrapping her arms around him, breathing in the smell of autumn that clung to his clothes, the faint scent of smoke still hanging around them both. "Truly where you do your best work."

His grip on her tightened even as he chuckled, and Vivi wished they could put off this bit just for a little bit longer. Just let her have him a little longer, one more night, maybe two.

But that wouldn't make this any easier. If anything, it would just make it harder. Because Rhys couldn't stay.

And she couldn't go.

"Look on the bright side," she said, as she pulled back. "At least this time I won't be cursing you. Might even set up a little mini–Rhys Penhallow shrine on my desk at work."

"Canopy bed included, I hope."

Vivi could feel the smile wobble on her face. She was making the right decision. They both were. This thing between them had always been built not to last. They were too different, wanted different lives, had different dreams.

That didn't make letting him go any easier.

But she did.

"Good-bye, Rhys," she said, brushing her lips against his one more time.

"Good-bye, Vivienne," he murmured, but he didn't kiss her again. He just turned and walked back down the porch steps and, for the second time, out of her life.

CHAPTER 35

Winter semester was always a little bleak.

If Graves Glen was at its absolute best in October, January was the flip side of that coin, the time of year when Vivi started wondering if she should move to a beach or something. The snow was never that bad, and it could even be really pretty when you were watching it from a porch up in the mountains, the snowflakes floating through the bare trees.

It was less pretty when you were sludging through a couple of inches of the stuff mixed with mud as you made your way to work.

Grimacing, she scraped off her boots before walking into the history department.

"January suuuuucks," she heard Ezichi call from her office as she passed, and Vivi ducked her head in.

"Agreed. But I hear you finally got the tenure track gig, congratulations!"

Unlike Vivi, Ezi had her Ph.D., and had been stuck in the lecturer trenches for ages, so Vivi was genuinely thrilled for her, and Ezi was, too, if her smile was anything to go by.

"And congratulations to you, too," Ezi said, coming up from behind her desk. "Hear you're taking on some extra classes in the folklore department?"

Vivi nodded, already feeling a little flutter in her stomach at the idea. After Halloween, she'd gone to have a talk with Dr. Arbuthnot about what had happened, the change to Graves Glen's magic.

She'd assumed the woman would be angry, or at least snotty about all of it.

To her surprise, she'd been offered a job.

As of this semester, she was teaching two classes over on the Witchery side of things, a History of Magic course focusing on Graves Glen's past, and a class on Ritual Magic.

And she'd even bought a new scarf.

But just one.

Saying good-bye to Ezi, Vivi headed to her office, flicking on the teakettle as soon as she got in, and setting her bag down on her desk. Reaching inside, she pulled out a heavy book, its cover bloodred leather, the title stamped in aging gold foil on the cover. It was a history of Wales as written by a Welsh witch over a hundred years ago. She'd gotten it in the mail at Yule, no return address, just a note scrawled in Rhys's handwriting:

For your office. Xx

No *cariad,* no *I miss you,* but he was thinking of her, and that was enough.

Or at least she told herself it was.

Shaking her head, Vivi made herself a cup of tea, and fired up her computer.

By the time she was done typing up notes for her afternoon history lecture, she realized she was due over at the Witchery side of things to meet with Dr. Arbuthnot, and sighing, she shoved her arms back into her coat and twisted her scarf around her neck.

It was quieter on that side of campus, and the snow was a little less trampled as she walked into the main building, her nose wrinkling slightly at the scent of patchouli—seriously, was there someone she could talk to about that?—but she made her way down the hall, glancing at doors as she went.

Other than the classier furnishings, it wasn't all that different from the history building. Same rows of doors, same frosted windows with names stenciled in black.

A. Parsons.
J. Brown.
C. Acevedo.
R. Penhallow.

Vivi was already past the door before it registered, and she slowly turned and looked back at it, her heart hammering.

It couldn't be.

It had to be someone else, some other Penhallow, first name starting with *R*. Rhys probably had a cousin, Richard Penhallow, or Rebecca Penhallow.

But she found herself reaching for the doorknob anyway.

Vivi knew it was horribly rude to just walk into someone's office without knocking, but she had to see, had to shut down this stupid little flutter of hope in her chest before it took flight.

The door opened, revealing an office that didn't seem all that different from Vivi's own. Small, one window, desk and a lamp, a filing cabinet, a bookshelf. The only difference was that the shelf was empty, and there was nothing on the walls, and there, sitting behind the desk, grinning up at her, was Rhys.

She almost wondered if she'd walked through some kind of spell when she came in here, or if this was a trick the witches were playing on her, some kind of faculty hazing thing.

But then he stood up and walked over to her, as warm and real as anything as he gently shut the door behind her and said, "Hello, *cariad.*"

There were a million things she wanted to say to him, to ask him.

But all that came out was, "You have . . . an office."

"I do."

"And a desk."

"Even so."

"And you're . . . here."

"Noticed that, did you?"

"Why?"

Blowing out a breath, Rhys put his hands in his pockets and shrugged. "Well, you see, I went back to Wales, business as usual, only the thing was, I was completely fucking miserable. Just the saddest bastard you've ever seen in your life. So sad, in fact, that Wells—*Wells!*—told me I was a sad bastard, and as he is president of the Sad Bastards Club, I found this very distressing."

Vivi's face was aching, and she realized it was because she was smiling.

Rhys was smiling, too, as he continued. "And so I thought what I could do to make myself less of a sad bastard, and I realized the only thing for it was to be with you. Or at the very least, near you. And it turns out that when a college is named after your family home, they're fairly willing to let you teach the odd class, so here I am."

"What about your business?" Vivi asked, still feeling a little dazed, and Rhys nodded.

"Still got it. Can run it from here, no problem, but Bowen said this moment needed a big gesture . . . I mean, I decided this moment needed a big gesture and received zero help from my brother at all.

"Besides," he went on, "I wanted to prove to you that I was serious about this, about staying here. Putting down roots. This isn't a lark, Vivienne."

He stepped closer, and Vivi breathed him in, her hands already going to his chest, where his heart beat a steady tattoo under her palms. "I realize that uprooting my life and moving to Georgia for a woman might fall into the reckless and ill-thought-out category, but the thing is, I'm very much in love with that woman."

He leaned in a little closer, lowering his voice. "That woman is you, by the way. Wanted to make sure that was clear."

Vivi laughed even as she felt sudden tears sting her eyes. "Okay, good, because I really can't compete with Aunt Elaine for your heart. My baking is atrocious."

"Your only fault."

Rhys took a deep breath, reaching out to cup her face, his fingers resting on the back of her head as he looked into her eyes. "I love you. So very, very much. And I know that I'm flippant sometimes, or make a joke rather than say the truth, but I want you to know that you're everything to me, Vivienne. Everything."

Leaning in, he rested his forehead against hers, eyes closing as Vivi reached up and put her hands on his wrists. "You've had my heart from the moment I saw you on that bloody hillside, and I hate that I wasted nine years without you, but I'm not wasting a single second more. If you need to be here, then I need to be here. Simple as that."

Stepping back, Vivi looked into those blue eyes. Rhys might have been The Fool, but maybe she was, too, because she realized that the image, a person walking merrily off a cliff, wasn't necessarily about being reckless.

It was about taking a leap and trusting something—someone—would catch you.

"I want to go to Wales with you," she blurted out, and Rhys's brow furrowed in confusion.

"Did you miss the part about how I've moved here?"

Laughing, crying, Vivi shook her head. "No, I mean . . . it doesn't have to be either-or. You here or me in Wales. We can do both. We can have both. And it's going to be messy and hard sometimes, but it will be worth it. Because I love you, too. You've had my heart just as long, and I trust you with it."

And as soon as she said it, she knew it was true.

She trusted Rhys with her heart. Reckless, capricious Rhys, who glided through life, but who loved her and had proved it over and over again.

The Fool and The Star, just like Gwyn's cards had shown. Leaping off cliffs and shining steadily, opposites who couldn't live without each other.

Who didn't have to.

And that, Vivi had to admit as Rhys leaned in to kiss her, might be the most magical thing of all.

Acknowledgments

As is fitting for a story about witches, this is my thirteenth published novel, and I have been lucky enough to have Holly Root as my agent for each and every one of those thirteen books. The magic a good agent can wield is a truly powerful force, and I am so lucky to have Holly spinning her spells for me.

Tessa Woodward understood this book from the very first, and thanks to her particular brand of magic, it is so much stronger than I'd ever dreamed it could be.

The entire team at William Morrow is, I'm fairly certain, comprised of wizards, and I am so grateful!

To my own coven, especially my Orlando Ladies (the Anti Go-Getters), thank you for listening to me when this book was still in its softest and squishiest stage. Next round of brie is on me!

This is, at its heart, a book about families, and I have been so blessed with mine, both the one I came from and the one I made. Love y'all.

HEADLINE ETERNAL

FIND YOUR HEART'S DESIRE...

VISIT OUR WEBSITE: www.headlineeternal.com

FIND US ON FACEBOOK: facebook.com/eternalromance

CONNECT WITH US ON TWITTER: @eternal_books

FOLLOW US ON INSTAGRAM: @headlineeternal

EMAIL US: eternalromance@headline.co.uk